TALES

D0063957

Alluring TALES

Awaken the Fantasy

VIVI ANNA, SYLVIA DAY,
DELILAH DEVLIN, CATHRYN FOX, MYLA JACKSON,
LISA RENEE JONES, SASHA WHITE

red

AVON

An Imprint of HarperCollinsPublishers

"Lover's Locket" copyright © 2007 by Cathryn Fox; "Kili's Ice Man" copyright © 2007 by Delilah Devlin; "The Hottest One-Night Stand" copyright © 2007 by Lisa Renee Jones; "Out of the Shadows" copyright © 2007 by Mary E. Jerningan; "Tempting Grace" copyright © 2007 by Sabrina Ingram; "A Familiar Kind of Magic" copyright © 2007 by Sylvia Day; "Quick Silver" copyright © 2007 by Tawny Stokes

HarperCollins books may be purchased for educational, business, or sales promotional use. For information please write: Special Markets Department, HarperCollins Publishers, 10 East 53rd Street, New York, NY 10022.

FIRST EDITION

Interior text designed by Diahann Sturge

Library of Congress Cataloging-in-Publication Data

Alluring tales : awaken the fantasy / by Cathryn Fox . . . [et al.].—1st ed.
   p.   cm.
ISBN: 978-0-06-117603-6
ISBN-10: 0-06-117603-6
1. Erotic stories, American. 2. Erotic stories, Canadian. 3. American fiction—Women authors. 4. Canadian fiction—Women authors.   I. Fox, Cathryn.

PS648.E7A45 2007
813.'60803538—dc22   2006021571

   07   08   09   10   JTC/RRD   10   9   8   7   6   5   4   3   2   1

Contents

Lover's Locket

Cathryn Fox

To Mark,
who loves me enough to accompany me to Atlanta
to hang out with two thousand other romance writers.
I love you.

One

"So . . . how did your date with Brian go?"

Caira glanced up from the three-tiered wedding cake she'd just finished icing and watched her best friend, Nikki, breeze in through the back entrance of her bakery.

Blue eyes wide with anticipation, Nikki rubbed her palms together and grinned. "Tell me everything. I want all the juicy details. Every last drop."

Caira quirked her lips and gestured toward the cake. "Let's just say I won't be making one of these for myself any time soon."

Nikki plopped herself onto a nearby stool and scrunched her nose. "Was it that bad?"

"I think the word *bad* is an understatement." Caira brushed powered sugar from her fingers and continued. "Try painful. I spent hours listening to Brian recite stories about how wonderful he is, and then he intimately introduced my tonsils to his tongue when he tried to give me a good-night kiss."

Nikki bobbed her head in agreement. "Yeah, I guess he does think highly of himself. But he's cute enough, and I heard he has a huge co—"

With a wave of her hand, Caira cut her off. "If *one* can get past his overinflated ego, *one* might enjoy his other attributes." She paused and carefully placed the groom onto the top layer of cake. "Unfortunately, I am not that *one*."

Caira stood back and admired the finishing touches on the wedding cake. As she adjusted the small groom figurine she sighed regretfully. Would she ever find her very own Prince Charming? She'd made enough cakes over the years to know other women discovered their true love. The one man they were destined to be with. Why couldn't she? Was she too picky? Too set in her ideas of what qualities her Prince should possess?

Was it too much to want a man with deep soulful eyes that looked at you, not through you? A man with long, midnight hair, a strong angular jaw, quiet confidence, richly bronzed skin, and a body that oozed strength and sexuality.

A man like the one in the portrait hanging in her living room. The one that had been handed down in her family for generations.

With his blond hair, blue eyes, and boyish twin dimples, Brian was the antithesis of her ideal man. Surely Nikki knew that.

Knitting her brow together, Caira glanced at her best friend. "Whatever gave you the idea that we'd hit it off?"

Nikki shrugged. "He's a wedding photographer." She paused and waved her hand through the air. "And you own your own bakery shop specializing in wedding cakes. I just thought you had a common interest."

"The only thing we have in common is we both breathe oxygen. And for a while there I wasn't even too sure about that. I had a sneaking suspicion he came from another planet. Planet Narcissist to be exact."

Nikki chuckled and jumped from her stool. "Come on, let's go shopping. I'll buy you something nice to make up for it. I hear there's a new boutique that opened up on Fifth Street and I'm just dying to check it out."

Caira uncoiled the apron straps from around her neck and eyed her friend. "No more blind dates okay?" She pulled the plastic clip from her nape, letting her blonde curls tumble over her shoulders.

Nikki raised one brow, a wry grin curling her lips. "Not even if he has a huge co—"

Groaning in exasperation, Caira nudged Nikki toward the back door. "No, not even if he has a huge cock." She tossed her apron aside, and followed her friend outdoors.

A short while later Caira found herself peering through the frosted, curbside door of a store called The Magic Boutique.

She shadowed the afternoon sun from her eyes and turned to Nikki. "What is this place?"

Nikki shrugged. "Let's go find out." Tiny bells jingled overhead when she pulled open the thick, opaque glass door and stepped inside. The small store was overcrowded with unique, antique items, rich in history, and undoubtedly, family secrets.

Caira's senses were immediately enticed by an exotic blend of jasmine and vanilla incense. Soft rays of light from an overhead beaded chandelier bathed the room in a golden glow, creating a cozy, somewhat mysterious atmosphere. Gusts of warm air from a ceiling fan rattled the dangling beads, the resulting noise similar to the soothing sound of raindrops falling on an old porch roof. Blinking her eyes to adjust to the dim light, Caira glanced around the room and noted the dark shadows dancing across the crimson-colored walls.

"Come closer, ladies."

Caira and Nikki both turned in the direction of the aged, smoke-roughened voice coming from the other side of the room.

In an attempt to avoid banging into any of the expensive items, they pressed their bodies together and carefully moved across the wooden floor until they found the old woman with the deep, gravelly voice.

Dressed in a silk chiffon flamenco skirt with a cut velvet ruffle and a peasant style top, wrapped and knotted at the waist, the woman looked more like a traveling gypsy than a store owner.

Sitting on an oversized stuffed chair, with her legs folded underneath her, she pressed her lips together and stared at Caira for a long silent moment. Her eyes bore into her with a gaze so intense and probing, Caira feared the woman could see into the depths of her soul. She found it most difficult to hold the woman's stare.

With weathered fingers the gypsy-woman lifted her hand and took a long, slow drag off her menthol cigarette. Tendrils of smoke billowed around her braided, waist-length gray hair.

Not wanting to appear rude, Caira blinked the smoke from

her eyes, weaved her fingers tightly together, and restrained herself from fanning the fumes away.

When the woman finally spoke she leaned forward and said, "*Ma Petite Princesse*. It is you. You have come."

Did this woman somehow know her? To Caira's knowledge they'd never crossed paths before.

"I'm sorry, have we met?" Caira asked.

Her question was left unanswered.

The woman barely spared Nikki a glance as she unfolded her legs, crushed her cigarette into a pink flamingo-shaped ashtray, and rose. Her joints moaned like a wounded animal with each jerky movement. Using small, measured steps she closed the gap between them and stood in front of Caira. Tension lines bracketed her mouth as her eyes roamed Caira's face. A moment later a wide smile split her lips as her violet eyes gazed at Caira as if she'd just discovered some long lost treasure. When she reached out and placed her palm on Caira's forearm, the tiny hairs on the base of Caira's neck began tingling. An uneasy, foreboding feeling closed in on her.

Feeling extremely uncomfortable, Caira took a distancing step back and reclaimed her personal space.

The gypsy-woman must have sensed her discomfiture. She positioned herself behind the dark, paneled counter and cut her hand through the air. The movement sent a fresh wave of jasmine and menthol before Caira's nostrils.

"Please browse, ladies." Returning to her previous position on the chair, she concentrated her attention on lighting another cigarette.

Caira made a move to turn. The woman's voice stopped her mid-stride. "I must forewarn you that each antique piece comes with its own unique magical power. You must wield that power wisely, *Ma Petite Princesse.*"

A shiver skittered down Caira's spine as she turned and stared wide eyed at her friend. Remaining silent through the entire bizarre encounter, Nikki nudged Caira and gave her a look that suggested she too found the whole situation strange.

"Maybe we should get out of here," Nikki whispered as they inched toward the exit.

Caira readily agreed. Wrapping her arm through Nikki's, they both quickened their footsteps. As they approached the opaque glass door, a strange almost surreal sensation washed over Caira. It was as if someone had physically cupped her chin and turned her head in the direction of the antique oak cabinet in front of the store window.

Her steps slowed and time seemed suspended. She felt her body turn as though she no longer controlled her movements. Suddenly, she found herself standing before the cabinet, even though she couldn't recall crossing the room.

"I see you have found the Lover's Locket."

"What?" Startled by the woman's sudden appearance, Caira jumped back. She hadn't even heard her approaching footsteps.

The woman gestured toward the beautiful silver necklace enclosed behind the protective walls of the glass case and motioned for her to take a better look.

"The Lover's Locket," she repeated. Her aged voice cracked like brittle bones causing goose bumps to pebble Caira's flesh.

Palms open, Caira placed her hands on the glass. She was so mesmerized by the beauty of the exquisite piece of jewelry she almost found it impossible to speak. She fought to recover her voice. "It's magnificent."

"You're searching . . . yes?"

"Searching?" Caira didn't understand the question.

"For your true love."

She was surprised at how perceptive the old woman was. Uncomfortable talking about her personal life with a complete stranger, Caira turned the discussion back to the locket. "Is it antique?"

The woman ignored her question and asked one of her own. "Should you wish to have it?"

Caira gave a quick shake of her head. "I can't afford—"

The woman cut her off. "It is not for you to argue." She opened the glass case, removed the locket, and placed it in Caira's hand.

The second the locket came into contact with her flesh, an odd tingling began in her bloodstream. She was strangely fascinated by the piece. Strangely fascinated by the way her pulse kicked up a notch at first contact. Curious about its origins, she stared at the antique locket in awe. She'd never seen anything more beautiful.

The woman touched her arm, bringing Caira's attention back to her. "You feel it don't you?" she asked.

Uneasiness closed in on her as she met the woman's challenging gaze. She felt something, an unexplainable strange pull toward the locket, but she wasn't about to admit it. She lowered her lashes, hiding her emotions from the woman's probing eyes.

"I have no idea what you're talking about," Caira responded quickly, turning the locket over in her hand. A ribbon of sunlight burst through the window and reflected off the unusual intricate design etched in the silver. Caira squinted and stared at the inscription until the words in front of her blurred together.

The gypsy curled her weathered fingers around Caira's and squeezed until the locket was tightly enclosed in the safety of her small hand. "With this locket comes great power, but with all great power there comes darkness."

"What do you mean?" Caira asked, indulging her for a moment.

Her gravelly voice became as smooth as silk as she recounted the tale of the Lover's Locket. "It is said that if one recites the incantation etched in the silver, their true love will be revealed." Suddenly, an anxious expression crossed the gypsywoman's beguiling violet eyes. "The incantation also awakens the Keeper of Darkness from his eternal slumber." Frowning intently, she looked deep into Caira's eyes. "The person who recites the incantation is the only one who can defeat the Keeper of Darkness. It is said that death is the price of failure."

Caira blew out a breath she hadn't realized she was holding. She remembered the old legend well. It was only a few years ago while babysitting her niece that she'd recounted the story herself. She almost laughed out loud at the foolishness of it all. She took a moment to recall the legend.

It was believed that centuries ago on the eve of her arranged wedding to a man she didn't love, a rebellious princess had fled her father's castle and secretly met her lover. Their plans to elope were foiled when one of the Lord's vassals captured them. The all-powerful Lord had a curse placed on his daughter's lover. In retaliation, the princess acquired the help of an old gypsy woman. She had an incantation etched on her most precious possession, a locket given to her by her lover. Should the locket find its way to her in another lifetime, the princess could read the incantation and break the curse. But unfortunately, as the old woman had already said, with great power comes great darkness. The princess must battle the forces of evil to free her lover forever.

"You know the story . . . yes?" The worry in the woman's voice gained her full attention.

Caira forced a smile and addressed the old woman's concerns. "It's just a legend. A story told at slumber parties. The legend also says that *only* the princess can unleash its power," she pointed out. Rolling her shoulders she continued, "So if this ever fell into the hands of the original owner—"

A frown formed on her forehead as the old woman sealed Caira's protest with her fingers. Caira repressed a shiver as a chill rushed through her. "What makes you think you're not the original owner, Bella?" the woman asked.

Caira's skin prickled. The air almost seemed to crackle with electricity. Bella? Obviously the old woman had her confused with someone else.

"My name isn't Bella, it's Caira."

The woman gave a slow nod. "Yes, of course, Caira. Forgive my slip. Perhaps this belonged to you in the past, Caira."

She met the woman's glance and tried to placate her. "It's ridiculous to believe the legend." Waving her hand over her worn jeans and t-shirt, she said, "Besides, I hardly think I was a princess in another lifetime."

"Yes, well, you'll never know unless you recite the incantation." The look in the woman's eyes caused her skin to grow cold.

Caira gulped, her stomach plummeted. Good Lord, what was going on with her? What was she getting all worked up about? She shook her head to clear it. It was just a silly legend.

Wasn't it?

Two

Night had closed around her as Caira restlessly toyed with the locket draped around her neck. Padding softly across the carpeted floor of her small living room, she glanced out her bay window and gazed at the dark sky. It was nearing midnight, yet sleep continued to elude her. Earlier in the evening she'd had a warm, relaxing bath and dressed in her most comfortable two-piece silk pajamas, but to no avail, she still couldn't seem to unwind.

Grabbing a new book from the stack of paperbacks on her coffee table, she decided to settle herself into her cushiony recliner. Perhaps that would help her relax and fall asleep. Misty, her cat, jumped onto her lap and curled up on her outstretched legs.

"Hey, girl." As Caira stroked her cat's silky fur, her glance wandered to the portrait overlooking her sofa. Drawing a deep breath, she stared at the beautiful man for an endless moment.

Zarek. His dark eyes seemed so intimate, so possessive as she gazed at him in rapture.

She drummed her fingers on the wooden armrest. Who was this handsome man? And what was her obsession with him? Years ago when she had posed that question to her parents, they had no concrete answers. All they could tell Caira was that the portrait had been in the family for generations. She only knew his name because it had been carved into the back of the picture frame.

As her hand tightened over her new locket, the old woman's words rushed through her mind like a windstorm. "It is said that if one recites the incantation etched in the silver, their true love will be revealed."

Even though she thought the whole idea of the legend was silly, Caira took a moment to imagine what it would be like if the man in the portrait was her true love. Closing her eyes she fantasized about how wonderful it would be if he came to her, in person. His strong hands cushioning her in his arms. Chest against chest, skin against skin. His full, sensuous mouth taking possession of hers while she touched the hard planes of his magnificent body. His long midnight hair sweeping against her naked flesh as he laid her out and buried himself deep in her welcoming sheath.

Lust swamped her as she played out the provocative mental image. Her breasts tightened in bliss and she reached out and cupped them in her palms, gently massaging and brushing her nipples, attempting to relieve the ache.

A needy, not quite satisfied sigh caught in the back of her throat as she stood and walked closer to the portrait. Rocking on her heels, she fingered the aged canvas. Her hand traced the pattern of his face and surfed the outline of his jaw. There was something in his eyes. Something hauntingly familiar. As her fingers glided over his sculpted chest, she could feel a heavy, sexual pressure building in her body. Her toes curled, her heart pounded, and her skin came alive. Her entire being reacted as though she was touching the man himself. She bit her lip as a rush of heat moistened her silky pajama bottoms.

Good Lord, she had to pull herself together and find a way to get over her strange fascination with the handsome, mysterious man that watched over her every night. A man who continually invaded her thoughts, even in sleep.

He was always with her.

In her.

In her head, her heart, and her soul. It was like she was waiting. Always waiting. But for what, she didn't know.

She inched back and steepled her fingers. No wonder all her dates and relationships had ended in disaster. How could any guy possibly live up to the rich, erotic fantasy life she'd created with the sexy man from her portrait?

Returning to her recliner, she flicked on her lamp and propped opened her book. Soft rays of warm light danced off her silver locket and drew her attention. Heat seemed to radiate off it and electrically charge the air around her.

She gathered it into her hand and turned it over to see the incantation. The silver felt warm to the touch. Rubbing her thumb in a circular motion over the engraving, she concentrated on the words.

No time, no earth, no sky, or place shall ever thwart our way. To right a wrong, to change the past, I bring you back to stay.

Of course the whole idea of the legend was ridiculous. And

how could the old lady possibly think she was a princess from the past? *A princess.* She resisted the urge to throw her head back and laugh. Instead, she threaded her fingers through her hair and rolled her eyes heavenward. The idea was simply ludicrous. And with the so-called Lover's Locket draped around her neck, Caira was presented with the perfect opportunity to prove it. Ignoring the sudden pounding of her heart, she moistened her lips, drew a fueling breath, and read the inscription out loud.

Holding the locket tightly in her fist, she waited. Seconds turned into minutes. The only sound in the room was coming from the antique grandfather clock ticking in the alcove behind her. Another unique piece handed down through history.

She glanced out her open living-room window, watching the leaves on the oak tree bristle in the warm night breeze, and continued her wait. The streetlamp cast golden shadows on her walls.

Nothing.

Silence.

No true love appeared. No Keeper of Darkness threatened her life. She had to admit, she was rather grateful for that. She'd much rather cuddle up with her book than battle the forces of evil, she mused.

She shook her head and laughed at the foolishness of it all. It was well past time to forget her bizarre encounter with the strange lady from The Magic Boutique.

Pushing herself deeper into her cushiony chair, she opened her book and proceeded to read the first line. *"What makes you think you're not the original owner, Bella?"* The book fell from her fingers. Her heart pounded like thunder in her ears and her mouth went suddenly dry.

She squeezed her eyes shut then blinked them back into focus. She scooped the book up, flipped to the beginning, and concentrated on reading the passage again. This time the line read as it should. Obviously the old lady had shaken her up more than she cared to admit and now her mind was playing tricks on her.

She diligently tried to shrug off the gypsy-woman's warning and force her focus back on her story. A short while later her eyes grew heavy and soon fatigue overtook her. She felt herself slip away.

"Caira."

The voice was soft, hypnotizing, pulling her awake. She sensed a movement in the shadows. A gasp caught in her throat as the air around her seemed to stir with energy.

"Caira. Wake up," he commanded in a gentle voice.

As she took in the hazy vision before her, she had difficulty remembering how to breathe. Although he moved in the deep shadows of the room, she instinctively knew it was him.

Zarek.

Her pulse jumped in her throat. Excitement coiled in her veins.

She drew a breath and said calmly, "I'm awake." Of course she wasn't awake. She'd obviously fallen asleep while reading. She wasn't about to admit that to him, or herself, and risk the possibility of spoiling a perfectly good, erotic dream.

His voice was like a rough caress. "Caira come to me." He held his arms out to her.

She reacted to the intensity she heard in his deep sexy tone. Her body buzzed to life as she rose from her recliner and crossed the room, slipping into the dark shadows with him. There appeared to be a highly charged, glowing blue aura of energy radiating from his magnificent, muscular body as he stood over her.

He wrapped his thick arms around her small waist and crushed her body to his. She sucked in air, raised her gaze to his, and gripped his shirt. His steel gray eyes blazed with heat and hunger. The way he looked at her with such need and desire made her insides quiver.

He slid his fingers through her hair and brought her lips close to his. A smile touched his mouth as his eyes moved over her features with tender warmth, appraising her.

As he breathed his words over her face, she could taste the sweetness of his mouth. "I have waited centuries to hold you like this." The heat in his voice licked over her skin. Her body liquefied under his smoldering gaze, forcing her to lock her knees to avoid collapsing.

Sexual energy leapt between them as she arched forward and pressed her breasts into his firm chest. He wedged her legs open with his knee, her pussy pressed hard against his thigh. She began trembling, with need, urgency, and utter excitement. His thick cock curved her stomach inward as she leaned into him.

"I want you, Caira."

"Then take me." Nestling closer, she gyrated her hips and rubbed her pelvis against his leg. "I am ready," she added. A surge of heat rushed through her veins when his cock throbbed in response to her bold touch and words. "I've always been ready, Zarek."

She'd dreamt of him before, of course. But it had never been like this. It had never felt so real, so vivid. Her senses seemed to be amplified. Everything about her was heightened, even the hairs on the back of her neck were alert. She didn't need to touch him to know how his hard muscles would feel beneath her fingers. Nor did she need to draw a breath to bask in his arousing, heady male scent. Instinctively she knew his skin would taste sweet and salty, and at the first delicious touch of her tongue to his naked flesh, she'd lose herself in him, body and soul.

Her hands shook as she put her palms flat on his chest. She could feel his blood surging though his veins. She could feel his every breath, his every heartbeat as though it were her own.

As though they were connected.

As though they were one.

Those thoughts vanished when he lowered his head. His eyes fixed upon her parted lips as the pad of his thumb brushed her cheeks. The artist who painted his portrait should have been commended for capturing the sharp angles of his face to perfection. He was so beautiful, so flawless. He slanted his head sideways. It was then that she noticed a deep, purple scar on his face. Every sculpted angle and plane of his face was burned into her mind forever, yet she'd never seen this mark before. It didn't exist in the portrait but gave off a hazy, violet glow in her dream. She reached out and traced the pattern of it. Her mouth formed a question.

His brow puckered into a frown as he grabbed her hand and anchored it to her side. The smile faded from his face. "There will be time for questions later. Right now I must taste you and hold you as I have so desperately longed to do." The depth of urgency and emotion in his voice made her shudder.

Caira knew it was her dream, hers to control, but she could no more control her dream world than she could control the man in it, a man who gazed so deep into her eyes she thought she'd burn from the inside out.

All thoughts were forgotten when his hands stole up her silky night shirt, his rough fingertips heating her body to near boiling. His fingers climbed higher until he skimmed the underside of her breasts. Heat and energy transferred from his fingertips to her puckered nipples. They tightened with arousal while an explosive wave of pressure began building deep inside her. Sexual energy whipped through the air around them.

"I am going to make love to you, Caira." She trembled as his rich voice rolled over her. "As your true love I can bring your mind and body to a higher level of passion that will leave us both sated and drained."

She nodded, unable to find her voice. She closed her eyes, wanting nothing more than to listen to the sound of his hypnotic voice. It seeped into her skin, flooding her with desire.

"Are you prepared for me?" His voice was dark, seductive.

"Always." He swallowed her response as his mouth closed over hers. She moaned and drew his tongue inside to mate with hers. She could feel herself burning up in his strong arms.

Pressure.

So much pressure.

Deep in her body.

Fighting for release before she melted all over him.

His hand slid over her breasts, kneading them, caressing

her nipples with deft manipulation. His other hand began a slow descent, over her flat stomach, until he dipped a finger below the band on her pants. She pushed her pelvis against him, wanting to rub her entire body over his. She ripped at his shirt. Buttons popped and fell to the floor. His chest was magnificent. She stroked him, unable to keep her hands from his naked bronzed flesh. With much greed, she shoved at his shirt until it rolled off his shoulders.

"You are so very responsive, Caira." He brushed his tongue over her bottom lip and drew it into his mouth, tasting her. With seemingly practiced, controlled patience, he worked the buttons on her shirt. He eased it open until the curves of her breasts were exposed.

"Beautiful."

His words, his voice, and his touch made her insides shudder. Her entire body responded as though this dream was real. As though his hands were actually stroking her flesh with dark urgency, his mouth possessing hers with hunger. God, she never wanted to wake up. Ever. Nothing in real life could ever feel so good.

"Your lips are even softer than I remember." The low growl of longing was deep in his throat. Barely audible. Had she not been so in tune with his every breath, his every emotion, she would have missed it.

He shifted his position, dipped his head, and drew her breast into his mouth for a taste. His warm, wet tongue glided over her trembling flesh, raising her passion to new heights just like he promised. Her body shook and her heart pounded as his mouth moved over her skin. His touch was erotic, intimate. God, she felt so safe, so cherished in his tender arms. She now knew why no other man appealed to her. She was made for Zarek.

He growled and sucked harder. "Yesssss," she hissed. Throwing her head back, she drove her fingers through his long hair. "Oh God, that feels incredible."

"And it tastes incredible, Bella, just as I remembered," he added, curling his tongue around her engorged nipple.

Bella!

Deep in her arousal-fogged mind she fought to make sense out of it. Why would he call her Bella? Had the old woman's stories seeped into her subconscious, rattling her more than she realized? Caira knew at that moment, as she floated on some level between sleep and awake, her brain was too foggy to rationalize anything. She pushed it far from her mind.

All thoughts were forgotten as his tongue continued its gentle assault. Biting, nipping, and ravishing her with hunger. Her whole world was pulsing, throbbing. She'd never been so desperate, so needy.

She could feel an orgasm pulling at her as he lapped at her breasts with demanding strokes. He dipped a finger between her moist folds and stroked from front to back, his finger bathing in her syrupy arousal.

"Zarek," she cried out breathlessly as pleasure forked through her. The room began spinning as a rainbow of colors danced before her eyes.

"You are nice and wet for me." He swirled his finger through her slick heat. "I must taste your sweet juices, Caira."

"Please . . ." she begged, needing him to answer the urgent demands of her body. There was no time for him to taste her. She needed him to bring her over the edge now. Before she burned up inside. "I need to come." She could hear the impatience, the greed in her voice.

When she reached out and cupped her hand over the bulge in his pants, he groaned and burrowed a finger deep inside her. Her pussy muscles gripped him and held him high in her tight, moist fissure. His tongue climbed up her neck until his lips were a hairbreadth away from her. His long hair tickling her ultrasensitive flesh.

"Ahhh my sweet Caira, you are much closer than I thought. Your body is quivering."

He pressed a kiss over her mouth and eased another finger inside her while his thumb circled her clitoris. "Let me take the edge off for you, sweetness. Then I'll make passionate love to you all night long. Let me make up for all the years we missed."

She could barely make out his words. She could only hear the raw ache of lust in his voice. His need drove her into a heated frenzy. She was desperate, frantic for an orgasm. She pressed her face against his chest. His masculine scent curled around her.

"Are you ready to come for me, Caira?"

"Yes, please . . ."

She shifted her hips and snaked her arms around his neck when his thumb applied the perfect amount of pressure to her clitoris. At the first sweet touch, her body pulsed and throbbed and responded with a hot flow of release.

He held onto her and absorbed her tremor as she rode out the gripping waves of her orgasm. Minutes later when her breathing finally regulated, she gave a small satisfied purr and loosened her grip around his neck. She touched his cheek and looked deep into his haunted, dark eyes.

Zarek pulled his hands from her damp bottom and drew his glistening fingers to his mouth. He inhaled her feminine scent and suckled his finger with sheer delight.

"Mmmm, you are as sweet as ever. Taste with me, Caira." He cupped her chin and drew her face to his.

She closed her lips over his mouth as his finger played between their tongues. His cock throbbed against her stomach. She ached to taste his juices, to feel his thickness in her mouth.

It was her dream after all. She could do as she pleased.

His mouth dropped to her neck and did magical things to her nerve endings as her hands slid down his body, touching him, absorbing his heat and energy. She eased away from his kiss, her mouth following the path of her hands until she sank to her knees before him.

God, he was so beautiful. He looked down at her. His long thick hair fell forward, shadowing his handsome face, hiding his scar. He smiled. A perfect smile that made her insides turn to liquid.

"Zarek, let me love you as I've longed to do." Her voice was a hoarse whisper.

He threw his head back and moaned softly. "Yes Caira, as I have longed for this too."

She leaned into him, mesmerized by his sensual voice. Lowering her head, she worked the button on his pants. His low groan of pleasure stirred the fire inside her. Easing his pants past his hips, she let his thick cock spring free. The scent of his arousal stirred her blood. Her hunger for him grew to new heights. She sheathed his cock in her small hand, stoking his smooth, silky skin as blood pumped through his swollen veins.

He was so magnificently huge. Fire licked over her loins and her mouth salivated, eager to sample his male juices.

When she flicked her tongue out to taste him, something stirred in the back of her mind.

Sometime from long ago.

Something distant.

Something forgotten.

She tried to grasp onto it but it slipped away much too quickly, leaving her with no time to examine it further.

Three

As her sweet silken tongue glided over his length he clenched his jaw and fought to hang on, wanting to prolong the exquisite pleasure longer, wanting to bask in the heat of her erotic mouth. Her hands cradled his tight balls, gently massaging them with the pad of her thumb.

Although he'd spent centuries watching over her, aching to hold her in his arms, he knew they were playing a dangerous game. By reciting the incantation she had awakened a great darkness and soon that darkness would try to consume her. Zarek could feel danger all around them, lurking nearby, waiting, just waiting to destroy their love once and for all. He needed to tell her, to warn her, but first he needed to love her the way she so desperately needed to be loved.

As her sweet mouth drew him in deeper, his orgasm mounted. Threading his fingers through her long golden hair, his hands followed the motion of her head as it swayed back and forth.

His need for her consumed him. A growl of longing lodged in his throat. Knowing his time with her would soon be over filled him with a hollow ache. He wanted to hold her, protect her, have her stay with him for an eternity. He gripped her shoulders, possessively, as her tongue swirled around his cock.

He pushed his hips forward, burying his cock in her throat, needing to get deeper. Not wanting to ever let her out of his grasp, he squeezed his hands, tightening his grip, bruising her delicate shoulder. She winced and he forced himself to release his hold.

His blood raced as she smiled up at him, gauging his emotions. He returned the smile, letting her know that passion, not anger, stirred his soul. He mopped at the beads of sweat trickling down his face as the pressure of an orgasm made him quake.

He closed his eyes in sweet agony, tension building, coming to a peak. "Caira, I'm going to come." His voice sounded strangled, barely recognizable. He began trembling from head to toe as his groin throbbed. Sparks multiplied and shot through his body as he gave in to his orgasm.

She parted her lips and poised his cock at the opening. Her hands continued stroking, coaxing his release. He bucked, driving his cock between her lips. Her teeth scraped his sensitive skin as her mouth closed over him like a vacuum, milking every last drop from his body.

She looked up at him. He reached out and held her face between his palms. The blue glow emanating from his body made her moist skin glisten. The love he felt for her rushed over him, slamming the air from his lungs.

He sucked in a tight breath. "Come here, Caira."

As he drew her mouth to his, a flash of anger coiled through him. So much time had been lost. The ache inside him gathered around his heart. They'd lost so many loving, caring moments like this together. To think her own father, Lord Montright, had purposely destroyed her happiness, and her future, by placing a curse on him and forcing her to marry a man whom she didn't love. Rage welled up inside him and he fought to control it. His time with her was coming to an end. He didn't want his anger ruining their last minutes. He wanted to make this night perfect for her, in case it was the last. He'd been in her mind for centuries and knew all her secret fantasies and desires, and was about to fulfill every one of them.

He tried to control the tremor in his voice. "Take me to your bedroom where I can lay you out and taste your body in its entirety."

Nodding anxiously in agreement, Caira swallowed. There was nothing in the world she'd rather do. She forced her rubbery knees to carry her down the hall. Keeping pace, Zarek walked beside her. The blue glow emanating from his body guiding the way. He walked silently, with easy, fluid movements that were both sensual and confident.

She pushed open the door and stepped inside. Before she could walk toward her bed, Zarek grabbed her and spun her around to face him. There was an ache of longing in his dark eyes. Powerful emotions tore across his face as his gaze glided over her. "So beautiful," he whispered. "I want you to remove your clothes, my sweetness. Let me see you. All of you. Naked."

She nodded, her voice lodged somewhere deep in her throat.

Taking two steps back, she slid her pants down her thighs, letting the silk pool at her feet. She eased her shirt from her shoulders, her pert nipples alerting him to the heightened state of her arousal. The material kissed her skin as it feathered to the floor. Awareness flared through her as she stood before him naked, needy—for his touch, and his love. Her chest heaved as his ravenous gaze dropped to her damp, silky curls.

She watched him come toward her. His cock was so thick. It excited and frightened her at once. She'd been with men before, of course. But those encounters were always fast, awkward, and uncomfortable and had left her feeling used and unsatisfied.

This man, however, was different from the rest. He was skilled. Patient. Concerned about her pleasures. Eager for her pleasures.

He cupped her bare sex in his hand. Her muscles clenched as fire shot through her body. She couldn't believe that with one simple touch, he made her burn up inside. Now she understood why she had never been able to find pleasure in another man's arms. Because none of those men were Zarek.

With the utmost ease, he gathered her into his embrace and in two long strides, carried her to her bed. As he laid her sideways on the mattress, across a splash of silken sheets, her long hair fanned her face. She moaned, her eyes beckoning him to take her. But he didn't take her. Instead, he straightened and took a long moment to admire her body. Her breasts grew achy under his tender gaze. She stroked her fingers over them and then her hand wandered lower, to touch her inflamed clitoris.

He pitched his voice low. "Open your legs for me."

She did as he requested.

"Wider."

Moaning softly, she opened her legs as far as they would go. When she brushed her fingertip over her clitoris, his nostrils flared, his dark hair fell forward. She almost came just from the heated look in his eyes.

He licked his lips, and she shivered in anticipation. He stepped closer, knelt on the floor before her, and spread her open. "That's good." His finger breached her opening. "Your scent is driving me wild, Caira." His warm breath feathered over her quivering sex and made her skin tighten. He pushed his finger in deeper. "Ahhh, you are very swollen."

He didn't move his finger at first. It remained motionless inside her, driving her into a frenzy of sexual frustration.

She threw her head to the side and arched into his touch, driving his finger in deeper, urging him to stroke her, to touch the spot that made her quake all over. He wiggled his finger, ever so slightly. Her breath came in a gasp as she concentrated on the tiny points of pleasure.

"Oh God." Her throat went dry as he slowly drew it out. The nerve endings in her pussy screamed in protest. She wiggled and writhed on the sheets trying to drive him back inside.

He held her down gently. "Don't move," he commanded. "Remain still while I kiss you."

She fisted the sheets in her hands and bit her lip to stop herself from crying out. He was so commanding. So in control. It was thrilling, exhilarating. How did he know she liked it this way? She hadn't even known herself until this very moment. He seemed to know her desires better than she did herself.

"If you move, you shall have no pleasures."

None too gently he gripped her inner thighs and pushed her legs open further. Her hips ached, but it felt incredible at the same time.

Using his fingers, he parted her labia and inhaled her feminine scent. A shiver passed through her when he growled his approval. His tongue touched her damp folds. It felt rough and cool and so deliciously wonderful against her scalding flesh. She wanted to move, ached to move, but remaining pinned to the bed, knowing she was forbidden to budge pushed her desires beyond anything she'd ever known. It thrilled her to know he was in control of her pleasures.

"You're dripping, Caira."

Her heart thudded. She could feel her juices pouring between her thighs. It tickled but she didn't dare squirm.

His finger followed the path of her liquid heat. "Ahhh, I believe you are ready for me, my sweetness."

"Oh God." Both fear and excitement coiled through her. She glanced at his magnificent erection.

His eyes softened as they met hers. "I will never hurt you, Caira. Ever." He responded as though he was in her head, able to read her every thought, her every desire.

Was it possible? Was he inside her head? Could he read her mind?

His hands brushed her face. His voice covered her like warm honey. "Yes, Caira. I know what you need, and I know how to give it to you. Now stop asking so many questions and let me taste you as I've longed to do." He breathed a kiss over her quivering pussy, making her incapable of coherent thought.

His warm tongue slipped back between her folds, stroking her with expertise. The warmth from his mouth spread out over her skin. He pressed his mouth over her clitoris and drew it between his teeth. He nipped at her until she cried out in pain and pleasure. His fingers slipped inside. Her pussy muscles clenched, driving him deeper into her hot sheath, and she fought the urge to buck against his hand. His powerful muscles bunched as he shifted position, pushing his tongue as far up inside her as it would go. Her mouth opened in a silent gasp as a powerful, overwhelming, all-consuming orgasm washed over her. She began panting, drawing in his warm, masculine scent, letting it curl over her.

"That's it, Caira, let me taste your sweetness."

She bit down on her lip as the room blurred before her. A stab of pleasure made her cry out his name. Her orgasm hit so hard the room darkened before her eyes. She couldn't think, she could only feel as Zarek moaned and licked every last drop.

He lifted his gaze to hers. "I love the taste of you."

He took one more long, luxurious lap at her, then grabbed her hips and positioned her into the center of the bed. He climbed over her, his eyes were darkly seductive, and his breath was labored. Juices pearled on the tip of his cock as he prepared her for entrance.

"Put your hands above your head."

She lifted her hands and gripped the headboard. "Like this?" came her breathy reply. How many nights had she laid in bed, arms restrained above her head, fantasizing about him? It was like he knew every fantasy she'd ever had.

"I do." His smile was wry.

God, he really was inside her head.

He crushed his chest over hers, twined his fingers through hers, and in one quick motion pushed inside. The fit was perfect and so deliciously full.

His fingers tightened over hers. "You feel so wonderful, Caira." His smoldering eyes glazed with lust and some deeper emotion that Caira didn't recognize.

She wrapped her legs around his waist and drew him in deeper. She gave a sexy moan. "Kiss me." Her voice trembled with emotion.

Zarek closed his mouth over hers, angled her body for a deeper thrust, and pumped into her. She met his every loving push with one of her own as she swiped her tongue over his. Their bodies moving in perfect unison.

Blinding pressure began building inside her as moisture pebbled her skin. The scent of their lovemaking saturated the room and closed over her. Fire burned through her, driving her beyond the brink of sanity. Her heart pounded, her body buzzed. It had never been like this before for her. So perfect. So right. So intimate. He rotated his hips, massaging her sensitive spot with the tip of his cock, bringing her as high as the moon and the stars.

She was close, so close.

"Zarek I . . ."

He buried his mouth in the crook of her neck. "I know, sweetness, let it go, come for me. Come with my cock inside you, and let me feel your liquid silk." His voice was a rough whisper over her skin.

Her pussy muscles tightened and gripped his cock. Zarek let go of one of her hands and slipped a finger between their bodies. He stroked her clitoris, his touch scorching her body as he pulled an orgasm from her. She let out a gasp, writhed on the bed, and locked her legs around his hips. Tightening her grip on the bedpost, she began quaking. Heat poured through her as another earth-shattering orgasm ripped through her body. Everything around her seemed to fade. Zarek clenched his jaw and she sensed he was struggling for control. His eyes darkened, his breath came in a burst as her pussy massaged his thickness.

He didn't even give her time to catch her breath before he flipped her over onto her stomach. "I'm going to make love to you the way you've imagined in your fantasies." His voice was thick, urgent, filling her with desire and apprehension.

She tried to twist around but he gently anchored her to the bed. She'd never tried this position before. It made her feel exposed. Vulnerable. Her alarm was obvious in her tone. "I don't think—"

Her resistance melted when his finger probed her wet pussy. Her whole body tightened in pleasure. As his finger moved deeper inside her another wave of desire engulfed her. She wiggled, her swollen clitoris scrapped against the soft sheets. She felt her face flush with heat and desire.

He pulled his finger out and gripped her hips, lifting her ass in the air, exposing her swollen cleft to him. His fingers brushed the length of her. "So perfect." There was so much emotion in his voice.

Caira took a deep gulping breath and gave herself over to him completely. Heart and soul.

Zarek slipped two fingers into her pussy and slathered her juices over her heated, fleshy opening. He placed a pillow under her curvy hips and gently pressed on her shoulders, easing her breasts onto the bed.

His voice dropped to a whisper. "Wiggle your backside for me, Caira. I promise you this will be better than any fantasy you've had."

She gave a low moan as he eased his cock into her pussy. Slowly, steadily, inch by inch, until her lubricated sex swallowed up his thickness. The depth of penetration nearly made her explode from sheer pleasure. Heat rushed through her.

She'd never experienced anything so magnificent, so intimate. She bucked against his body, lifting her hips higher in the air to give him better access.

He groaned and gripped her hips harder, driving his cock impossibly deeper.

"You're so tight, Caira, I won't be able to last long if you keep that up."

She bucked again, wanting him to give himself over to her.

He began panting. A low growl rumbled in his throat as she wiggled. A sweet moan filled her throat as his cock throbbed inside her tight warmth.

Everything about what they were doing felt so right, so familiar, like she had experienced this before.

"I want you to come inside me, Zarek. Let me feel your juices inside me."

"It's too soon. I want to give you pleasure first." His voice fell over her like a soft blanket.

She arched her back, giving him deeper access inside her body. "I cannot even begin to tell you how much pleasure you've given me, Zarek. This is for you. For your pleasure now. I want to give you what you need."

Groaning in ecstasy, he eased his cock out until only an inch remained inside her swollen sheath. He pulled her delicate folds open wider and in one quick trust he pushed into her. Hard. She gasped with euphoria and pitched forward as he rode her with the utmost expertise. His fingers bit into her hips and would surely leave bruises. Every erotic sensation running through her body heightened.

She moaned.

He growled.

Her muscles tightened in bliss as she indulged his cock. She ground her clitoris and whimpered as another orgasm tore through her.

As her muscles tightened around his cock, air rushed from his lungs. He pushed into her then stilled his movements, joining her in orgasm. "That's it Caira. Come with me." He came so hard she could feel his seed pulse through her body.

Caira dropped onto the bed, Zarek laid over her. He whispered into her ear. "You are amazing."

She drew a breath, trying to regulate her voice. "You are too," she whispered back. She'd had sex before but it had never been like this. "That was the most wonderful, intimate thing I've ever done."

He brushed her damp hair off her shoulders. He eased his cock out of her and rolled onto his side, pulling her with him. The look in his dark, passionate eyes turned serious. "I love you, Caira." The love in his eyes took her breath away.

And she knew, even though he was her dream lover, she

loved him too. She touched his face and pressed a light kiss over his sensuous mouth. "I love you too, Zarek."

Caira snuggled in closer, resting her head against his chest. Zarek pulled the blankets over them and tipped her chin until their eyes met.

She stifled a yawn and smiled up at him. Her eyes felt so heavy. She could no longer keep them open.

"Rest now, Caira. When you awake you will have much to understand."

Four

Zarek stared at the beautiful women asleep in his arms, a woman who'd been in his heart and mind for centuries. The love he felt for her rushed to his heart, making it difficult to draw his next breath. His gaze moved over her features as he ran his hands over her silky soft skin. Although she needed to rest, he couldn't let her sleep long, not while evil lurked nearby. Threatening to destroy their love.

He had to warn her. Prepare her.

He touched her chin. "Caira."

She stirred and snuggled in tighter. "Yes?" Her voice was whispery soft.

"Look at me, Caira. I need you to understand what I am about to tell you."

Caira perked up. She lifted her gaze to his. Her blonde brows puckered. "What is it?"

Zarek drew a breath. "You shouldn't have recited the incantation, sweetness."

She smiled. A slow sexy smile that stirred his blood. "Why? Didn't you enjoy being with me?"

"You know I did. But now you are in danger." Zarek sat up on the side of the bed. He gathered Caira in his arms and held her tight.

She rested her head against his shoulder. Her heavy lids fluttered. "Danger? Why would I be in danger?"

"Your father placed a curse on me, Caira." He touched the scar on his cheek. It ached. It always ached. It was a deep scar crafted by her father's sword. A reminder that Bella was never to be his.

She glanced up at him and placed her delicate hand over his.

"He placed a curse on me, banishing me to an eternity inside your portrait. To watch over you yet never be able to claim you as my own. By reading the incantation, you broke that curse, but you've also awakened the Keeper of Darkness."

She let out a heavy sigh. "Oh yes, the legend. It's not real. None of this is real." She closed her eyes, slipping back into sleep.

Zarek looked at his hands. The blue glow was fading. His time was almost up. He touched her cheek, bringing her back around. "It is real, Caira." He made his voice harsh so she would understand the seriousness of the situation. "My time is up, but before I go I must warn you." He felt his body grow cold, his movements were slow, his speech harder to come by. "You have awakened the Keeper of Darkness from his slumber and now a great evil will soon descend upon you. I cannot help you. The battle is yours and yours alone. You are the only one who can vanquish him."

Alarmed, her eyes sprung open.

He gently tilted her face up so he could look at her. "Just remember, I am with you." He reached out and placed his hand over her heart. "Here and always."

She blinked. The look on her face alerted him to her fear, her confusion. Zarek's heart ached for her. He fisted his fingers and fought down the anger raging inside him. He hated that he was so damn helpless.

"How? What if I can't?" There was desperation in her voice.

Zarek buried his face in her hair and inhaled her fragrant scent. "Then I fear death is the price of failure."

Hours later, Caira awoke, blinked her eyes open, and stretched her naked body. Early morning rays of sun burst through her window and warmed her bare flesh. She rolled onto her side. Her whole body felt lethargic, exhausted, as if she'd just climbed the world's highest mountain. Ignoring her discomfort, she drew in a rejuvenating breath and glanced at her clock. Just enough time for a quick shower before she had to deliver the cake to the reception. Rubbing her sleepy eyes, she twisted and threw her legs over the side of the bed. As she stood up, her shoulder throbbed, and her hips ached.

Suddenly, her mind filled with memories of last night's dream and the way Zarek's strong hands had gripped her hips and squeezed her shoulder.

The locket!

The incantation!

Dear God, it was a dream. Wasn't it?

Her heart slammed against her chest. Her mouth went as dry as burnt toast.

She quickly jumped from the bed and ran into the living room. Zarek was in the portrait, looking exactly like he always did. His dark haunting eyes stared down at her.

She blew out a breath she hadn't realized she was holding.

Of course it had been a dream. A very real, vivid, sexually satisfying dream. She must have simply kinked her shoulder in her sleep. Her mind urged her to believe none of it was real, because the alternate was much too scary to consider. Yet something in her gut compelled her to examine this further.

Desperately trying to shrug off her worries, she showered and grabbed a quick bite for breakfast. Before she headed out her front door, she took a moment to look at the locket draped around her neck. A cold shiver ran through her veins as her hands closed over it. When she brushed her fingers over the incantation a movement in the corner of her room caught her eye.

She turned in time to watch her cat jump up on her side table. Misty sat perfectly still, staring at the portrait of Zarek. The tiny hairs on the back of Caira's neck tingled as Misty starched her spine in apprehension.

The poor animal looked spooked. Caira crossed her arms and hugged herself. The cat wasn't the only one spooked. "Misty, come here."

The cat didn't budge. She sat there, immobile. An uneasy feeling closed in on Caira as she glanced around the room. Her gaze settled on the clock. If she didn't get moving she was going to be late. That wasn't good for business. She'd have to deal with her cat when she got home.

Stepping outside her apartment, she locked the door and made her way to her car. The whole time something in the back of her mind kept nagging at her. She'd never seen Misty act like that before.

But that wasn't what was bothering at her. It was something else. Something else in her apartment. Something wasn't right.

With her thoughts consumed by Zarek, Caira's day flew by rather quickly. She'd delivered the cake to the wedding reception and had run a few other errands. Before she went home for the night she wanted to speak with the gypsy from The Magic Boutique. She needed to find out if she was crazy, like her mind urged her to believe, or if the Legend of the Lover's Locket was indeed real, and her life was in danger, like her gut instinct suggested.

Darkness had fallen as she quickened her pace and turned the corner onto Fifth Street. She stopped in front of the antique shop, wrapped her fingers around the metal door handle and tugged. It didn't budge. Caira stepped back and looked for a sign indicating the store hours. Perhaps they were closed for the day. She moved to the window and peered inside. A small lamp burning in the back of the store gave sufficient light for her to see inside. Except for a few old crates, the store was empty.

Her heart lodged in her throat.

How could everything have been moved so quickly?

She needed to get home. To sort matters out in her mind.

She wanted to call on Nikki, but if any part of this legend were true, she didn't want her best friend's life in jeopardy. She rushed back to her car and hurried to her home. Drawing a deep breath, she knew she needed to get hold of herself and gain control over her emotions.

As her fingers closed over her doorknob she drew another deep breath. She needed to be able to think with a clear, rational head. She twisted the knob open and stepped inside. The minute she walked into her apartment she became instantly aware that all was not right. An uneasy, foreboding feeling closed in on her. Danger. Evil. Lurking nearby.

She felt it. It was all around her. All over her. In her skin. Crawling over her flesh. Her gazed fixed on the portrait.

"I am with you, Bella."

Zarek. She heard him. Clearly. He was in her mind. Reciting encouraging words of love. Her mouth opened in a gasp, her hand closed over her stomach. Oh God, it was real. The legend. The locket. The curse.

It was all real.

A dark figure moved in the shadows of her room.

Caira gripped the doorknob, ready to bolt.

"You can't run from him, Bella. He will find you no matter where you go."

She could hear the helplessness in Zarek's voice.

Caira swallowed past the lump in her throat. "What do you want?" she cried out, searching the room for something, anything to use as a weapon.

The figure moved out of the shadows. Caira's heart nearly failed. Her knees went weak, and she locked them to avoid collapsing.

Cloaked from head to toe in a black hooded robe, his face was masked in darkness. For that she was thankful. At least she didn't have to see the evil that lived beneath.

"Why have you awakened me?" His deep insidious voice crept over her flesh. She shivered.

Caira took a breath, centering herself. "To break a curse. To right a wrong."

"Be strong, Bella. Do not let him smell your fear."

"And you have no fear of the darkness you have brought forth in order to right that wrong?"

She did. With every fiber of her being, but she heeded Zarek's warning and fought to conceal her fear.

She worked to keep her voice steady. "No."

"Then you are most foolish, *Ma Petite Princesse.* Your lover's soul is the price you must pay to right a wrong and change the past." He moved toward the portrait.

Her pulse leapt, her heart skipped a beat. Her vision went fuzzy around the edges as light-headedness overcame her. She couldn't let him harm Zarek and steal his soul. She wouldn't allow it. She'd fight to her death to protect him. He had died because of her, and now she would die to give him back his life.

She gathered every ounce of courage inside her. "No!" She challenged with an unwavering stare as she took a threatening step toward the dark shadow.

"No?" There was amusement in his voice.

She knew she was no match for the Keeper of Darkness. She did not possess the strength or the wisdom needed to defeat him. He would leave here tonight with a soul and there was nothing Caira could do to change that.

"No. Let him live. Take mine."

"Bella, no. Let him take mine."

There was a long moment of silence before the cloaked darkness spoke. "You will sacrifice your life for your lover's?"

"Yes." Her voice was unwavering.

"Very well then."

"Bella, I love you."

"I love you too, Zarek."

She took a step closer to the Keeper of Darkness and stood proud. "Take me." The last thing Caira saw before she fell to the floor was the sharp blade of his sword cutting through the air.

"Wake up, Bella." Zarek touched her cheek and ran the pad of his thumb over her lips.

Slowly, her eyes fluttered open. "Zarek. Am I in hell?"

He gave a soft chuckle. "No, Bella, look around, you are in your apartment."

Her voice was not quite steady. "I don't understand."

He held his hand out to her and she eagerly accepted it. "The Keeper of Darkness could not take your soul." Zarek brushed her hair from her eyes.

"Why?"

"Because you showed him the true meaning of love."

Her beautiful eyes softened as they met his. "I did?"

"Yes, sweetness. You were willing to sacrifice your life for mine."

Her blonde brows puckered. Panic rushed across her features. "I couldn't let him hurt you, Zarek. I love you too much to allow anything happen to you." Her voice ended in a soft whisper.

Zarek's body shook as his heart filled with the love he felt for her.

Her small, shaky hands reached out to touch his cheek. "You're no longer blue."

He smiled and gathered her into his arms. "That is because the curse is broken. I am here, Bella. In the flesh. To stay with you. Forever." He carried her to the bedroom and laid her on her bed.

Her eyes fixed on his mouth. "What we did last night. The lovemaking. It was all real." It was more of a statement than a question.

"Yes, Bella. It was all real." He moved in beside her, resting his chin on his palms.

She laughed softly. Desire flickered across her face. "So that is why my body hurts all over."

He laughed with her. "Perhaps I should kiss your aches away."

Her eyes opened wide. She pushed her pelvis into his and he immediately hardened as heat and desire whipped through his blood. "Yes, perhaps you should," she purred.

Zarek planted his mouth over hers and kissed her possessively. She matched the passion and intensity of his kiss.

Joy sang through his blood. He'd waited a lifetime to claim her, to have her back in his arms, his life, and his bed.

And now, armed with the gift of true love, they would have the power to fight and destroy any evil that tried to come between them.

He inched back to gaze at her beauty. "I love you, Bella."

She gave him a wry smile and whispered into his mouth. "The name is Caira."

He chuckled. "Yes, of course, Caira."

She grinned. "But you can call me Princess."

This time Zarek laughed out loud and smothered her smirk with a kiss.

CATHRYN FOX graduated from university with a Bachelor of Business degree, majoring in accounting and economics. Shortly into her career Cathryn quickly figured out the corporate life wasn't for her. Needing an outlet for her creative energy, Cathryn turned in her briefcase and calculator and began writing erotic romance full-time. Cathryn enjoys writing dark paranormals and humorous contemporaries.

Kili's Ice Man

Delilah Devlin

One

$\mathscr{K}$ili couldn't help it. As Ice Man's exhalations came sharp and harsh, her own shortened and rasped. Perspiration gathered on her upper lip. Each powerful thrust caused muscles along his glorious arms, buttocks and thighs to bunch, then stretch, as he reached to deliver another mighty drive. Kili's body tensed, her nipples tightening hard as diamonds, heat coiling low inside her belly—

"Are you feeling all right, sweetie?"

Kili fumbled to flip off her bio-plasma screen before looking up at her best friend and cubicle mate, Willa. "Fine!" she said, her voice a little sharp and high. She cleared her throat. "I'm fine. Why do you ask?" Did her arousal show on her face? She plucked away her blouse from her chest.

"You look a little hot and bothered. Got a fever or something?" The sparkle in Willa's green eyes contradicted her concerned words. Willa knew full well about Kili's dirty little obsession. "Honestly, I don't know how you can watch that stuff—those gladiator matches are so barbaric," she said, shivering delicately.

"I was just prepping myself for the pitch to the Centurion reps. Have to know what I'm selling, right?" she said, reaching for her purse beneath the desk.

Willa lifted a finely arched auburn brow. "Uh huh, and that outfit's what you usually wear to a marketing meeting?"

Kili glanced down at her short-skirted suit. "It's black and covers everything." She tugged down the hem in back. "Mostly. It's slimming. 'Sides, I'll be seated the whole time."

Willa shook her head. "You know they're probably going to send the home office management boys—pencil necks—to the meeting. Don't get your hopes up they'd take anyone off tour for a little sales pitch."

Kili stifled a twinge of disappointment. "A girl's gotta dream," she muttered.

Willa looked beyond Kili's shoulder and stiffened. "Come to Mama!" She pursed her lips and whistled softly. "Spoke too soon. Looks like they sent at least one gladiator."

Kili glanced over her shoulder just in time to see her boss, Wilson Pickering, and an entourage winding their way down the aisle. Behind Wilson strode the pencil-neck management team, but bringing up the rear was the man who set her pulse quickening faster than a starship caught in Black Hole gravity—

The Ice Man! The man she'd fantasized about for weeks since he'd been drafted into the major leagues. As he towered above the men in the lead, she forgot how to breathe, staring at his chiseled jaw and the unbelievable shoulder span that just got wider the closer he came.

"This is Kili Wilder," Wilson said, smiling although he lifted one questioning eyebrow in her direction. "She'll be presenting our pitch for the new network spots after lunch."

Kili clamped shut her slackened jaw. Now was not the time for her to go starstruck over arms that looked like they could bench press a hover car. She shook hands with the management team, and then drew a deep breath to fortify her jellyfish legs as Ice Man reached for her hand.

She thought she was ready, back in control, until his large hand engulfed hers. One look up into his ice blue gaze and her tongue stuck to the top of her mouth. "Uhmmmm."

Humor wrinkled the corners of his piercing eyes. "Nice to meet you, too."

Kili almost melted into a puddle of goo. The low timbre of his voice wrapped around his words like a caress as his gaze swept over her face and down her body, lingering on the length of her bare legs.

Wilson cleared his throat, drawing her attention away from the way the gladiator's blond hair brushed the shoulders stretching his wine-colored team jersey.

"We'll meet back here at one o'clock sharp. Right, Kili?"

Wilson said the last with just enough emphasis to make her flush. Lord, had her lust been that transparent?

As the men walked away, Willa snickered behind her. "Wow, you sure made an impression."

Heat flushed her cheeks as she stared after Ice Man's amazing ass. "Some friend you are—you could have warned me he was coming."

"And spoil the surprise? Oh my God, the look on your face!" she chortled, and slipped her arm through Kili's. "Come on. Let's do lunch. Give you time to lower your blood pressure. Think about it—he uses brute force and a saber. You'd be bored talking to him inside an hour."

Checking her makeup in the mirror hanging on the cubicle wall, Kili snorted. "Remember, I've had smart. Daniel was clever enough to figure out how to date three women from the same department without any of us catching on. I don't want smart. I want . . ."

"Ice Man?"

Her stomach still quivering, Kili assumed a bland expression. "Someone *like* that, yeah. Not too bright. But strong enough to make me feel overwhelmed." She closed her eyes and sighed. "Can you imagine stroking those arms?"

Willa leaned into her side and snorted. "I'm thinking his ass would be even finer."

Kili groaned. "This isn't helping. I need to get my mind off those glutes."

"Girlfriend, I have just the thing to get him out of your system."

Staring through the shop window, Gunnar Thorsson didn't know whether to strangle the woman or haul her from The Lunch Break chair and kiss her breathless. The way she wriggled to snuggle her butt deeper into the contoured, black-upholstered chair succeeded only in raising the hem of her little black skirt centimeters higher. He wasn't the only man in the vicinity to notice.

The technician in the lab coat who'd fitted her virtual-vacation helmet to her head had to readjust electrodes glued to her temples and chest because he couldn't stop ogling her long legs.

Gunnar swore again. A perverse throb centered in the knot of flesh rising between his legs. Perverse because he shouldn't be here. Shouldn't be lusting after a woman who was as shallow as a mud puddle.

One thing for sure, he'd liked her better before she'd untangled her tongue to speak. The way she'd stared with those chocolate eyes when they first met, a blush rising above the collar of her pale blouse to flood her face with hectic color—her lips parting as she'd moaned—had him hard in an instant.

Instinctively, he knew she'd wear the exact same expression when he took her to bed.

He'd left Pickering and the management team and circled back to Kili Wilder's desk, intending to ask her to lunch and arrived just in time to hear a mention of his name. Curious about her first impression of him, he'd ducked into a neighboring cubicle, feeling foolish as a boy with his first stirring of lust, and listened to the tail end of her conversation with her friend.

So she wanted him . . . or someone just as *dim-witted*. Disappointment, unaccountably sharp, pricked his irritation. She was just like all the "gladiator groupies" who'd thrown themselves at him since he signed. They wanted the "fierce warrior" fuck, not the real man inside.

He'd almost blown her off. But then he recalled her soft brown hair, slender figure and endless legs and thought, why the hell not? He'd give her exactly what she wanted—while taking his own pleasure.

So he'd followed the women to the food court in the belly of the office building, keeping well behind and taking a separate elevator so they'd never know their next meeting wasn't an accident. When they'd passed the food kiosks, he continued to hang back, curious about their destination.

"Wow, you're the Ice Man! Can I have your autograph?"

Gunnar started, surprised to find another Lunch Break tech standing beside him, his face flushed with excitement. The younger man must have rushed out of the store when he found a sports celeb gawking through the window.

A thought, reprehensible as it was delicious, crept into his mind.

"Tell you what"—Gunnar paused and glanced at the tech's name tag—"Oscar, I'll do you one better. Can you hook me up with her?" he asked, nodding toward Kili. "But sit me somewhere she can't see me?"

The technician's eyes widened. "I don't know, sir. Co-vacation is supposed to be consensual. She's already engaged with the computer."

Gunnar reached into his pocket and pulled out his wallet. "Want ringside tickets when the Centurions come to town? I wanna surprise my girlfriend."

Kili sucked in a deep breath and blinked as her eyes adjusted to white, searing sunlight. Her first glance at her vacation setting sent her stomach plummeting. Where was the desert island with the horseshoe strip of pale sand and navy sea? Sure, heat radiated off the ground in suffocating waves, but where was the cabana boy in the Speedo?

Instead, an endless savannah stretched in front of her with tall, golden grass waving in the hot breeze and gnarled, stunted trees dotting the horizon. "What the hell?"

Stones skittered behind her and she spun to find a large, male figure standing on a rocky knoll. At least the program had gotten that much right. The Ice Man's incredible, burly physique was nude except for a furry loincloth that draped from a slender cord at his waist, leaving the sides of his tanned hips and his massive, sleek thighs bare.

The breeze ruffled his pale hair as he strode toward her, his sharp gaze sweeping down her body, a predatory gleam in his eyes.

Kili's heart thudded and her nipples tightened, the sensitive tips pressing into supple fabric. She glanced down and noted she too wore an animal's skin, tanned and buttery-soft. The miniscule top barely covered her breasts and was knotted between them. Another soft garment draped around her hips, and the breeze licking up her thighs revealed she was totally nude underneath the crude clothing. "Now, that's attention to detail," she murmured. But if this was her fantasy, why weren't her hips slimmer?

When she brought up her head again, Ice Man's attention was directed behind her and his entire body tensed. He hefted a spear in one hand, holding it above his shoulder.

She followed his gaze and saw an enormous creature crouched low in the grass staring back at them, cat-like with long fangs curving like tusks from its gaping mouth.

Before she could gasp a warning, Ice Man let loose his spear and snagged her wrist, dragging her behind him as he ran back up the knoll.

A hideous, snarling scream erupted, and Kili forgot that none of this was real—her heart accelerated and her breath rasped as she ran like the wind, flying up the rocks behind the gladiator, grateful for the fur-lined booties that shielded her feet from the harsh terrain.

Just as they crested the knoll, the sound of heavy paws thundered behind them. She didn't dare look back, but Ice Man dropped her hand and drew another spear from the leather sheath strapped to his back. With a lithe twist, he turned and launched the spear straight into the large cat's chest.

The animal dropped like a rock without a sound, dead before it hit the ground.

Kili shivered and reminded herself, *This isn't real.* All that blood spurting in a gurgling stream from the creature's gaping wound was just part of the program hooked up to her brainwaves to deliver a virtual adventure. She'd never really been in danger, but her racing heart didn't seem to know the difference. The trembling that shook her body felt authentic, as did the excitement that thrummed through her veins.

She drew a deep, steadying breath and lifted her head to find Ice Man's gaze leveled on her.

His chest gleamed with sweat, his jaw was taut, and hunger glinted in his hard eyes.

"I'm guessing this is where we're supposed to share celebratory sex, huh?" she quipped, already feeling her body soften and moisten in anticipation.

A slow grin stretched his sexy mouth, revealing a flash of startling white teeth. His arm snaked around her waist and pulled her close, his mouth descending toward hers.

Kili let her eyelids droop, shutting out everything but the curve of his firm lips as she tilted back her head to await his kiss.

When his breath brushed her mouth, she shivered and

snuggled her aching breasts against his naked, sweaty skin. He smelled earthy—of wood smoke and healthy *man!*

A masculine growl rumbled from deep inside him, and he paused, opening his mouth to speak.

Kili melted, clinging to his rock-hewn arms, a breath away from heaven.

He inhaled, pressing his brawny chest ever closer, and said, "Ugh!"

Two

$\mathscr{G}$unnar jerked back his head and tried again. This time, "Urgha!" was all he could manage to cram past vocal chords that had forgotten how to function. *Fuck!* Now, how was he supposed to convince the woman he was smarter than the average caveman?

Kili's lips stretched into a grin, and a wicked light danced in her dark eyes. "They must have downloaded my personality profile," she murmured. "Do they know what I want or what?"

He almost dumped her on the ground, but their bare midriffs were fused by sweat, and his barely clothed cock snuggled in the well of her soft belly—the possibilities were way too tempting for him to overlook for pride's sake.

Besides, "Little Gunnar" didn't seem to care that Kili thought he was the brains of the operation and unfurled beneath the loincloth, straining against the contrary woman's body.

Big Gunnar hoped like hell his southern brain hadn't forgotten how to function, too, because it sure looked like she was warming up fast to the idea of that celebratory sex.

Her palms molded the contours of his chest, and she rose on her tiptoes to glide her lips along his chin. "Mmmm, I've wanted to do this since the first time I saw you clobber the Zoltan Twins in the 'Rumble in Orion.' " Her arms encircled his shoulders as she strained upwards.

Aware more beasts might be lurking in the grass, Gunnar knew he had to take the party indoors. He silently cursed the idiot who thought a caveman fantasy was the way to turn the tables on the woman. Never mind he'd bribed the tech to place them in the scenario of *his* choice. At this point, he figured he'd earned a little reward for all the earlier aggravation she'd put him through.

The same program that had robbed him of speech flashed a picture into his mind of a route to his abode. He gripped Kili's hair to get her attention, and then took advantage of her gasp to kiss her mouth hard, stroking inward for a quick taste of what was to come.

Jesus, she was sweet—and hot! She mewled and rubbed on him like a kitten, until he seriously considered lifting her to fuck her where they stood.

Her mind must have traveled the same sexy path, because she hopped up and wound her legs around his waist before he had a chance to come up for air.

Unable to resist a quick feel, he slipped his hands beneath her suede skirt to clasp both bare cheeks. Her ass filled his palms—soft and round, yet surprisingly muscular. He clutched it tight and ground his cock against her open sex. Now, only the supple hide of his loincloth separated him from heaven.

A distant roar reminded him they needed to find shelter. "Nnnnn," he protested, as he let her slide down his body.

Swaying, she held onto his arms for a moment then stepped away, her eyes blinking. "All right, I'm thinking they should have given me at least a few verbal commands you would understand. How do I say 'fuck me' in cave lingo?"

Gunnar growled his frustration, and then quicker than she could gasp, he bent and shoved his shoulder into her abdomen, forcing her to fold over his shoulder. If he was doomed to play a ravaging caveman . . .

Kili screeched and scissored her legs. "Put me down, you Neanderthal!"

Grinning, Gunnar reached up to swat her delectable bottom, and took off in the direction of the cave just beyond the next rise. With the sun resting on the horizon, he broke into a lope, not wanting to be caught in the dark with whatever creatures the program had decided should populate their adventure.

As a bonus, Kili stopped her caterwauling and held on for dear life, grunting softly as her stomach bounced on his hard shoulder. However difficult their communications issues, she understood he meant business. Nothing was going to get in the way of his seduction now.

The ground beneath them blurred as Ice Man picked up speed. Kili grabbed for his waist to save more abuse as she flopped like a rag doll.

Thank God, this was a fantasy! The last rays of the sun struck her naked upended bottom, but thankfully there was no one around to witness the sight. She could just imagine how ridiculous she looked from a frontal view—all wide, glowing ass cheeks. "Twin Moons over the Savannah" could have been her pitch line.

At the base of a tall rock outcrop, they passed an open fire where the grisly remains of some small creature roasted on a spit. Suddenly, he slowed and ducked low, scraping her ass along the roof of an overhanging rock.

Kili gasped, and then let loose a shrill shriek when he dumped her onto a bed of furs. Tossing back her hair, she came up on her elbows and glowered.

The object of her "Fantasy-Gone-Wild" grinned, looking entirely too pleased with himself as he pulled the strap of the spear case over his head. Not that she could blame him. He had her exactly where he wanted her, and she was hotter than a rocket in reentry.

And that was before he reached for the knot at the side of his loincloth.

Kili *almost* opened her mouth to give him a scathing set down just to keep him humble, but remembered he probably wouldn't understand a word. *Plus* she'd just paid half a week's wages for the privilege of taking a look beneath that furry flap. She licked her lips and stared as it slid down his thighs to pool at his big feet. Then she took a deep breath and followed the length of his braced legs back up to their juncture. "Wow!" she whispered.

His cock was as thick as her wrist and slightly darker than his bronzed skin. Uncircumcised. That wasn't something you saw very often, except in men from the farther reaches of the galaxy. Primitive, barbaric men.

Her body expressed its enthusiastic approval with a wash of

silky delight. But that wasn't the end of the spectacular show! His glorious cock rose slowly as though hoisted by an invisible crane. No way should something that heavy lift under its own steam. And holy shit! It was still expanding—in both width and breadth.

"They didn't have to exaggerate that much," she said, feeling a little breathless. "I was all ready to be impressed—but wow!"

"Hrmph!" He snorted, bringing up her gaze to find him staring at his cock with a frown on his face.

"I'm thinking I'm glad this is my fantasy, because that's actually going to fit, isn't it?" she said, gulping.

Ice Man's gaze returned and one dark brow rose—mocking her unease. His glance dropped to her breasts, lingering for a moment before sliding down her body to rest on her legs.

A thrill of excitement poured into her loins, a pure adrenaline rush of super-heated lust. "I'm thinking I'm overdressed."

"Hrmph!"

The man certainly had a way with snorts. His hands went to his hips in a universally male "I'll give you five seconds to start stripping" pose.

"Well, this is what I came for, right?" she said, her confidence lagging by the second at the heat staining his face and the sharpness of his gaze.

This was *her* fantasy, so naturally he'd be just as impressed with her overblown physique or her money back! However, her *ass-nemesis* made it impossible for her to feel comfortable stripping in front of perfection. But how could she distract him as she shimmied out of her clothes? "Maybe . . . we should have some of that . . . roast meat, before we—"

Ice Man stepped over her, placing his feet on either side of her hips. The man obviously had no body-part-nemeses to give him any insecurities.

As well, he seemed awfully proud of the cock-that-could-choke-an-elephant. This close, it seemed to stretch above her—endless, and well, damned intimidating.

"You know, I'm thinking we should take a little time to get to know each other first," she babbled, alarmed when he dropped to his knees and leaned forward on his arms, his wagging appendage tapping her belly before he eased down.

Closer now, she noted the flare of his nostrils, like he was taking in her scent. Was scenting a stone-age mating ritual or was he sniffing out his next meal? Her nerves jumped when a low growl erupted from deep inside his wide chest, and he leaned down.

Her hands shot up and braced against that wall of solid muscle, but he seemed as immoveable as the rock ledge on which she lay. "Um, I don't suppose you're the kind of guy who just likes to lick his food first, huh?"

The corners of his lips twitched, making her wonder if her expression had clued him in to her nervousness. His downward momentum didn't stop until he lay on top of her—every overwhelming inch.

She forgot how to breathe. Instead, she wheezed, afraid to inhale too deeply and accidentally press upward against the long erection. Already, it burrowed between her legs and lapped over the top of her miniscule mini.

The fat, bulbous tip of him burned her quivering belly. "This is nice," she said quickly. "Maybe we could stay like this for a little while?"

"Uh ugh," he murmured, and dropped his head to nuzzle her neck. Again, he inhaled, sniffing her like she was a tasty treat. A thick thigh nudged between hers.

Despite her misgivings, her nipples dimpled and she relaxed her knees to let him slip between them. The base of his cock settled against her pussy, and she couldn't help the little gasp that escaped her lips or the liquid pleasure that bathed his heavy sac as he rubbed against her. Her body softened instinctively beneath his.

No less breathless, now she opened to him, lifting her knees on either side of his hips to help him snuggle closer to the part of her drowning in excitement. "Maybe you *are* the kind of guy who licks first, hmmm?"

As though he understood her need to slow things down, he nudged beneath her chin and mouthed her skin, sucking softly as he followed the column of her throat.

"Yes, please. Just like that," she whispered, her arms creeping around him to slide her hands up his neck and into his thick, blond hair.

She'd never considered herself easy, *exactly*, but going with the flow of this fantasy felt natural—even right—and if The Lunch Break had conjured the object of her daydreams to deliver the ultimate lunchtime getaway, why should she resist?

Slowly, Ice Man worked his way to the bare expanse of her upper chest, sliding his body downward so she missed the feel of his balls nestled against her pussy. She may even have moaned a protest, but he quickly substituted new delights that blew the loss right out of her mind.

His wicked mouth suctioned and nipped at her mounds until she gasped and moaned according to his will. Soon she was mad for him to remove the garment knotted between her breasts. Her nipples swelled and tightened, aching for his caress.

However, he seemed content to trace the edges of the garment with his tongue, licking over the tops of her breasts and between, then nosing the spiking nipples pressed against the thin suede fabric. When at last he sucked them through the cloth, her belly jumped and quivered, and moisture seeped to wet her swelling labia.

But it wasn't nearly enough. "Please," she moaned and tugged at his hair, trying to gain his attention, trying to urge him to get to "the points" a little faster now.

Rather than unknotting the garment, he tugged it lower, freeing her breasts, but trapping them above it, so they were squeezed over the top.

The constriction excited her almost as much as the heavy-lidded look he gave her rosy, dimpled areolas. Each shallow breath she managed to drag into her air-starved lungs lifted the distended tips like offerings.

Please, please suck them! She'd never known her breasts could be so sensitive, so attuned and eager for one man's attention. Foreplay involving her breasts had always been nice, but only an appetizer.

Now, she'd gladly skip the main course if he'd just *suckle*—his wicked mouth to her taut stems.

His fingers closed around one peak, plucking, squeezing, twirling—igniting a firestorm that raced from her breast to her womb.

Kili's breaths shortened, each exhalation a soft groaning sob as her body undulated, seeking to bring him toward her center. Her fingers threaded through his hair and wrapped tight around his skull as she tried to pull him down and bring his lips to her throbbing crests, but he resisted.

Frustrated, she curved her belly, craving more connection, and ground her mons against his belly.

Motionless, he stared at his fingers plucking her ripening nipple. Finally, he grunted, a harsh and fiercely masculine sound, and swooped down to take her breast into his mouth, drawing so hard her toes curled into the furs.

He didn't stop suctioning—not when she keened high and sharp, not when she clamped her legs around him and bucked, her belly shivering and jerking as he tortured her.

Kili stared at the jagged ceiling of the cave and savored the sensations of the rhythmic pulls of his mouth, the weight of his solid body pressing her into the fur, and the coiling heat building deep inside her. She thought she might come from just his mouth on her breast—*a first.*

But he released the tip and glanced back up at her face. The darkness creeping into the cave painted deep shadows beneath his sharp cheekbones and cast his eyes in an almost sinister light. Again, he seemed a predatory animal, pausing to gauge whether the mouse he teased still had the strength to play.

Kili panted, unable to rally her mind to wonder what he planned. She trembled, anticipating what he'd kiss next and hoping for something even more breathtaking than what she'd already experienced. "Please, Ice Man."

Perhaps her urgent tone and the way her nails dug into his flesh gave him the message. The corners of his lips curved upward, forming a slight, satisfied smile. Rather than moving lower down her belly, he simply switched to the other breast, clamping hard on her ruched nipple.

Her back bowed beneath the unrelenting pressure of his lips. Her head thrashed, every sensation painfully intensifying. His hot mouth surrounded her; his teeth grazed and chewed the hard, swollen tip. Even the fur beneath her felt erotically charged—soft, yet prickly on her back and bottom, a counterpoint to the sleek, smooth chest and belly pressing her deeper into the bedding.

She was so wet—so unbelievably hot! *Everywhere*! Moist, humid heat. Sweat, slick and searing, bonded their bodies where skin met skin. Her sex wept, the swollen folds clasping around nothing, aching to be stretched and filled with his cock.

Teeth bit into her nipple and Kili arched her back, crying out. Ice Man wasn't just a gladiator—he was a love god!

Three

*G*unnar ground his cock into the fur and groaned. Sweet Kili was killing him—coming apart in his arms—and he hadn't even entered her yet.

Her body shuddered, and she was making those kittenish sounds again—the ones that made his balls so hard he thought he'd explode. Each little jerk and rolling wave of her hips had him ready to slide back up and slam inside her tight, hot cunt. Well past ready, she was hotter than a saber burn.

He didn't know why he'd drawn out his lovemaking so long. Kili seemed eager enough to get on with it, but his hunger drove him to explore her body and discover every erogenous secret it withheld.

With the women he'd enjoyed before, foreplay had been pleasant, but strictly a preliminary round building to the Grand Slam.

However, Kili's breasts seemed more delicious and velvety

than any he'd ever tasted and miles more responsive. Even her cries were more compelling, building a painful urgency in his loins. One he knew he had to temper or he might hurt her.

Never mind this was just a fantasy—*a real mind-fuck.* They'd share the memory of this wild-ass dream. Gunnar grew determined she'd never forget him.

So, he curved his tongue around one beaded little point and pushed it against his teeth, rearing his head back to tug it, side to side, pushing her past comfort into the pleasure-pain zone.

Her sexy little gasps and groans quickened like the panting of a cat and he smiled, wondering if she'd purr or snarl when she came.

The scent of her drove him crazy. Her arousal, a mix of wild exotic musk and clean woman, blended with the flavor of her skin—every bit as appetizing as a cinnamony sticky bun.

He released her breast and rose up on his elbows to admire his handiwork. Both nipples were reddened, the tips thick and engorged. Confined above the shelf of her little top, they looked like presents ready for unwrapping.

Because he felt every inch the primitive male, he growled, letting the sound rumble through him, and lowered his eyelids to half-mast before glancing up at her face. Then he reached behind his head and drew down one of her small hands and placed it on her breast.

Kili needed no coaching. Her graceful fingers fluttered over the straining peak, cupping the heavy mound then concentrating her caresses around the blushing areola. Her breaths puffed between her pursed lips as she stared down at what her fingers teased.

He leaned close and tongued her nipple between her fingers. He stroked along the appendages, sucking on fingertips and fluttering against the erect bud that peeked between them. Then he slid down her body to lick along the bottom of her ribcage, all the while holding her fascinated gaze.

Her gaze unknowingly held a touch of innocent wonder, while the teeth nibbling at the corner of her mouth betrayed more than a hint of worry.

He wished he had the faculty to reassure her, but then again, it was empowering knowing he held her entire attention and her body was his for the taking—and so attuned to his lovemaking he'd have her purring before he finished.

He growled again, deep in his throat, loving the way her eyes widened and her breath caught.

From fear or arousal? The latter, he thought, because her legs clamped around him tighter.

He scooted down again, his face now level with her rounded belly. He planted kisses and licked the salt from her moist skin, loving the way her belly jumped each time he surprised her with a sexy bite.

Her navel drew him, the opening a tender little hole that fit the tip of his tongue perfectly. He stroked inside, rimmed it, and pushed on the soft button at the center and her thighs splayed wider as her hips slammed upward against his chest.

Almost there, sweetheart.

He slid down further and grasped the edge of her little skirt and rolled it down to the top of her mons, exposing the first dark hairs peeking from underneath. Feeling a little more teasing was in order, he traced the edges of the skirt with his tongue and fingers, dipping beneath the band of fabric. Her hips wriggled, and he guessed she was ready to lose the skirt entirely.

So was he. He rose up, moving to the side, and pushed the skirt down. She lifted her hips to aid him, and once free, she sighed. She spread wide her legs. An invitation to play he couldn't resist.

Gunnar lay down beside her and trailed his fingers from her breast to the top of her cunt, twirling his fingertips in her dark curling hair, while his gaze drank in the sight of her white thighs and moist, swollen cleft.

Her hips rose from the fur, and a hand wrapped around his fingers to urge him further down between her legs.

He resisted the pressure and smiled to let her know he wasn't dense—just teasing.

Her answering frown caused a rumble of laughter. At least he hadn't forgotten how to do that.

She must have taken his laughter as a challenge, because she lifted the same hand and reached over to cup the head of his cock, squeezing it gently.

His reaction was impossible to deny—pre-cum smeared her palm, and she used the moisture to glide around his head, rubbing and squeezing harder.

He slid a finger deep between both sets of soaking lips and tucked its length into her opening to stroke in and out. *Christ*, she was wet!

Her inner walls clasped his finger, and her hips tilted up again to take him deeper. Her hand smoothed over the plump head of his cock and beneath to grasp the shaft. She squeezed up and down his length. "What's it gonna take to make you understand? I need you inside me," she said, her voice tight, strained.

Gunnar understood all right. His own body was primed, ready to cover hers, ready to thrust inside and find release. Instead, he drew a deep breath to calm his racing heart and speared her cunt with a second finger, easing inward, twisting to scrape his knuckles against her inner walls. He wanted her screaming for it.

Kili turned her body toward him and lifted a thigh over his, pressing closer to scrape his cock against her belly as she stroked up and down. "Didn't they program you to fuck?" Her look of desperate determination undid him.

He pushed her back on the furs and mounted her, shoving her thighs wide apart to settle his cock against her pussy. He stared at where their bodies met, thinking nothing could look sexier, and nearly groaned when she slid her fingers down to part her folds and position him at her entrance. Her hand tightened around his shaft and pulled him closer.

Poised above her on one arm, he burrowed a hand beneath her bottom to clutch her ass and slowly pushed himself inside her, cramming past the furled lips into her moist, clasping channel.

Sweet Jesus, she was tight and hot as he worked his way into her, flexing his hips to push forward then pull out, loving the drag and pull of her inner muscles on his penis. Gritting his teeth, he fought the need to slam into her and tunneled slowly inward, eager for her heated walls to surround him.

In. Out. Digging deeper with each stroke. Sweat gathered between his shoulder blades as he concentrated on the measured motions, finding a rhythm that kept him sane, under control.

The obstruction, when he butted against it, shocked him.

Kili's eyes flew open, and he knew the program had given them a gift—a little "celebratory" first for both of them. His whole body shuddered as he paused, cursing inwardly at the evidence of this incredibly erotic beginning.

His body clenched as he fought to regain control, but he was too far gone, too aroused to be gentle. Holding her wide-eyed gaze, he pulled back his hips and slammed back inside, tearing through the thin membrane.

Kili gave a strangled scream, but her arms encircled him, pulling his torso closer as he crammed his cock inside her silken sheath, pressing relentlessly forward, forcing himself as deep as he could reach. Only then, could he gather the strength to halt his movements.

He hovered above her, dragging in deep breaths while his arms and thighs trembled as he fought to hold himself back. He squeezed his eyes shut to close out the sight of her with her brown hair glinting from the firelight, her features strained and taut.

Her hands smoothed up his back, sliding easily in his sweat, then glided back down to trace his spine, widening as they reached his hips. When her fingers splayed to cup his ass, he opened his eyes.

Her tremulous smile was sweeter than any he'd ever seen. "I'll have to ask them to rerun this program," she whispered, her voice a little unsteady. "But I'll ask them to do a few things differently—like get you here on top of me, inside me, faster. You feel . . . incredible."

He hated the reminder this was only a fantasy, and that at any moment they could both be plucked out of their bed of furs and parted. Time was only relative inside the program. Half an hour on The Lunch Break time clock couldn't last. His aggravation was tempered only by a feeling of overwhelming tenderness at the echoing sadness he read in her moist eyes.

Would she miss him? *The real him?* The one trapped inside the monosyllabic Cro-Magnon.

However, now wasn't the time to dwell on partings. His body clamored for release. Since she didn't betray any signs of further discomfort or pain, he pulled slowly out, almost free-ing the crown of his cock, then thrust forward again.

Her cheeks billowed around a gusting breath. "Oh yeah. Again," she said, urging him to move with her hands.

Another series of pulls and thrusts, the same as before, earned him a deep sigh and a quivering response from deep inside her inner walls. He increased the speed of his steady strokes, varying the angle of his hips, seeking, testing, until she gasped—and he knew he'd found that little spot of hyper-sensitive nerve endings inside her vagina. The one he'd heard about, but had never taken the time to find with any other woman.

Scraping slowly over it, he delivered shallow thrusts, careful to rub the spot with the ridged crown of his cock. He gauged her rising excitement by her shallow gasps and the way her fingernails dug into his ass.

"Ice Man," she keened, her back arching and her eyes squeezing shut. "It's happening! *Jesus*, now!"

He withheld himself, continuing to stimulate the spot, want-ing to draw out the moment as long as he could.

"No, no, no! Please, fuck me!" The rising pitch of her voice and the desperate way she thrashed her head told him she neared release.

Over the edge himself, he lengthened his strokes and hooked his arms beneath her knees to push them up and forward, tilting her hips at just the right angle to slam an inch or so deeper.

His cock became a hammer. Hard as steel.

Unleashed, he pounded against the cradle of her thighs. Driving his cock hard into her hot, juicy cunt. His thrusts quickened, sharpened—until tension gripped his thighs, tightened his balls. His jaws locked, and every muscle of his body strained toward release.

Kili's hands dropped from his shoulders and clutched the furs. Her sweet mouth opened around a scream as she arched her back. Convulsive ripples, like waves of liquid heat, caressed his shaft.

He was lost. He slammed into her hard one last time and felt his balls erupt, jetting cum through his cock in a pulsating wash of fire.

Afterward, he was loathe to release her legs and continued to rock his hips against her. Tension slid from his body while the last ripples rolled along his cock, slower now, fainter.

Slowing like the rhythm of his heart.

He removed his arms from beneath her knees and lowered himself on top of her, easing her legs alongside his thighs, while he rested most of his weight on his forearms.

Bodies aligned but still connected, they stared into each other's eyes for a long moment, until Kili's gaze fell away.

She drew a deep breath and blew it out. "Wow. Think there's

time for a second round?" Her attempt at lightness sounded forced.

He hated the reminder their time was nearing an end.

Apparently, she did, too. A shadow crossed her face, and she brushed his hair back with her fingers and tucked it behind his ears. "If you were real . . . if this were real . . . I'd want to stay like this forever." The admission seemed real as the breathy catch in her voice.

Gunnar didn't want to let go either. He hoped she'd say more and give him a key he could use later to unlock the soft, sexy side of Kili when next they met.

Here inside the program, he though he could see the heart of the real Kili, the one inside the brassy, smart-mouthed career woman. Here, she had no need for sexual subterfuge, no reason for sarcasm. She believed her thoughts and words were private—between her and a virtual reality program regulated by law to provide confidentiality. Here, he could eavesdrop on her heart's desires.

He just wished he could ask her outright what the hell they were.

Four

$\mathscr{K}$ili framed his face with her palms and stared into his blue eyes. Now that her breath had caught up with her, she was content to stay like this—physically linked, blanketed by his large body. She felt truly surrounded.

Finally, overwhelmed.

This was the feeling she'd been seeking, although she hadn't really known how wonderful and all-consuming it would be.

Now, she just wished she could figure out a way to find it outside the cave—back in her real life.

If only she could find another man like this caveman.

Knowing she'd never find his likes again, she sighed. "This is pretend, right?" she said softly. "I'm your cavewoman. You're my caveman-boy-toy," she quipped. She knew he didn't understand and was glad for it, but she babbled away just the same. She liked to talk after having explosive sex—and saying whatever came to mind helped her keep from thinking too much about what lay ahead. "Although I think I'll leave the grunting to you. Your delivery is quite masterful, by the way."

His lips twitched and a growl rumbled in his chest.

She tilted her head to the side, trying to read the intent behind his ice-blue gaze. "You understand me, don't you?"

He lifted his chin, and his gaze speared hers. "Ugh!"

Her breath caught. "Then every time I asked you to fuck me and you didn't, you were just playing, right?"

His lips stretched around a wide, wicked grin.

"Oooh!" She smacked his chest and laughed. "I'm almost mad at you. But I really like where we ended up, so I think I'll forgive you."

When he ground his hips into her, she knew he understood her point. He punctuated it with a nip of her earlobe, which turned into sexy licks that rimmed her entire ear. Finally, he lifted his head to press a quick kiss to her mouth.

"Yeah, I know," she said, slipping her arms around his shoulders to snuggle closer. "This feels great. You feel . . ." She lifted her shoulders in a shrug. ". . . incredible!" She giggled. "For a woman who makes her living finding just the right words, my brain seems stuck on one so far as you're concerned."

His head lowered and he nibbled at her chin, then nudged it up to suck the soft, ticklish skin along her neck.

"Oooh, you know exactly what I love," she said, biting her lip, when he sucked particularly hard.

His hips circled over hers, and his cock stirred slowly back to life inside her.

Kili rubbed her inner thighs restlessly alongside his. Round Two was underway! "But I wish I had another name for you. I feel kind of silly calling you Ice Man all the time." She grabbed a handful of his thick hair and pulled his face back. "Will you understand if I tell you I'm Kili?" She pointed to herself. "Kili." Then she pointed to him.

He leaned to one side and lifted a hand to point a finger at himself, "Gnnnn." He appeared frustrated, and his eyebrows lowered as he tried again. "Ggghhhhn," was all he could growl out.

"Ghhnnn. Guuun? Shall I call you Gunn? Do you like that?"

He huffed a breath and nodded. "Ugh!"

She grinned. "I like that so much better than Ice Man. It's not like you're really him. But it's not like you'd make great date material in real life, either. I know guys don't like to talk, but a 'yes' or a 'no' every once in a while is essential." Only that was a lie. If only she *could* find someone like this caveman. Her "Gunn." She had no illusions the real Ice Man was anything at all like this roughly tender man.

One blond eyebrow quirked upward and his head canted to the side.

"This virtual dating—I've never considered it before. A girlfriend turned me onto the vacation aspect, and thought a quick fling was just the thing I needed." She traced the edge of his sharp cheekbone, not wanting to meet his gaze when she spoke so intimately about her inner thoughts. "I'm awfully glad she brought me here. I was feeling a little nervous. The guy you look like took my breath away, and I knew I wasn't going to get an intelligible word out if I didn't do something drastic to get back in control.

"Now, I think I'll have no problem at all, because I'm not going to be the least bit attracted to him. He's not anything like you. All beating his chest, ape man, growling at the cameras. You're perfectly matched to my personality. I wanted a man who was less talk/all action, and they gave it to me."

It must have been a trick of the light because it looked as though he crossed his eyes.

"Next time I come here I'll definitely ask for some adjustments. Although, I may have to mortgage my house, because I think you're going to be an addiction."

His lips curved and he dipped down to nibble at her cheek.

"I know I'm talking your ear off, but I'm still feeling chatty like I always do after a really wild bout of sex—and this was the wildest I've ever had, so I have lots to talk about. I used to drive my old boyfriend nuts when all he wanted to do was sleep."

His hips lifted and surged back inside—hard.

"Are you jealous? Or ready for me to shut up?"

Another sexy thrust had her lifting her knees to let him ease deeper. "A little of both, huh? No wonder Willa is always in a good mood after lunch," she said, her breath getting lost again as her body revved up. "But I'm thinking I should have brought a change of underwear. I bet I'm soaked through."

A low-pitched growl sounded from outside and Gunn's head drew back sharply, his expression instantly hardening.

"We could ignore it," Kili said, trying to turn his face back toward her. *My time can't be up! Please, not now!*

He glanced back down, looking as though he was about to say something. Instead, he shook his head and leaned down to kiss her hard. When he ended it, he withdrew his cock, sliding it slowly out, his jaw tightening as though the effort was killing him.

She held him with her legs a moment longer, and then let him go. Despite the balmy air inside the cave, her skin dimpled at the loss of his heat.

He rose to his feet and grabbed the sheath of spears.

Kili's breath caught on a moan. Standing near the mouth of the cave, red gold firelight flickering over his sweat-slick skin, his cock still erect and glistening from her juices—she knew she'd carry that picture with her for the rest of her life.

And then he was gone—and she was sucked back into the black dream-void, a low whooshing sound filling her ears.

Kili waited, feeling numb as the tech removed the electrodes from her chest and then slipped the helmet from her head. She accepted his hand to help her out of her seat and tugged at the bottom of her skirt.

Willa came bouncing from around the corner of a booth. "Well? How'd you like it?"

Kili gave her a thumbs up, although inside she felt like howling. "I think that did the trick."

When the management team filed into the conference room, Kili steeled herself—and fought the urge to tug once more on the bottom of her skirt to make sure everything was covered. Her undies were tucked safely into her purse, and she hoped like hell she didn't drop anything she'd have to bend down to retrieve.

Wilson nodded and proceeded to direct the men to the sideboard where drinks and snacks awaited. Kili stood beside the projection screen, ready to run through her prepared spiel.

Then Ice Man entered the room.

She thought she had herself back under control, but one

look at his silvery blond hair and bluer-than-blue eyes and she forgot how to breathe again.

She forced her gaze away and gripped the papers in her hand hard, deciding then and there she wouldn't look at him once during the presentation.

Her heart was too vulnerable, her emotions too raw. She'd had the adventure of a lifetime during a thirty-minute lunch break—and nothing would ever be the same.

She'd found—if not love—connection. Something she'd never known with a man before. But her lover didn't exist.

Now that she knew how that "connection" felt, she wanted to find it again—with someone. But at the moment, it hurt too much to look at the man whose face would forever be etched on her heart.

"Ahem, Kili," Wilson's voice broke through her thoughts, bringing her back to the purpose for the meeting. The management team had all taken their seats and waited with pencils poised above pristine white pads of paper.

She gave him a nod and cleared her throat before sweeping her gaze over the men assembled to hear how she was going to increase the number of female viewers who tuned in to watch the Centurion Gladiators' matches.

But her gaze snagged on Ice Man who remained standing beside the snack table, his arms crossed over his chest, his gaze boring into hers—wearing the exact same expression as her "Gunn."

Swallowing, she tried to remember what she'd scripted for herself to say, but mortification settled around her like a heavy blanket of embarrassment when she couldn't remember a word she'd rehearsed.

She dropped her gaze to her papers, realizing she couldn't go with the pitch she'd prepared if she couldn't remember it.

She drew a deep breath and decided to go with her gut. "Ever wondered what makes a woman hot? She'll tell her girlfriend it's an animal—a monosyllabic caveman in a loincloth—all bulging pecs, thick neck, and rippling abs. That man will certainly catch her eye—make her pause and stare. But how does he keep her interest?" She paused to swallow and wet her dry mouth.

"Is that a rhetorical question?" Ice Man's deep voice came from the sideboard.

Finally, she was forced to meet his gaze. Her heart skipped a beat at the smoldering warmth she found there. "I am inviting . . . your answer," she said carefully, pushing the words past stiffened lips.

"Gunnar Thorsson is the team's elected rep," her boss added. "He's got final approval on the spot. He has a dead-on instinct for what people want."

Gunnar? Her eyes opened wide.

His gaze didn't waver. "A woman likes the danger and strength the warrior embodies, but she really wants more than a simple 'yes' or 'no'—or a primal grunt. She wants the warrior to unstop a clogged sink, or teach a child to play ball . . . and to tell her roughly, but eloquently, how beautiful she is to him." The last seemed like a caress.

Christ, it couldn't be him. Her Gunn. But he was giving her back her words . . . and more.

Had what happened in the cave been real, or at the very least, mutual? And who would she kill later—Willa or The Lunch Break staff for hooking them up? If it really was him, he'd remember every stupid thing she'd said.

Her throat tightened around a lump at the back of her throat. It couldn't be true. She was just projecting her desires onto him.

Her eyes filled. She shook her head as she stared at him, hearing the murmured questions from the management team as she tried and failed to pull herself together.

Ice Man's arms dropped to his sides and he stepped forward.

Alarm filled her. *Christ, don't let him get too close or I'll fall apart!*

But he opened his arms and enfolded her next to his rock-solid chest. His hands caressed her, soothing up and down her back.

She inhaled, dragging in his now familiar scent—not the wood smoke part, but the manly musky part. She clutched the front of his jersey and tried to make sense of her reactions and figure out a way to run from the room before she made an even bigger fool of herself.

His hand cupped the back of her head, tugging on her hair to tilt back her face. His gaze held hers for a long, intense moment, and she wished like hell she understood what it meant.

Then his lips slammed down on hers in a searing, mind-blowing kiss.

His lips ate hers, molding, sucking, drawing her back into a familiar firestorm of searing emotions and lust. Finally, his tongue thrust inside her mouth to stroke hers, and she was helpless to resist. She tangled her tongue with his and moaned.

Christ, the man could kiss!

"Oh, I see you already know Gunnar," Wilson said from

somewhere behind Ice Man, an edge of dismay in his voice. "He has an excellent track record, actually, for gauging what consumers want. Kili?"

She lifted her hand, one finger extended, telling him to wait just a second. Her heart pounded as she recognized the sound rumbling from the chest pressed to hers.

Ice Man drew back and settled his forehead against hers, his breath hitching every bit as raggedly as hers. "Sweetheart, it's gonna be all right," he rasped.

"But, I don't understand," she said. He kissed like Gunn, growled like Gunn . . . Her heart accepted him as Gunn.

Ice Man snorted and kissed the tip of her nose. Then he bent to whisper in her ear, "Ugh!"

DELILAH DEVLIN has lived in Saudi Arabia, Germany, and Ireland, but calls Texas home for now. Always a risk taker, she lived in the Saudi Peninsula during the Gulf War, thwarted an attempted abduction, and survived her children's juvenile delinquency. Creating alter egos for herself in the pages of her books enables her to live new adventures—and chronicle a few of her own (you get to guess which!).

The Hottest
One-Night Stand

Lisa Renee Jones

To Diego,
who believes in dreams coming true.
This story wouldn't have been possible
without your support and influence in too many ways to detail.
Thank you.

One

He made her think of sex.

Hot, wet, blow your mind kind of sex. The kind she hadn't had in far too long. Correction. Ever. She had never, ever had the kind of sex this man made her want.

Suddenly, the dingy little roadside bar she had stopped at because her cell phone had no signal seemed a darn good decision. It offered a damn delicious distraction from her long hours on the highway.

Standing at the bar, dressed in all black, dark hair touching his broad shoulders, he looked like a wild, exotic form of Zorro. He was the kind of man that made women pant. Even her, conservative little Jessica Montgomery, was ready to jump his bones.

She leaned against the railing behind her, forgetting the irritation over the bartender ignoring her. Her eyes dropped to his truly stellar ass just as he turned and looked at her. There wasn't time to avert her gaze, nor did she really see the point. They were in the middle of nowhere Texas, two strangers, likely to never see each other again.

She was checking out his ass and didn't plan to hide it.

What she didn't anticipate was the intensity of his gaze. Dark eyes assessed her, taking her in from head to toe. He inspected her with such completeness, she felt exposed on some carnal level. Yet, oddly, she was at ease with the feeling.

She couldn't help but notice the contrast in their appearances. He was dark, where she was light. His hair was black, as were his eyes, and his skin was a perfect light chocolate brown. She was fair, with hair the blondest of blond, porcelain skin, and eyes the palest of blues. Something about their differences made her feel a little thrill inside. The thought of her fair skin contrasting against his dark, her blond hair draped against his black, was enticing.

She watched him watching her. Those eyes of his, those deep, dark eyes, only served to enhance his quintessential sex appeal.

For the briefest of moments, she had the oddest sensation of being touched. Goose bumps spread across Jessica's skin, her nipples tingled and then hardened, and a light ache spread between her legs. Shocked at the utterly sexual response he evoked in her, Jessica found it difficult to catch her breath.

No man had ever aroused her so easily.

Perhaps, it was her lifestyle that made her respond so readily. After her divorce, she joined the district attorney's office and had since been burning the candle at both ends, with little to no time for social affairs. Not that she was eager to jump into a relationship after her ex-husband's nasty comments about her overall appeal. As hard as she tried to dismiss his harsh words, they had stuck with her. Especially the part about her being undersexed and outright boring in bed.

Funny, the wetness clinging to her panties didn't make her feel undersexed. Quite the opposite. This stranger had her feeling quite ready to get naked and take him on in a little game of one on one.

She laughed and broke eye contact with him.

What in the hell was she thinking? She hadn't had sex in eighteen months, and she was wet and wanting a man she didn't even know. Was she insane?

Apparently, because her eyes moved back to her Zorro as if she was desperate for another glance. But it was too late. He had turned away and was paying the bartender, preparing to leave. Seconds later, his boots scraped the floor as he started toward the door.

She watched him saunter across the floor, his walk graceful but masculine at the same time. His hair fell down his back, not too long, not too short. It made her long to run her hands through it, to touch it and feel it draped across her body.

As he reached the door, she fought the desire to run after him. It was crazy, but she wanted this man in a powerful way. Willing herself to stay in her chair, Jessica took a deep breath. And that's when he turned, fixing her in a hot stare. In his eyes, she saw the potency of a desire she had never experienced.

If only he wasn't leaving. Inwardly, she laughed. Not that she would ever have a fling with a stranger. She bit her bottom lip. But if she ever did, she'd want him to look exactly like the man who just walked out the door.

The last two putters of the car engine dispelled any hope that her trip would be a good one. It was bad enough that she had let the sexiest man she'd ever seen slip through her fingers. Now, only a mile up the road, Jessica was stranded.

Of course, she had made it into some dingy motel parking lot. For that she should be thankful. Still, from the looks of the building, it was no great find.

Shoving open her door, she stepped out into the hot Texas night and stared at the blinking red sign. The wind whipped around her shoulders, dirt blowing at her feet. A storm was coming, and she had car trouble. Looked like she would be sleeping at a place with no name other than *Motel*.

"Great," she muttered as she slammed her door shut and began a stomp toward the office door. She didn't know a damn thing about cars. What kind of help was she going to get in a place like this?

Stepping into the tiny lobby that held only a dirty chair and a counter enclosed in glass, Jessica didn't feel any more optimistic about staying here. She wouldn't be sleeping much this night.

There wasn't a person in sight as she stepped toward the counter. "Hello?"

No response.

Jessica looked around her, hugging her body with her arms. Deserted and a bit eerie was the only way to describe the feel of the room. She just wanted a warm bed and some sleep, dreadful as they might be. Tomorrow, with a broken-down car, she already knew she would be in hell.

For tonight, she just wanted someone normal to come to that glass window and give her a room. Then, she would snuggle under the blankets and dream of the sexy Zorro-looking man from the bar.

If only he were here, getting a room with her. To be alone and naked with that man would more than make up for the challenges of the night and tomorrow. She could practically feel his body next to hers. Hard muscles pressing against her body, his hand on her breast, kneading and teasing . . .

Jessica mentally shook herself. What in the heck was happening to her? She never fantasized about men. Yet, now, in the middle of a crisis, she could feel her panties, for the second time in one night, wet with wanting.

She needed a room and sleep. She knocked on the glass. "Hello?"

Just as Jessica opened her mouth to call out again, an old man with a cigar hanging out of his mouth shuffled, feet in slippers, through a side doorway.

"We're full," he said grumpily, his wild eyebrows making him look like some kind of spook.

Jessica felt a wave of panic. "But my car is broken down, and I can't get anywhere else."

The cigar stayed in his mouth moving up and down. "I don't know what to tell you, lady. First come first serve around these parts. Should have been here ten minutes earlier. I had one room left." He laughed. "Not no more though."

Sleeping in her car didn't sound like a good option. "How far to the next hotel?"

"Three miles."

Three miles . . . she could walk three miles.

"It's the land of nothing between here and there. Pure ghost town."

She frowned at the man and shoved a strand of her long, blond hair from her face. "But you won't give me a room?"

"Told you, lady," he said and had the gall to have a hint of irritation in his voice. "Don't got one to give."

Mumbling not so nice words under her breath, Jessica turned toward the door. Talking with this rude man was getting her nowhere fast. Pushing open the exit door, she stepped outside and was instantly slammed with a gush of wind and rain. Droplets of liquid gathered in her hair and on her cheeks.

"Can this night get any worse?" she whispered into the darkness, feeling very alone and on edge.

As she moved toward her car, the wind seemed to pick up several notches, throwing wetness and dirt around her body.

All Jessica wanted to do was get to Brownsville in time for her nephew's party. She had to be back in court in two days. If she didn't get to her sister's place soon, she'd have to shove her present at her nephew and turn around and leave.

By the time she yanked open her door, she was dripping wet. The wind blew so hard she could hardly get into her car. Panic was building as she slid inside. She sat in her seat, darkness surrounding her, and for the first time since the night she found her husband with another woman, tears began to fall.

The turbulence that erupted took her by surprise. So long suppressed, her emotions seemed to simply invite themselves to explode. Her hands clenched onto the steering wheel, and she rested her forehead on her knuckles. For long moments, she could do nothing but let the tears fall, trying to understand what she was feeling.

This wasn't like her. She didn't cry. Getting to her family had just felt so important. She'd been working night and day at the DA's office, trying to forget the past, and focus on career. But now . . . she needed more. Seeing that sexy man in the bar had jolted her a bit, reminding her that she had to stop hiding from her personal life. She needed one. Fear over the past was holding her back from exploring any new relationship and she knew it.

Thunder rumbled around her as rain fell hard against the windows. She sat in the middle of it all and had her own storm. Swiping at her cheeks, she reprimanded herself. Tears were not going to solve her issue of being stranded. She needed to think through her options.

Jessica was pondering her thoughts when a loud knocking made her scream. There was a man at her window. Her hand went to her chest, shocked at the presence. But more so because it was a familiar face. "Oh my God."

It wasn't just any man. It was a dripping wet version of Zorro from the bar.

What should she do? Let him in? Lock the doors?

She decided to crack the window. A little. "What are you doing in the rain?"

"You can't stay in your car all night. It's not safe."

"Getting out isn't either."

"You're under a tree in lightning."

"You're in the rain," she argued.

"Trying to get you out of it."

"I *am* out of it."

"I'm not," he said testily. His long hair was plastered to his face. "Come inside with me. I promise it'll be safer than here."

Water was splattering in her face. "How do I know I can trust you?"

He gave her a steady stare despite the water splashing around him. "You don't." Pause. "Room 112."

Then he turned and walked away.

Two

She called after the stranger as he walked away. "How'd you know I was out here?"

But he didn't turn, didn't answer.

Jessica sat there, fretting. Had she not wished for an opportunity to be alone with the very man who just welcomed her to his room? A man who offered to spare her a scary night alone in a car, under a tree, in an electrical storm?

Then thunder boomed overhead. She jumped and reached for the door.

Somehow, a night alone with her sexy stranger sounded better than a night alone in her car. Not thinking, just acting, she stomped through the rain, her purse the only item she carried with her.

Once she was at room 112, she stood before the door, dripping wet, hair stuck to her face and stared at the number sign.

Maybe this was a bad idea? What if he was a serial killer, or a rapist, or . . .

The door opened.

Her mouth dropped. There stood her stranger with no shirt on, looking like a poster for the world's sexiest man. His hair hung in damp strands around his face, barely brushing the tops of his muscular shoulders. He held a towel in his hand and interest in his eyes.

"Come in," he said, stepping backward and holding the door open for her. For the first time she realized he had a distinct Hispanic accent. Not too strong, but evident enough to slip into her mind and entice a response.

She was so soaked in rainwater that she literally dripped.

"I'm wet," she said, feeling the need to state the obvious.

He smiled, a slow, sensual smile that said he read into her words. "Thanks for the warning." He held up his towel, offering it to her. "I think we'll manage."

The room was lit by only one small light. In a quick glance over his shoulder, Jessica took in the shadows created by the light dancing seductively on the walls. She barely glanced at the rest of the room, so mesmerized was she by this man. One thing she was now certain of, he was alone.

Licking the wetness from her lips, she accepted the towel, the intimacy of sharing it hard to ignore. Rubbing her hair, she stepped tentatively through the doorway.

His eyes, dark and mysteriously sexy, followed her path. He stood directly in front of her and didn't seem inclined to move. Arm reaching over her shoulder, he pushed the door shut.

The action put him so close their faces came mere inches apart. The towel was forgotten. She could feel him even without ever physically claiming to touch. His scent, a woodsy, clean smell wrapped around her, enhancing the feeling of invisible touches.

Their eyes locked. Slowly, he took the towel from her hand and wrapped it around her, holding it on either side of her body and cocooning them together. "I'm glad you decided to come inside, mi Hermosa."

She gulped. He had said something complimentary in Spanish. She knew that much. And for some reason, it really got to her. Someone else could have said those words and they just wouldn't have set her on fire the way they did from him.

Soft, sexy and incredible arousing, his voice danced along her nerve endings. She reached for words, struggling to speak coherently. "I'm still not sure I should be here."

"No?" he asked, his eyes searching her face. "I think you want to be here." He let the towel rest on her shoulders and ran a finger down her cheek.

The touch should have scared her. The whole situation should have. Instead, she felt oddly exhilarated; in fact, she had never felt so alive and eager. Eager for what? was the question. A question she definitely wanted answered.

A tiny little light flickered in her mind. Maybe this man, this incredibly alluring stranger, held within him a means of escape from her past. Alone in a hotel with a man she hardly knew wasn't her style. But then neither was divorce.

Circumstances had delivered her here, alone in a motel room, with a man as sexy as any of her best fantasies. Looking into this man's obsidian eyes, she began to wonder if he could take her beyond her insecurities.

This seemed a rare opportunity to find a new her. And

damn, she needed a new her. She hated how her ex had made her feel. In her professional world, she knew how to put on a show. How to seem strong and secure. But when it came to intimacy between a man and a woman, the past didn't let go. Insecurity ruled.

A knowing look slipped into her stranger's eyes. He repeated his words, an edge of understanding now in his voice. "Yes," he said softly. "You want to be here."

For the first time, in far too long, everything woman in her was awake and alert. She wanted this man. She didn't know his name, didn't know a thing about him, but she wanted him. "I have to be here."

One corner of his mouth lifted, and his finger slid down her neck. "Not so. You have choices." He paused a beat. "You're in no danger with me." His eyes, which had been following the path of his finger, lifted to hers. She felt his hand settle around her neck, gently touching her. "Whatever you want, you can have without fear. Comprendes?"

She didn't know what to say. His face was slowly descending, and her moment of decision was upon her. If she kissed him, she would want more. Did she want to? Could she abandon reason and fall into this man's arms?

Head swimming in confusion and desire, she couldn't think. Just knowing his lips were about to be upon hers, she felt her nipples harden and throb. Wet and now aroused, they pressed against her bra, begging to be touched. The feeling sent a wave of heat across her skin and settled with a not-so-subtle impact between her thighs.

She wanted this. She wanted him.

His lips lingered above hers, breath mingled with her own,

teasing her anticipation. And she understood the purpose. Understood his hesitation was a question.

Yes or no?

Thoughts, fears and a few remnants of logic raced through her mind. It was her body, though, that held the answer. Desire and physical need was controlling her, not rational thought. She let her purse slide off her shoulder, onto the ground. Then, she inched forward ever so slightly and pressed her lips to his.

Her decision was made.

It was a gentle kiss, lips pressed to lips.

He leaned back and looked at her and then whispered something in Spanish before feathering kisses on her lips. One, two, three . . . . and then he dipped his tongue into her mouth. She felt the light brush of it against her own. She whimpered.

Jessica's eyes fell shut and he slowly, perfectly, seduced her with his kiss. Hands at her sides, she longed to touch him. He closed the remaining space between their bodies, bringing them thigh-to-thigh and hip-to-hip.

Proof of his arousal pressed against her stomach. A thought, provocative and arousing, danced in her head.

He was hard *for her.*

It was an empowering realization. This sexy man wanted her. She had aroused him, made him hot for her. Suddenly, a one-night stand, no strings attached, felt liberating.

Her hands went to his waist, and the feel of his skin under her palms ignited the need to feel more. She touched him freely then, feeling the flex of muscles under her palms.

She wanted him. Really wanted him, like she had never wanted before. What was so wrong with that? It had been so very long since she had felt such need, such heat. Maybe she never had. He deepened the kiss, and a heavier fog of desire built, threatening to consume her.

No, she had never felt this kind of arousal before. It was as if a magnetic force pulled her to him, making her yearn to feel his body next to hers.

And they had only just begun.

His power to make her ache in places he didn't touch was nothing short of amazing. This was new. This was incredible. This couldn't be missed.

To hell with her conservative, good-girl lifestyle. For once in her life, she wanted to let go and feel. If her ex-husband had made her feel these things . . . she shoved the thought away. Thinking of him, her past, might mess with her head and rattle her confidence and cool the desire her Zorro was so effectively building.

Instead, she sank into the kiss, sliding her palms up his back. Giving into the need to be closer to him, she pressed her chest to his, her nipples aching sweetly as they brushed against him.

He held her close, touching her face, her hair, her neck. Gentle caresses etched with sensuality and tenderness. This was not a man who acted as if he wanted only sex.

He was a man intent on *making love*.

And she was intent on experiencing *all he had to offer*.

He pulled back slightly, softly wiping the wetness from her bottom lip with his thumb and then taking her hand in his. "Come, mi Hermosa, you are going to catch cold. We must get you out of those wet clothes."

Heart racing at mega speed, she let him lead her across the room. When they were in the bathroom, standing at the sink, he turned her to face the mirror. He stood so close to her, she could feel his hardness pressing against her bottom.

What would he do next? Nervous anticipation laced with excitement had her trembling ever so slightly. Not knowing what to expect from him should have frightened her. Instead, it seemed to heighten the excitement.

Using the towel, which he still held in one hand, he began drying her hair. "I noticed your hair back at the bar."

Her eyes lifted, locking with his in the mirror. "You did?"

"I noticed a lot of things," he said, tossing the towel on the counter.

Her eyes widened. "Like?"

One of his hands spread wide on her stomach. "There is loneliness in your eyes."

"I choose to be alone," she said defensively.

His hand inched its way upward and then stopped. "I have no doubt." He studied her lips as if he wanted to kiss her and then slowly raised his eyes back to hers. "But not tonight."

She digested his words. He was right. *Not tonight.* Tonight she wanted to be with him. But she didn't have the courage to say it out loud.

His hand began inching upward again. She could feel anticipation building in her stomach and in the tingling between her legs. Where was that hand of his going?

Courage. She repeated the word several times in her mind, even as she fought through her sensual fog. "No," she said softly. "Not tonight."

Jessica wondered if he knew how much it had cost her to say those words. To admit she wanted to be here. How much she had to overcome to stay. Here. With him.

Somehow, she thought he might. His body knew hers in ways no one ever had. Could he read her so easily through and through?

His mouth settled at her temple, pressing lightly as his hand moved up the line of buttons on her shirt.

He unbuttoned it slowly, using both hands and then sliding the wet material off her shoulders. Tossing it on the counter, as he had the towel, he looked at her in the mirror.

Jessica stood facing her own reflection in a lacy black bra. She was covered, but not. Her attention shifted to him. She watched him in the mirror. His hands and eyes moved over her shoulders. The darkness of his skin against hers stirred something inside her.

"Such fair skin," he murmured and then lifted his eyes to hers, clearly thinking the same thing she was. Their differences aroused him as well. Holding her gaze, he reached for the clasp at her back and unhooked her bra.

Nervously, her hands went to cover her breasts, holding the material in place. His hands slid up her back, warming her skin with their caress, as they returned to her shoulders. "It's your choice," he said.

Nerves and old fears were haunting her. Her ex-husband's harsh words about her sexual performance, and even her body, were like demons in her head. But she wanted this man. He made her feel sexy and adventurous.

And she wanted to be all that and more.

Wanted it with all her heart and soul. The ghost of the past was destroying her, and she wanted them gone. "No," Jessica said, though her voice quivered. "I don't want a shirt. I want this." Her hands dropped, and she shrugged out of the bra. Moments later it lay with her shirt.

She didn't look in the mirror, averting her eyes downward, as she took a deep breath to calm her nerves. She could feel him looking at her.

"You are truly lovely." His fingers ran down her neck, but still she didn't look up. "Such full, beautiful breasts. And your nipples . . ." He stopped speaking, and she looked into the mirror, locking eyes with him. She could see the depths of his arousal in his eyes.

He looked down at her nipples. "They are very aroused, are they not?" He looked back up at her. "Because you are cold or because you are thinking about what I might do to them?"

She wasn't used to talking about this type of thing. Her ex's words raced through her head. Boring, sexless. "I'm . . . not cold."

One of his hands ran the length of her hair, and his lips nuzzled the sensitive spot behind her ear. "Meaning, you are thinking of what I might do to you?"

Her lashes fluttered. "Yes," she whispered.

"Open your eyes, mi Hermosa." She forced herself to comply, meeting his gaze. "Now. Tell me what you want me to do to you. Wht is your desire?"

Three

Tell him what she wanted him to do? She'd never told a man what to do during lovemaking. She clenched her teeth at the words and corrected herself. This was sex. Just sex. The thought of telling this man what she desired, both scared and excited her. She swallowed and wet her lips. "I . . . I don't know."

His eyes narrowed in reprimand. Bringing his mouth to her ear, he nipped her earlobe ever so gently. "Yes, you do. Tell me."

Their eyes locked in the mirror yet again. His face was still low, cheek pressed to hers. She could smell him, enticingly male with a hint of spice. Her senses were so alive she could still taste him, even though it had been long minutes since they kissed.

There were so many things she could do with this man. "I want . . ."

"You want what?" he asked as his hands moved back to her stomach. "Tell me. You want what?" He repeated the words.

"Touch me." Jessica's voice was barely audible.

"I am touching you."

"No." She swallowed, no, gulped. "Touch my . . . breasts."

He didn't so much as hesitate. His hands cupped her breasts, taking their weight and ever so softly kneading. But he didn't touch her nipples, and she knew it was on purpose. He was teasing her and it was working. Her nipples ached, begging for relief. For satisfaction.

"Like this?" he asked.

"No." He started to move his hands, but she covered them with her own. "I mean yes, but . . ."

His brows inched up in the mirror. "Tell me what you want."

She took a deep breath. What she wanted was the courage to be bold and spicy and everything a sexy woman would be with a man like this. "Touch my nipples."

He murmured something in Spanish, kissing her neck and then lightly pinching her nipples between his fingers. She moaned as a rush of sensation washed over her.

Her nipples throbbed with painful bliss, his hands now more diligent in their exploration. No longer was he holding back, waiting on her. He seemed to be acting on his own needs.

Jessica's head fell back on his shoulder as ripples of pleasure controlled her, forcing her eyelids to her cheeks.

Unexpectedly, she felt herself lifted and turned. Now, sitting on the counter, eyes open, she found him at her feet, removing her shoes. It was an incredibly erotic sight, him at her feet, hair half dry and shirtless.

Sliding up her body, hands trailing up her calves and thighs, he seduced her perfectly, teasing her with what was to come. He brought his mouth to hers, kissing her with slow, erotic strokes that made her feel as if she might melt from the heated need building in her body.

Never, ever, had she been kissed the way he was now kissing her. Arms wrapped around his neck, she was lost in him, kissing him with equal hunger.

Against her lips, he asked, "When was the last time you had an orgasm, mi Hermosa?"

Her ex had never cared if she came or not. He blamed her if she couldn't, and that was always. "Does a vibrator count?"

He laughed, a deep, sexy sound. "No, but that answers my question." Leaning back he looked into her eyes. "Tonight you will have many."

Jessica's eyes went wide as her stranger's words replayed in her head. *Tonight you will have many.* She'd never had an orgasm that wasn't self-induced. She would have told him as much, but he moved, distracting her. His mouth had found its way to her nipple, and he was doing a delicious combination of licking, suckling and nibbling.

She allowed herself the luxury of doing what she had longed to do for hours. Her fingers sunk into his wonderful mass of hair. Even as she laced her fingers into his silky strands, she moaned. His mouth was doing such deliciously perfect things to her body.

With each suckle, she felt it not only in her breasts but between her legs. There was no question, she was beyond wet. After equal time devoted to each nipple, he moved to eye level with her. He nipped at her lips, ran his tongue along her bottom lip. She was reaching for him, wanting more, as he in turn reached for her pants.

"I am falling down on the job," he said in a deeper voice than before. "You still have wet clothes on."

More than willing to get undressed, she lifted her hips to allow him to slide her slacks and panties down her legs. Hands on her thighs, he inched her legs apart. She sat there, nude, legs spread wide and became his eye candy. For long moments, he took her in, eyes growing hotter, more potent. It felt as if his hands were on her, touching her. But it was only those eyes, those amazingly dark, expressive eyes.

Unbelievably, she felt empowered and sexy rather than shy or awkward, as she would have felt with her ex. This stranger made her more comfortable, yet at the same time more turned on and excited, than her ex or any other man ever had.

"I want you," she said boldly, proud of how confident her voice sounded.

He tilted his head ever so slightly, studying her, assessing and probing. Then he smiled. "And you shall have me, mi Hermosa." His fingers began walking up her inner thighs. "As I shall have you."

Her lips parted as one of his fingers slid across her inner core. "You *are* wet."

Despite the pleasure and the intensity of the moment, he managed to make her smile. He was referring to that moment in the doorway when she had announced she was wet. Only this time it wasn't her hair and clothes that were wet. "Yes," Jessica told him. "I would never lie about something so important."

A second finger slid along her sensitive flesh, circling, spreading her own liquid. He stepped closer between her legs, bringing his mouth so that it lingered just above hers. "Are you wet for me?"

"Yes," she whispered in the midst of a gasp as his finger slid inside her. He kissed her then, swallowing her sound, feeding her need.

His tongue pressed along hers as his finger found the upper wall inside her core, mimicking the same motion. She felt like she was falling into a haze of pure desire. No longer were her actions thought out. She simply responded.

"Do you like this?" he asked her.

Her mouth barely formed a word as he slid yet another finger inside her. "Yes."

Her head fell against the mirror as he leaned back and pressed her thighs open a bit further, looking at her as he touched her. Eyes shut, she felt the climb of heat in her body, tingling and wanting.

And it just kept getting better.

He dropped to his knees and focused his tongue on her nub, shocking her with the warmth of his mouth. "Oh God," she moaned, looking down at him, aroused by the sight of him between her legs, tasting her so intimately.

The journey toward ultimate satisfaction was almost complete as he licked, suckled and delved his tongue into the sensitive core of her body.

All she could do was lie back and experience what was to come next. And as he lifted her legs over his shoulders, dipping his tongue yet deeper into her body, his motions more frenzied, she arched her back, feeling the need to be closer.

His fingers slid inside her again, caressing just as his tongue flickered. It was just the right combination. It made the impossible happen . . .

The first ripple of orgasm shook her body. The second made her tremble. On and on, the feel of pleasure seemed to inch its way through every nerve ending in her body, until she felt completely sated from pleasure.

Her stranger was only just beginning, and she was already putty in his hands. He hadn't even found his way inside her.

Boneless from satisfaction, she sank against the mirror and sighed. An instant later, she found herself in her sexy stranger's arms being carried toward the bedroom.

As he laid her on the bed, he spread her legs and slid between them. Instinctively her arms went around his neck. Weight on his elbows, he stared down at her, eyes brimming with heat.

"You are beautiful when you come," he told her in a low, deep voice.

Any other time, words such as his would make her blush. Tonight, with him, they didn't. Still she chose not to respond directly. Despite having just had an amazing orgasm, she felt the distinct sensation of arousal already building again.

Feeling his hard body pressing against her own turned her on. "I still want you." In some far corner of her mind she wondered how she could feel so much desire, and yet, complete comfort within that passion, with a stranger.

His mouth, full and sensual, lowered toward hers. It drew her away from her thoughts, pulling her into the anticipation of what was to come.

"I want you very much," he said in a voice so thick with his need that it sounded almost hoarse.

His lips brushed hers, gently, but with such electricity, she felt it in every inch of her body. When finally his tongue parted her lips, brushing past her teeth, she eagerly met it with her own.

Within seconds they were kissing passionately, pressing their bodies together as if they couldn't get close enough. Her breasts pressed in the hard perfection of his chest, even as her hands caressed the muscles of his bare back.

She melted into his kiss and knew that if this was a dream, she didn't ever want to wake up.

Four

*H*e didn't remember ever wanting a woman the way he wanted this one. Even as he kissed her, pressing his tongue against hers, savoring her flavor, he knew he shouldn't be here with her.

He was dangerous.

She was like an innocent angel, too pure for him, and too tempting for him to walk away from. He kissed her neck, nipped at her ear and touched her nipples.

Her soft sighs only provoked his urgency.

He wanted out of his pants and anything else that served as a barrier between them. Pushing away from her, he met resistance as she clung. "Where are you going?"

"Nowhere." He leaned back down and pressed his lips to hers. It was a quick kiss, but not lacking in passion. "I'm going to get rid of these pants."

She pressed her lips to his for a brief moment, and then a bit breathlessly said, "Good."

He couldn't help the smile that played on his lips. There was no doubt this woman was allowing him to see a side of her others didn't. He had watched her struggle to maintain control, sensed her internal battle. Had she not held so tightly to her inhibitions, he would have made her come sooner.

Quickly unsnapping his pants, he shoved them over his hips along with his underwear. Stepping out of them, he kicked them aside. Ready to remove all obstacles, he stood at the end of the bed, fully aroused, and stared down at her.

Her skin was as ivory and pure as new fallen snow. It made him want, no need, to touch and kiss her all over. This woman got under his skin, made him hungry for more. It didn't seem to matter how much he'd already had of her.

"What about birth control?" he asked, addressing the final obstacle that kept him from taking her in his arms and sinking deep into her body.

She lifted her weight up on her elbows, giving him a delicious view of her breasts, nipples aroused. "I don't have a condom."

"A condom," he repeated flatly, feeling impatient. Damn, he wanted to feel her skin to skin, no barriers, but a condom was necessary and he knew it. "I do."

He moved, reaching impatiently for his pants and yanking his wallet from the back pocket. Moments later, he rolled the condom over his throbbing cock.

Her eyes dropped to his erection, her tongue wetting her lips and making him want to moan with the images it evoked. Her gaze lifted back to his. "What are you waiting for?"

He laughed, but it was laced with passion, thick and rich in tone. "You," he said. "Come here."

A combination of surprise and nervousness registered on her face. "As in where?"

Not wanting her to feel uncomfortable, he dropped to his knees on the bed. His hands settled on her legs, and gently, careful not to hurt her, he pulled her closer.

He spread her knees, moving between them. The action put his cock directly between her thighs. As much as his body begged for him to find her wetness, he resisted. Instead, he ran his hands up her inner thighs.

His thumb touched the slick folds of her core, lightly spreading the moisture. She made a soft sound of pleasure. It inched its way through his body, spurring his need for ultimate satisfaction. He wanted desperately to bury himself deep inside her body.

Still he resisted. He would only have her one night, and he wanted to make every second count.

He moved so that his hands rested on either side of her shoulders, holding his body just above hers. Their hips touched in a tantalizing tease. He kept his arousal carefully tucked between her thighs, but not quite at the point of total satisfaction.

Her hands moved under his arms, over his shoulders, as her body arched upward, her breasts pressing into his chest. She was like a cat curling up to her master, practically purring with the pleasure of body-to-body contact.

His mouth closed over hers, hungry to swallow her moans, and just as eager to taste her desire. Never before had he kissed someone and felt the potency he did at this moment. His body sank down on top of hers even as she arched into him yet again.

Their need for one another was like a living creature with

its own agenda. It controlled them both, blocking out everything else. There was no question they were both lost in one another.

"I can't get enough of you," he said, biting her shoulder and then licking. His urgency made him rougher than normal; yet, she seemed to get more aroused, crying out with pleasure at his actions. He nipped at her shoulders over and over. Then he soothed each spot with his tongue.

One of his hands explored her nipple, pinching and tugging, before rolling it with his finger. He cupped and kneaded her breasts, one at a time and together. All the while his mouth explored her shoulders, her neck and her mouth.

She touched him, feverishly stroking, fingers exploring and bringing him pleasure. She begged for fulfillment. "I can't wait anymore." It was a strangled whisper against his lips.

His mouth claimed hers yet again, his tongue stroking hers, seducing her with its long, soft caresses. Adjusting his hips, his hand slid between their bodies. He wrapped his fingers around his erection and allowed the tip to slide across her wetness.

"Ohhh," they both moaned at once.

He moved his cock back and forth, slowly, feeling the sensations it created in every nerve ending of his body. It took absolute willpower to keep from sinking inside her body . . . but every second he waited would make the completion hotter, more intense.

"Now," she cried out, urgency in her voice.

"Soon," he said, barely keeping a grip on his restraint.

Without warning, he moved, maneuvering her to her side. "What are you doing?" she asked, surprised.

He didn't say a word. She'd see soon enough.

Rolling onto his back, he pulled her with him. Her hands pressed on his chest, as he urged her to straddle him. Realization and a touch of nervousness flickered in her eyes.

Briefly, he wondered at the insecurities he glimpsed within her. Gently he urged, "Come, mi Hermosa. I want to see your passion."

Moments later, she was willingly climbing on top of him. He was damn happy the lights were still on, because what an erotic sight she made.

Her skin was like a painting, pale and perfect. And her hair . . . long, silky strands danced around her shoulders. A blond veil of silk dangled over one of her sexy, round breasts, drawing his eyes to the red bud. He wanted it in his mouth.

Before she could hesitate, he took his cock in his hand and urged her to lean forward. He slid the tip along her wetness and then slowly slipped inside. His breath caught in his throat as she moaned softly.

Inch by inch, he felt her slide down his length, watching as her eyes fluttered shut in pleasure. Forcing a breath, his hands settled on her hips. His eyes feasted on the sight she made, gloriously naked and sexy. "You're beautiful."

She bit her bottom lip, her hands moving in a circular motion over his chest, timidly at first and then with more hunger in her touch. "So are you." Her voice was low and heavy with arousal.

Their eyes locked and held. It was then, at that moment, that he felt a connection to her beyond what he had experienced with any other women. It was something he neither understood nor recognized as familiar.

Something passed between them . . . emotions, passion,

perhaps even a deeply rooted understanding of each other. It was a connection of souls, deep and unexplainable. He felt it in his stomach, in the rapid beat of his heart, and in the arousal of his body.

"Come here," he said taking her hand and pulling her forward. Her breasts pressed against his chest, arousing something primal inside, his mouth claiming hers in a hungry kiss.

Slowly, they began to move. Their bodies pressed close, each movement part of a sensual dance. Every stroke more frantic. Faster and harder. Sweet sounds of pleasure slid from her lips as she buried her face in his neck. Her hands were all over his body, hips pressing harder and harder against his.

"Come for me, mi Hermosa," he whispered in her ear. "I want to know I please you."

"You . . . do," she replied in between strokes. "You . . . oh . . . um . . . do."

His body begged for release, but he fought back his orgasm, wanting her to come first. His hand found one of her breasts, kneading and stroking. His lips found her neck.

She was close. So close. Breathing deeply, he filled his lungs with the delicious tang of her arousal.

He felt her rotate her hips, taking him deeper. She arched her back and cried out as he felt her first spasm grab his own. Seconds later, he gave into his own need for release, pushing deep into her body and pulling her down hard on his cock.

Spilling himself inside her, his body shook from the waves of pure pleasure racing through his body. Moments later, completely sated, he wrapped his arms around the amazing woman now still on top of him.

He stroked her hair and told her again how beautiful she was. Silently, he wished for so many things he couldn't have. If only he could ask her name and tell her his. If only he could get to know her beyond this one night.

But he couldn't. He knew he couldn't. Instead, he would have to be satisfied with holding her and making love to her now. He could only hope she didn't want sleep because this night had to last a lifetime.

Rolling her to her side, he pulled her close against his shoulder. She started to move. "I need to clean up."

He kissed her forehead. "Don't move. I'll get you a towel."

She stared at him, eyes wide, and then nodded. He returned only seconds later and pressed the small hand towel between her legs. He stretched out beside her again and pulled her into his arms.

Crazy as it seemed, he already wanted her again. "Rest a few minutes," he told her, willing himself to contain his desire.

She laughed and looked up at him. "Only a few minutes?"

He smiled. "I see you have never experienced the desire of a Latino man."

"I must admit," she said, resting her chin on his chest, "you are the first."

"You are pleased with the experience?" He already knew the answer, but he couldn't resist asking. "Yes?"

She shifted and snuggled under his arm. "Yes." The word was like a sigh of satisfaction. "I am quite pleased."

His fingers found her hair, sinking into it, and enjoying the feel of the silky strands. "And I have only just begun, mi Hermosa."

★   ★   ★

Jessica's hand lay on top of the muscular chest of her Latin lover.

She inhaled the sexy, male scent he wore, feeling the first hint of newly forming arousal. Amazing. She sure wasn't feeling sexless and boring.

Not one bit.

This man, whose name she didn't even know, had helped her discover a new, sensual side of herself she wanted to explore. Her fingers curled in the dark hair on his chest, her hand itching to explore.

And why shouldn't she?

This was a once in a lifetime experience. She'd never see him again. The only consequence she would have to live with would be regret if she didn't take advantage of the time she had with this.

With that thought in mind, her decision was made. Her hand slowly began exploring his chest. She felt a tiny warmth begin to build inside as the muscles under her palm flexed.

He was awake.

Her head tilted and she found his skin with her mouth. Lips pressing against his chest as her tongue darted out to taste him. His hand slid down the back of her hair, a tender, sexy caress that spurred her into action with the approval it offered.

Hungrily, her tongue, lips and teeth explored, lingering at his dark, flat nipples and pulling a moan from his mouth.

She smiled inwardly, loving the ability to arouse this man. Sliding her body closer his, her breasts pressed against his side, she kissed her way up his chest to his neck.

His hands inched into her hair as he urged her mouth to his. She met his tongue with her own, needing the connection, loving his flavor. Enjoying the tantalizing way he used that tongue of his to seduce.

But this was her seduction, as much as she enjoyed his. It was her turn to take control, and she wanted it. For far too long, she had played the submissive in her personal life.

Not now. Not here. Not with this man.

Her hand slid down his stomach and flat, taut abdominals rippled beneath her touch.

Seeking . . . She found exactly what she was looking for. He was hard and ready for her. But she wanted to play a while. No rushing. Briefly, purposely, she ran her hand along his erection.

Teasing.

His body jerked at the touch, and he made a sound, much like a growl, deep and aroused. Just like his body.

"I want you," she said against his mouth, being bold about her desire, even verbally. Something she normally didn't do.

He nipped at her bottom lip, breathing with her, as one of his hands pulled her tighter against his body. She nipped back, and ran her tongue along his bottom lip, imitating his action.

His head lifted slightly as he tried to claim her mouth, but she resisted, feeling empowered. This was a new her, a stronger, bolder, spicier woman.

Her hand flattened on his chest as she sat up, giving him a full view of naked breasts. His eyes dropped, heated. Body reacting to his stare, her nipples puckered, eager for his touch.

For a split second, she felt nervous, but this was a little fantasy. One she had the pleasure of living rather than dreaming. One where she was sexy, confident and free to explore her sexual side.

"Hermosos. Los quiero tocar." His voice was low, and laced with arousal.

She wasn't sure what he said, but the way he said it was sexy as hell. It made her whole body heat.

Then in English, he said, "I want to touch."

A slow smile turned up the corners of her mouth. "Not yet." He had made her wait earlier.

This time he could wait.

Five

*H*er stranger reached for her, and Jessica moved, maneuvering so that she was between his legs. Leaning up on his elbows, he looked at her, surprise and a hint of excitement in his eyes.

Or maybe it was anticipation.

She reached forward, eyes dropping to the focus of her attention, as her hand circled his cock. For long moments, she stared at her hand as it held his body. It felt liberating and sexy to feel him throbbing in her palm.

Her gaze lifted to his, wanting to see his reactions, his passion. And it was indeed there for her viewing. His eyes held his desire like a frame would a picture, displaying it for her viewing.

She loved this. Watching him watch her. Wanting to see his reaction. She kept eye contact as she lowered her mouth. Her tongue dashed out, touching the tip of his erection. He moaned, and she felt a rush of empowerment.

Gently, she circled the tip with her tongue and then took it into her mouth. He flattened onto his back, his body taut with the tension of pleasure.

Teasing him, she held her mouth there, tongue swirling in a seductive little dance. Amazingly, she felt incredibly turned on by the act. With her ex, she had hated sex in general. Pleasuring him in this way had been a chore.

With this man, she wanted to linger. She wanted to make him feel pleasure under her ministrations. Slowly, she began sliding back down his body. Desire played on her nerve endings as his fingers settled in her hair. It made her tongue explore, even as she began sliding up and down his length.

Her hand tightened around him, her tongue licking and teasing. As she increased the speed and pressure of her mouth, he lifted his hips, and he moved with her. She reveled at her success, loving the way his body responded, clearly eager for more of what she offered.

What she so wanted to give.

Low moans came from his mouth, feeding her own actions, making her taste him with deeper strokes. But she also wanted to come with him inside her. Greedy though it might be, she didn't want him to come and have this be over.

In one long stroke, she slid down his length and released him from her mouth. Her tongue lapped at the tip, circling it one last time.

She pulled herself upright, balancing on her knees, wanting a good look at his gorgeous body. He put one arm behind his head, looking at her, eyes dark with passion. For long moments, he allowed her to look her fill, and she did so with hungry eyes. As much as she yearned for him to be inside her, she also loved looking at him. What if it was her only chance?

He was nothing short of a work of art, broad chest, with a narrow waist that tapered to rippling, deliciously defined abdominals. Her hands ran the length of his strong thighs, feeling them flex beneath her touch.

He murmured something in Spanish and moved suddenly, taking her by surprise. His hands slid up her back, sending a rush of sensation to all parts of her body. He was kissing her neck, and his hand slid to one of her breasts and kneaded.

She moaned, her nipple tightening against the rough texture of his palm. His touch threatened to take her control, and she pressed her palms on his shoulders.

"Not so fast," she said urgently.

He responded to her tone, leaning back to see her face, but not releasing her. "No, porque."

"I'll tell you when you can touch."

His eyes narrowed, and then a slow smile slid onto his lips. There was a challenge in his voice. "If I can't touch, mi Hermosa, you touch."

A flash of insecurity made her freeze, eyes dropping to his chest. Could she do that in front of him? But she didn't have time to think. His hand was over hers, and the next thing she knew, her hand and his were on her breast.

Her eyes lifted, his darker ones pinning her in a hot stare. "You are very sexy, mi Hermosa."

It was as if he sensed she needed the reassurance. But she didn't want to need it. Her hand moved beneath his, gently applying pressure to her breast. His hand dropped from hers, his gaze shifting to take in her actions.

She brought her other hand to her other breast, squeezing and kneading. She could feel the impact of her actions on him, so thick was the sexual tension in the air. It empowered her, pressing her to release her inhibitions.

His head bent and kissed one of her hands, tongue slipping between her fingers to one nipple. She moaned, head tilting backwards. He eased her hands to the sides of her breasts, pinching her nipples with just enough pressure to almost be painful. Deliciously so.

"You do it," he said in a soft voice. She looked at him, wetting her lips as she did, her heart beating double time. She didn't hesitate, sliding her hands to replace his and pinching as he had done.

A low growl escaped his throat as she felt his fingers slide between her legs. She was wet with desire, her body begging for satisfaction. He fed that need, stroking her sensitive flesh with his fingers and then dipping one inside her.

Her hands went to his shoulders. "I want you," she whispered hoarsely, needing him inside her.

His hands slid to her waist, and he maneuvered so his erection settled between her legs. "Then what are we waiting for?"

She wasn't sure how, but they were almost at the headboard. Palms against his chest, she pressed him backwards, so he ended up sitting against the wood, legs in front of him. But they needed a condom. She had seen an extra on the floor where he had dropped it earlier. The temptation to skip it, knowing she had the pill as protection, was extreme. But she forced herself to move. To retrieve the small package.

Tearing it open, she watched him. Hungering like she never had before. And then she wrapped her fingers around his cock, loving the hard pulse beneath her hand. Quickly, she rolled the protection down his length. And then, able to wait no longer, she straddled him.

The tip of his erection met her wetness, and she bit back a moan. She needed him. Her body cried out impatiently, and she responded by taking all of him in one quick movement.

They both gasped, her head falling backwards, lashing floating down to her cheeks, pleasure dancing along nerve endings. She couldn't ever remember feeling this aroused.

"Mi Hermosa," he said huskily, when she didn't immediately move.

Her head tilted downward, eyes opening, as she responded to his plea. Hand on his chest, she arched her back and slowly began moving.

It was a mad rush of passion then, hands on each other's bodies, mouths meeting, tasting, teasing. She couldn't get enough of him. Something was between them, an unusual attraction that seemed to make them hunger for each other. It was as if they were trying to become one.

They clung, her breasts pressed to his chest, tongues meeting hungrily, until a rush of heat sent her over the edge.

She trembled and shook with the impact of release, fingers pressing into his back, body contracting with force. His hips seemed to buck as he joined her, body thrusting into hers, a moan escaping his mouth.

When finally they stilled, neither moved for long moments. It was as if neither could completely believe the full force of what had happened between them.

Or maybe they simply didn't want it to end.

Six

It was nearly time for sunrise when Dominic Montez forced himself to slide out of the bed, careful not to wake his sleeping beauty. Usually, leaving was easy. This time it was not. This time this woman had gotten to him in a way no other had before.

But he couldn't stay, even if he wanted to. He had an informant to meet in Brownsville, a job to do. And his job as a DEA agent was exactly why he made a better one-night stand than future lover. The nastiness that touched his life wasn't meant to be shared.

Yet, the connection between him and this woman enticed him to linger, wishing things could be different. He stared down at her, her blond hair a mass of silk on the pillow. Inhaling, Dominic could almost smell the floral scent it held. So sweet. So alluring.

The temptation to crawl back into the bed and hold her just

a little longer enticed him. To feel what he had just moments before, as she'd slept in his arms, relaxed and far too trusting.

He had made love to her over and over, determined to embrace every second he had with her. In the back of his mind, he knew his motivation. He wanted this unique woman to remember him for what they shared.

Regret for what would never be burned his soul. There was something about this beautiful white woman that called to him. But he would only be trouble and pain for her. Not that she would want someone like him.

For Dominic, the options were limited. His career ruled his life. A fact that had begun to bother him lately. At thirty-five, he barely remembered his own name, he was undercover so much. He had nothing to offer a woman like this one. Nothing of value.

Dominic knew he had to leave and he had to do it while she slept, without saying goodbye. He grabbed the hotel notepad and pen from the nightstand, pausing a moment as he tried to decide what to say.

Mi Hermosa,

I will never forget our night together.

He paused, struggling with how to sign the note. Using his name wasn't an option. Finally he wrote,

Adios,

D

He started toward the door, note in hand, and stopped as he almost stepped on her purse where it still lay on the floor. Squatting, he hesitated, and then gave into his urge. He unzipped her purse, determined to find out her name. Identifying a business card holder, he withdrew a card, and then returned the purse to its normal order.

Standing, Dominic left her purse on the floor, not wanting her to think he'd done what he had, and looked inside. Dominic gave her a quick look, confirming she was still sleeping, and then eased the door open, the note wedged into the closure.

He paused outside the door and read the name on the card. Jessica Montgomery, Assistant District Attorney, Travis County. "No fucking way," he murmured. That meant she dealt with criminal types almost as much as he did.

On a timeline, Dominic had no choice but to head out. He couldn't risk missing his meeting. But as he started toward the office, intending to pay the bill, he couldn't get his mind off the "what ifs."

Sliding the card in the front pocket of his jeans, Dominic forced himself to think about the business ahead of him . . . for now.

Later he'd decide what to do about Jessica Montgomery.

Jessica woke slowly, eyes fluttering open, nostrils flaring with the scent of the man she had tasted and touched all night. She didn't move, knowing her time with him was now limited, wanting to enjoy it just a little longer.

Sunlight beamed through the windows, making certain

she knew her fantasy world was about to end. The absence of cloud cover told her the storms had ended.

She squeezed her eyes shut, mentally reliving the images of her and her stranger in heated embraces. After long moments, she forced herself to open them again. She needed to touch him just one more time. Reaching for him, her hand met the mattress. Lifting her head with a sudden rush of fear, she found herself in bed, alone.

Her eyes moved to the bathroom, hopeful that he was there, not gone. But the door was open, and the light was out.

He *was* gone. She was indeed alone.

Unbidden, a tiny ache of disappointment formed. She threw the covers aside and sat up, refusing to let the reality of the situation get to her. This was how it was supposed to be. A one-night stand ended in one night. That was the whole point.

And it wasn't like she wanted a relationship.

Shoving her feet off the edge of the bed, she stood. That's when she saw the piece of paper shut in the door. Her heart began pounding against her chest, anticipation thrumming in her body like a second skin.

Maybe he hadn't left. Maybe he had just gone out for a minute.

Gingerly, she moved toward the note, and with far too much eagerness, she opened the door. Securing the piece of paper, she shoved the door shut. And then she read.

It was short and to the point. He was gone. She was alone. "D" was how he signed it. She still didn't even know his name.

Jessica sank to the ground, back against the door, thinking about her past, and how much she'd allowed herself to miss.

Compliments of her stranger, she now knew there really was a sexual woman inside her. Now that it had revealed itself, Jessica had no intention of shoving it back into hiding.

Memories floated in her mind. Of her stranger. Of her ex saying nasty things. Even blaming her for his cheating. But this stranger, and her night with him, had proven she wasn't, as her ex had said . . . sexless.

So he might be gone, but she still owed her sexy stranger a silent "thank you." She was going to embrace the future feeling more confident. Certainly, she was now making room for some physical satisfaction. She smiled at that thought, and pushed to her feet.

Sex had certainly taken on a new meaning.

All she needed was the right man.

An hour later, Jessica entered the motel lobby—if the dingy box of a room could be called that. She needed to deal with her car and get on the road.

Approaching the counter, Jessica found a teenage boy so consumed by a handheld game of some sort he didn't notice her approach.

Delicately, she cleared her throat. "I'm in room—"

He slid an envelope toward her. "112," he said, glancing up at her. "I know. Your room's paid for, and your car is out back being repaired."

Jessica frowned and started to ask questions but the kid interrupted. "That guy you were with said he had to leave but wanted to make sure you were taken care of. Paid for an extra night so you could wait in your room while your car gets repaired. Just a bad alternator though. It'll be ready soon." The boy smiled. "That man, he sure was a good tipper. Tell him to come back anytime."

Jessica smiled. "I'll tell him," she said, thinking she wouldn't mind one more visit with her stranger herself.

One more hot night.

Seven

Dominic sat down on yet another hotel bed. After passing on the details his informant had delivered, he flipped his cell phone shut.

Until a week before, Dominic had been deep undercover with the Alvarez Cartel. The information he'd received today helped take down a motorcycle gang trafficking drugs over the border for Alvarez. It had been the final piece of evidence needed before arrests were made.

Eyeing the hotel room, Dominic took in the floral bedspread and picture of a rose over the particle-board dresser. In Brownsville, this was about the best accommodations available. The town wasn't known for luxury, but the beach and border nearby drew tourists regardless.

Dominic's mind went back to the dingy roadside motel he'd shared with Jessica. To the beautiful white woman he'd forced himself to forget while he attended business.

In truth, she'd been there, lingering just beneath the surface, begging for attention the entire day. Unsure why, but unable to stop the urge, Dominic eased backward, shoving two fingers in the pocket of his jeans and retrieving her business card.

He stared at it, still surprised at her title of assistant DA. Flipping the card around between his fingers, he considered the implications. She understood the nastiness of the criminal world, of his world. She'd know what DEA meant. What complications came with the job.

A frustrated sigh slid from his mouth, and he tossed the card on the nightstand. If she knew the complications, she'd know he was trouble. He scrubbed his jaw, still unshaven, a one-day growth soon to become two.

Pushing to his feet, he crossed the tiny expanse of the room which included a sink and mirror, the toilet being in a tiny closed hole of a room. He leaned against the counter, looking into the mirror.

"Chingado," he murmured, searching his image for answers.

Why was he even considering contacting her again? *Why?* He'd seen how his line of work destroyed relationships. No. It was more than just his job. It was the *impact* of his job. The darkness he'd seen. The things he'd allowed himself to become in the name of good. The undercover jobs that almost sucked him under and destroyed all he knew himself to be.

Things best kept to himself.

Yet . . . Jessica had touched him in some way he didn't quite understand. And now, her role in law enforcement seemed to almost invite a future connection.

Dominic let his head drop between his shoulders, trying to make sense of how much he wanted to see her again. Considering the road they'd both traveled, the likelihood she was right here in Brownsville seemed strong. So close. So easy to track down with one quick phone call.

Not giving himself time to think, Dominic shoved away from the sink and walked back to the bed and sat down. He grabbed his phone off the nightstand and dialed, taking advantage of the resources available to him.

A minute later, he was talking to a contact, a research specialist, from his base office. "I need everything you can get me on Travis County Assistant District Attorney Jessica Montgomery." He paused. "I'm fairly certain she's in Brownsville today, and I need to know where."

As expected, Dominic wasn't questioned. If he needed intel, he got it. Years of service and a track record of success gave him certain liberties. The specialist would simply believe he was tracking down a lead related to his assignment.

And though Jessica wasn't part of his job, she most definitely had become a distraction he had to deal with.

Hours later, Dominic pulled his bike into Beth Montgomery's driveway and killed the engine. He'd considered his choices and knew showing up and seeing Jessica in person was his only option. She'd think he was a stalker if he called and probably blow him off. Or she'd just let fear drive him away. He'd seen a lot of fear in her. Too much. Fear, he realized, he wanted to drive away permanently.

He knew this was nuts. He came with baggage she didn't need. On the other hand, he'd seen the ghosts in those blue eyes and knew he'd put them at bay.

Starting toward the front porch, his groin tightened at the

mere thought of seeing Jessica again. Of touching her and feeling her tight against his body.

No other woman had ever drawn this kind of potent response. He couldn't walk away without finding out if it had been a fantasy that the light of day destroyed.

Or if it was more . . .

Eight

Jessica had made it to Brownsville just in time for the birthday party which included dinner, cake and lots of friends and family. Her mother had lived with Beth, her sister, since their father's death several years before. It had done Jessica good to see her doing well with Beth.

Now, hours after the festivities, exhausted from travel and no sleep, Jessica sat on a wooden swing located on the back porch of her sister's small, country house. Wearing jeans, no shoes or socks, and a t-shirt, she felt relaxed for the first time in a long while.

Staring into the rich black of night, no stars in sight, a breeze lifted her hair from her neck, her nostrils flaring with the scent of rain. Another storm was headed toward them. The thought conjured erotic images from the night before.

Of her Zorro look-a-like, with long, dark hair, mesmerizing eyes and milk chocolate skin. She loved his skin color. Loved how intimate and perfectly he had touched her. How sexy and feminine he'd made her feel.

The screen door squeaked, snapping Jessica reluctantly back to reality. Jessica opened her eyes, unaware she'd even allowed them to drift shut.

Beth peered around the doorway. "What are you doing out here, alone?"

"Just enjoying the peaceful night."

Beth gave her a probing look, and then stepped past the door, letting it slam shut. "Why do I feel like you have some secret you're dying to tell but you aren't sure you should?"

Jessica laughed, hoping it didn't sound as nervous as she felt. Beth had gotten married, a virgin, right out of high school. Admitting to Beth she'd slept with a stranger, and didn't even know his name, simply wasn't an option.

Besides, part of Jessica wanted to keep her Latin lover a special secret. "I assure you anything I might share is incredibly boring," Jessica said, patting the seat beside her, the swing big enough for two. "Come sit with me."

"I'm not wrong," Beth said, tossing her long, blond hair over her shoulder. Several years younger than Jessica, they shared the same coloring, though Beth was much taller, a good three inches above Jessica's five foot four. "I know you. Something is going on." She sat down next to Jessica, and angled her body to study her sister. "I can see it in your eyes."

"You are as crazy as always, I see," Jessica teased, diverting her gaze, trying to act nonchalant as she stared out into the darkness. Pulling her knees up to her chest, she hugged them.

"Come on, Jess," Beth prodded. "Tell me."

"There's nothing to tell," Jessica replied, peeking at Beth.

Then, she held up a finger. "Wait. I go to trial on Monday. Want to hear about the case?"

Beth made a frustrated sound. "You are *always* at trial, prosecuting some bad guy. And no, I do *not* want to hear the details. You know I don't like all that law stuff. I run a flower shop for God's sakes." She crossed her jean-clad legs. "And you're trying to distract me anyway."

"I am not," Jessica insisted even though they both knew she was.

"Are too," Beth said. She made a humph sound. "Fine." Her lips thinned. "Keep the fun stuff to yourself." She reached out and pulled a strand of Jessica's hair through her fingers. "It's gotten longer. The last time I saw you it was barely to your shoulders, and now it's well past them."

Guilt tightened Jessica's gut as she turned to her sister. It also opened up the door for Jessica to say what was on her mind. "I'm sorry. I know I've been far too withdrawn from you and mom. I buried myself in my work after the divorce but that's behind me. I'm going to change that. I *promise*."

Beth laced her fingers through Jessica's. "Both mom and I knew you just needed time. All we want is for you to be happy." She narrowed her eyes on Jessica. "*Are* you happy?"

"I'm getting there," Jessica said, surprised at how much she meant her words.

Before her sister could respond, the doorbell rang. "Great," Beth said, a frustrated sound following the word. "Mom and the baby are sleeping. Who would be visiting now?"

Jessica glanced at her watch and shot an amused look at Beth. "It's eight o'clock. Not late by most people's standards."

Beth pushed to her feet and shook a finger at Jessica. "Wait until you have babies. Eight will feel like midnight. I'll be right back."

As the screen door slammed shut, Jessica laughed out loud. Beth hadn't changed. Always melodramatic. Always in crisis. She hadn't realized just how much she'd missed her until now.

Until this weekend, she hadn't realized how much of everything she'd missed. Her mind raced back to the motel. To the awakening of the woman inside. The one she intended to keep alive and well.

Jessica was just about to go check on the visitor when Beth cleared her throat from behind. "Jessica," she said. "You have a visitor."

Jessica's brows dipped. No one would visit her here. She'd barely kept in contact with her family, let alone anyone else. "What?" She rotated around in the swing to see the doorway. "Who?"

And then her jaw dropped because she could see exactly *who* herself. It was him. Her sexy stranger. Her lover for a night. And though she saw *him* there, in the doorway, looming above her sister by several inches, it didn't seem real. Her stranger couldn't be here, in her sister's home. She blinked.

No.

It wasn't possible.

With her back to the stranger, Beth proceeded to form the silent word "wow" meant for Jessica's eyes only. God, what must her sister be thinking? *Crap.* What had *he* told her?

Her gaze lifted to his, to her fantasy man, who'd suddenly invaded her real world, and the impact stole her breath away.

Those eyes . . . those dark, sultry eyes of his packed a powerful punch of pure heat. They seduced with a mere look, wordlessly promising pleasure.

And they demanded she remember.

Memories flooded her mind. Of naked bodies entwined. Of boldly telling this man what she wanted and needed. Even demanding it.

How long she sat there, unmoving, body getting all warm and wet, with the vivid play of intimate moments, she didn't know. It was him, the stranger no longer a secret, who broke the silence.

"I told you I might be in town today. Didn't you warn your sister I might drop by?"

His voice was both familiar and thick with the soft, silky accent she'd found such a turn-on. Still did, it appeared, because she felt the distinct ache of pleasure between her thighs.

Jessica swallowed, unable to think what to say. She didn't understand how he was here or what he was saying. "I . . . I guess I didn't."

Beth made a *tsk* sound. "Now I know what your secret was." She winked at Jessica. "I'll leave you two alone."

Her sister's words shook Jessica back into action. She scrambled to her feet, backing up against the wooden railing of the patio. Beth disappeared, and *he* stepped out onto the porch and under the one dim light above the door.

His long raven hair was pulled back at his neck, a tie holding it in place, his square jaw dusted with dark stubble. His black jeans and matching, snug t-shirt, along with boots, completed the renegade look.

The one that screamed sex and fantasies.

Only this wasn't a fantasy. He *was* real. And getting closer. Suddenly, he was moving, and in two long strides he stood beside the railing, and she rotated to face him. So close she could smell his spicy male scent. The same enticing scent she'd awakened wearing like a second skin just hours before.

But no matter how familiar her body might find this man, he was indeed a stranger. One who shouldn't know how to find her. "Why are you here?" she demanded, straightening her spine. "No. How? How are you here?"

A hint of a smile lifted one corner of his sensual mouth. "Hello mi Hermosa." A pause and a nod. "Jessica."

She should be scared. Damn it, she was no fool. She didn't really know this man. So why was her stomach fluttering with excitement and nerves instead of fear?

"How do you know me?" she asked.

He reached in his pocket and pulled out a wallet, flipping it open and exposing a badge. DEA. She knew it at sight. Quickly, Jessica found his name, trying to determine if it was familiar. "Dominic Montez," she said, reading it out loud, but not placing it. She narrowed her eyes on him, searching his masculine features, trying to think of a time they'd met. "Did we know each other before . . . um . . . ?"

He leaned closer. "Before we made love all night?" he asked, in a husky whisper.

Her nipples tightened at the words, and she felt the ache of undeniable lust between her thighs. She let out a breath and eased backward, afraid she was going to lose all rational thought. Normally, as an attorney who knew the courtroom well, she handled herself with grace. With this man instinct took over. Right now, getting naked and repeating last night sounded far too good.

She needed answers and she knew it. "Did we know each other before?" she asked again, leaning her palm on the railing to her right for stability.

He mimicked her action, resting his elbow on the wooden ledge to his left. The position put him closer to eye-level with her.

"Not before last night, mi Hermosa." He spoke the words precisely, emphasizing the familiar endearment he'd spoken so many times as he'd made love to her, his eyes holding hers as if he wanted her to see the truth in them. "I took the liberty of taking one of your business cards."

The idea of him going through her purse bothered her, yet, if he hadn't he wouldn't be here now. She was confused. The feeling made her snap. "You went into my purse?" Her voice held accusation.

His nod came slowly. "That's right, and I used my contacts to find out where you were tonight. I wanted to see you again." He pushed off the railing, his expression suddenly indiscernible, his mood darker. The barely there smile, gone. "You can report me if you like. I won't deny my actions."

There was no apology in his voice. In fact, his words felt like a dare. She searched his eyes, his face. An almost overwhelming urge to reach out and touch him overcame her. Like an urge to reassure. To comfort. An urge she didn't let herself act upon.

"Dominic," she said, trying to offer in that word what she hadn't been willing to in touch.

And just like that, he closed the distance between them. He reached out to do what she had resisted, to touch. Anticipation sent a shiver racing down her spine. But just as the reward, the desired feel of his skin against hers, was to come, he pulled back, his hand dropping to his side.

Her body ached for him. For the contact that never came.

"I broke the rules to find you," he said in a low voice. "I wanted to see you *that* much. But make no mistake, Jessica Montgomery. This isn't the only time I've broken the rules nor will it be the last. I'm no angel."

At that moment, all she wanted to do was kiss him. To taste that spicy maleness so unique to him. But she sensed the importance of his words. He was looking for something from her. Perhaps she held back because she wanted something from him too.

But what? She didn't know. Only that a line was drawn in the sand and it somehow, someway, had to be crossed. And she wanted to do it now, not later. To tear down the barriers.

She didn't even know this man, but what she'd shared with him had felt far more exposing and intimate than anything she'd ever experienced with her ex. Everything inside her wanted to trust him.

"These rules you break," she asked, forcing herself to be cautious, to act as she normally would. "Are they for the right reasons?"

One second. Two. "Is there a right reason to break the rules?" he asked.

There had been a time when she would have said no. Not anymore. Right and wrong weren't always black and white. She'd learned that after years of seeing criminals walk free on technical issues.

Besides, how could she convict Dominic for finding her when being found felt so . . . exciting? "Breaking the rules brought you here," Jessica said, not willing to say more, implying her meaning rather than speaking it out loud.

He didn't so much as move a hair, but the air crackled with the impact of her words. With his reaction. "Which means what?"

"I'm not sure," she said, and that was as truthful as it got. She was as scared as she was pleased to see him. "I'm . . . surprised."

"I needed to know," he said in a low voice.

"Know?" she asked, her stomach fluttering with nerves, anxious for his response.

"If what I felt back in that room was real."

He barely finished speaking the words when he reached out and brushed her cheek with his fingertips, and she felt it clear to her toes. Every inch of her body went warm and then turned hot. His palm settled on her face, and she found herself leaning into the touch, her lashes fluttering.

The way this man impacted her was as amazing as it was frightening. It also excited and aroused. And most of all, it left her wanting more.

"Mi Hermosa," he whispered.

She forced her eyes open, looking at him with what she knew had to be lust. "And what did you find out?" she asked. "Was it real?"

"I know how to be sure," he said.

His thumb brushed her bottom lip, and though Jessica knew her sister could walk outside any minute, she couldn't stop her reaction as she pressed her hand to that rock hard chest. Her panties were wet. Her body burning.

"How?" she whispered.

He looked down at her hand and then covered it with his own. After several seconds, he fixed her with a tormented look, and then, abruptly, stepped away from her, far enough to break contact, but close enough to speak for only her ears.

"I'll be in room 112 tomorrow at noon," he said. "If you show up we'll find out." With the words, he turned and started for the door.

Jessica wanted to call him back, but she didn't dare bring attention from her sister. Instead, she stood there, staring after Dominic, her body scorching hot from his touch. His presence. His promise of more than one night.

The soft breeze the only thing offering any relief from the loss of the man who set her on fire like no other.

Nine

*I*n front of 112 sat a motorcycle.

Jessica smiled, knowing it belonged to Dominic. Sleek and silver, it screamed of sex and power. It fit her image of her sexy Zorro lover like a glove. Just as her body had fit to his as if made for his.

Slowly, her eyes went to the cracked door leading to the room she'd shared with Dominic so recently. Her stomach fluttered with nerves. She'd called her contacts in Austin, and had Dominic check out. She assumed he'd expected as much. Only a fool would show up here, today, without such actions.

Dominic's parents were dead, his grandmother raising him from his teens to college years, before she too passed away. He had no siblings. He'd spent most of his adult life undercover.

Dominic was alone.

And deep inside, she knew he didn't want to be anymore. She had seen it in his eyes, and felt it in his touch.

As she walked toward the door, her boots scraping on the gravel, Jessica smiled. Dominic was nothing like her conservative attorney ex-husband.

And she loved it.

The idea of playing a little, and enjoying both Dominic, and life, felt exciting. And so did the continuation of her sexual exploration. She wanted to start there. She wanted to release her inhibitions and charge toward the future.

She eased open the door and found Dominic standing in the center of the room. Jessica stepped into the room and pushed the door shut. She leaned against the wooden surface.

Her eyes locked with Dominic's, and they stared at each other, the air sizzling with implication. With heat and desire.

Her gaze traveled his body. He wore faded jeans and a tight white t-shirt. Boots. Hair down around his shoulders. She pushed off the door and walked toward him, seeing the surprise register in his eyes at her forward action. She forced down the nerves that threatened to destroy her plan.

Stopping only inches from where he stood, she pressed her hand on Dominic's chest, feeling his muscle flex beneath her palm. Fighting the urge to explore his body. The time would come . . . just not yet.

Jessica started walking again, urging him backward until he hit the wall. He reached up to touch her and she waved off his hand. "Hands at your sides and against the wall." He hesitated. "Do it or I leave."

His brown eyes turned almost black. Potent. Hot. She could see the burn of desire in them. Feel the way her aggressiveness turned him on. She could even smell his arousal.

And she liked it. Really, really liked it.

Giving him a sultry look, she threw out her challenge. "You asked me what I wanted last night. In fact, you demanded I tell you."

"And then I made your wants and needs reality," he said, his voice husky with desire. "Did I not?"

She ignored his attempt at seduction. She'd come this far, Jessica wasn't about to hand over control now. "I want to know what you *want*, Dominic," she said.

"You," he said. "I want you."

She slid her hand down his body and palmed his cock, now hard and more than ready to be inside her. "I know that much." Her fingers traced the tip of his erection. "You don't really think I'm going to let you get off that easy, do you?"

A slow smile slid onto his lips. "I was hoping you wouldn't."

"What do you want, Dominic?"

"Everything you'll let me have, mi Hermosa," he responded. "All of you."

Lost in the game, the lust, the desire to simply feel his body against hers, she still didn't miss the implications of his words. "And what do I get in return?"

"Anything you wish," he whispered.

"Anything?" she asked, a coy smile slipping onto her mouth.

"Your wish is my command."

Jessica stepped away and took a seat on the bed. "Start by getting naked." She paused. "Slowly."

As Dominic reached for his shirt, prepared to do her bidding, Jessica inhaled, feeling the power. Loving the inner vixen come to life. She couldn't wait to see where it would take her.

Nor could she wait to see just how far Dominic was willing to go. Today and in the future. But whatever the outcome, she was going to enjoy the ride.

Prior to realizing her dream of becoming a writer, LISA RENEE JONES owned and operated a multi-state staffing agency, with sales as high as sixteen million dollars a year. She was recognized by many publications, including the prestigious *Entrepreneur Magazine*. In 2003, she sold her business to focus full time on her writing.

Since then, she has sold books to four major publishing houses in multiple genres. You can find out more about her busy release schedule at www.lisareneejones.com.

Out of the Shadows

Myla Jackson

Dedicated to my sister,
Delilah Devlin,
whose fanatical love of writing matches my own.

One

"They're cockier than usual tonight," TJ Evans whispered to his partner as a gang of five young men ambled down the deserted streets of inner-city Houston, kicking soda cans and talking loud enough to wake even the undead. "As expected. They're looking for anyone who might have ignored the mandatory evacuation order."

Ryan nodded in the dark. "Probably getting hungry."

"Good, when they're hungry they don't always think straight."

It was the witching hour, the time of night you didn't want to be out on the streets with all the creepy and dangerous people littering the hours between midnight and four.

TJ and Ryan crouched behind the abandoned automobile they'd chosen as cover for their mission. As cops assigned to the Houston Special Task Force, they were responsible for keeping the streets clean of the worst kind of riffraff, and the guys headed their way qualified—young, aggressive and vampires. He recognized them from the sketches at the station.

"Ready, Ryan?" TJ asked.

Ryan nodded and fitted a wooden dart into his crossbow.

About the time he was set, a woman emerged from an evacuated apartment building, carrying a laundry basket piled with belongs.

The vamps whooped and made a beeline for their first unwilling victim of the evening. Halfway to her car, the woman spotted the men, her eyes growing round. She darted a look from her car standing against the curb and back to the doorway as if debating which she could make faster.

"She's mine." The short, stocky vamp wearing a black T-shirt and sporting dragon tattoos on each arm led the way.

The woman dropped the basket and dove for the car, fumbling to fit her key in the lock.

"It's show time." TJ pressed the stock of his recurve crossbow against his shoulder. "Let's go."

The two cops stepped from behind the rusted-out vehicle.

Ryan called out, "Halt or I'll shoot!"

TJ snorted and sighted his weapon on the man in the lead. "You're such a rookie."

But the shout brought the gang of men to a standstill, and they turned toward the two cops. Their leader laughed out loud. "You're kidding, right? You want us to stop?"

"Houston Police, step away from the woman," TJ said, his weapon at the ready.

"And who's going to stop us? You?" The guy with the tattoo dragons threw back his head and laughed, his long white incisor teeth reflecting the light from the nearby streetlamps.

"Can't say we didn't warn you." With his hand firmly wrapped around the grip, his sights targeting the first man's chest, TJ squeezed the trigger, sending the solid wooden dart straight into the man's heart.

The laughter died on the tattooed man's lips and his eyes widened. As he glanced down at the wooden dart embedded into his heart, his body jerked and then jerked again. Within seconds he shook so hard he fell to the earth, screaming, his flesh dissolving into dust until the wind lifted his remains and blew them away.

The other four men stared down at where their leader had been. By the time they looked back at the two cops, Ryan squeezed his trigger, another dart flying into the chest of the nearest man.

TJ had already reloaded and fired off his next round when the gang of three remaining vampires turned and attacked. He was able to fire his last round into the heart of one, dropping him in mid-lunge. Neither TJ nor Ryan had time to reload. They moved back, pulling wooden stakes from the knife sheaths on their belts.

The two vampires left standing leaped onto the hood of the abandoned vehicle and roared, flashing their teeth. The bigger vamp growled and dropped to the ground, stalking toward TJ. "You're in luck. I believe the only good cop is a dead cop."

"Is that so?" TJ said. He braced his legs for the attack, adrenaline pulsing through his veins giving him an almost orgasmic rush. God, he loved his job! "We may have a bit of a problem. I believe the only good vampire is a dead vampire."

The vampire leaped at TJ, knocking him to the ground. For a moment, TJ's hand loosened around the stake. If he didn't get it into the vamp's heart quickly, he didn't stand a chance. Vampires had superhuman strength and resilience. TJ's only advantage was his ability to think under pressure. His opponent clamped clawlike hands into his shoulders and leaned forward, his lips peeled back from long, wicked teeth.

"No!" TJ yelled, acting as though the vampire had him now. But when the teeth neared his neck, TJ raised his hand in a sudden upward thrust, driving the stake through the man's ribs into his heart. He collapsed on top of TJ, his body shuddering and twitching as he withered into a cloud of dust scattered by the wind.

TJ rolled to his feet, brushing the dust from his shirt.

The other vampire had Ryan pinned to the pavement.

"Need help, partner?" TJ asked, retrieving the stake from the ground.

"Nope," Ryan grunted, straining to keep the vampire's teeth from sinking into his neck. "Got this one under control."

TJ chuckled. "Looks to me like he has you." He raised the stake and plunged it through the vampire's back into his heart. "Come on, quit playing around. It's nearing daylight and the end of our shift."

Ryan remained pinned for several more seconds by the dying vampire. Then he stood and brushed the dust from his shirt. "You take all the fun out of the job."

"You'll get over it." TJ glanced around for the woman in time to see the taillights of her compact car disappearing around a corner. He stared down at the dirt on his uniform and sniffed. "God, I hate the smell of dusted vamps. What say you and me head for the station?"

Ryan stooped to gather his recurve crossbow. "You're on."

★ ★ ★

The sun popped up over the horizon as TJ and Ryan left the station an hour later in TJ's pickup.

"Hard to believe a hurricane's headed our way," TJ commented. The wind was picking up, but the sunshine didn't give a clue as to what was headed straight for the coast.

"Know what you mean." Ryan stared out the passenger seat of TJ's F250 pickup. "Think it'll hit at category five?"

"That's what the forecast predicts." TJ turned left at the traffic light and drove down the deserted streets of his neighborhood. "I'm just glad most folks decided not to wait until tomorrow to leave Houston. The traffic on the evacuation routes was bad enough, yesterday. It's bound to be worse today. Glad I'm not on duty."

"I have a feeling we're in for another tough night." Ryan tapped his fingers on the armrest. "I'll bet the looters will come out in force."

TJ's lips tightened. "Yeah, and we'll be responsible for protecting the looters from the monsters. Doesn't seem right."

Ryan shook his head. "Should just let 'em have at it."

TJ nodded. "They deserve each other. But there'll be those who, for some reason or another, ignored the mayor's mandatory evacuation order. They're the ones we'll be out there for."

Ryan snorted. "Again, they deserve each other."

"I don't know. The elderly don't always listen to the news. They might not even know they're in the path of a hurricane."

"Yeah, I guess you're right." Ryan tapped his fingers on the arm rest. "Damned hurricanes. Seems like nothing's been right since hurricanes Katrina and Rita back in 2005."

Evacuation of New Orleans had not only inundated the housing market in Houston, it had also impacted the crime rates. Rape and murder were on the rise, as well as the addition of more frightening crimes.

At first, TJ had laughed off the rumors, but more and more people disappeared or were left dead, drained of blood. The problem couldn't be ignored—thus the need for the Special Task Force with the best of the Houston Police Department pulled from all over the city.

Because of their successful careers taking out the bad guys, TJ and Ryan had been reassigned to the Special Task Force, on permanent night shift. TJ was glad he'd finished night school before he took on the new assignment.

"Think your neighbor made it out?" Ryan asked. "You still seeing her?"

As the thought of Cassidy Jones's liquid brown eyes and smooth-as-cream skin crossed TJ's mind, his foot lifted from the accelerator. For a moment, he was back between the sheets, sliding inside her. His groin tightened and pushed against the hard metal zipper of his uniform pants. "I hope she made it out and no, I'm not seeing her anymore." TJ jammed his foot on the gas and the truck shot forward. Not because he didn't want to.

"Sorry I asked," Ryan said, clutching the "oh-shit" handle above his head.

Cassidy was the past, a one-night stand TJ still couldn't explain. After weeks of study-group sessions last semester and working together over her dinner table, she'd finally agreed to go out.

Their date had culminated in his bed—tangled in the sheets,

skin-to-skin and satiated from the best sex he'd had in . . . Well, the best sex ever.

He shook his head, still unable to figure out Cassidy. She didn't return his calls, didn't drop in like she used to and didn't even come out of her house. He should have known better than to date the girl next door. When the connection didn't work out, you still had to live next to her until one or the other moved. And TJ didn't plan on moving because of a ruined love affair.

As much as he liked to think he was over her, he missed her smile across a table loaded with books. Her laughter still echoed through his days, and the memory of her body beneath him haunted his sleep.

"Hey, don't forget to drop me off," Ryan said.

TJ hit the brakes and pulled into Ryan's drive. He slammed the truck into park, pushed the dark-haired beauty from his mind and stared at his friend's house. "You ready for the storm?"

"As ready as anyone. Got storm shutters installed after hurricanes Katrina and Rita. I'll be locking them tight before I report to work tonight."

"Need help?" TJ asked, not really interested in hanging around, but Ryan was his friend.

"Naw." Ryan climbed down from the truck, closed the door and slapped the open window frame. "Get going, we've only got a few hours before the wind gets really strong." He shook his head as he opened the door. "Tonight's going to be one long one and tomorrow even longer."

How many times had they had the hurricane warnings this year? Often enough to make TJ want to skip attaching storm shutters and go straight for the beer in his refrigerator.

The drive to his house five blocks away was completed in a surreal silence. The deserted streets were mostly still, only a few families, with cars loaded to the gills, hurried to flee the city.

In the short time involved in dropping off his friend, a line of clouds appeared in the southern sky, rolling in from the Gulf of Mexico. Trees shuddered as the first gusts of wind buffeted branches and shrubs, a little teaser for what was to come.

As he rolled to a stop in his driveway, a slight movement caught TJ's attention and he glanced up at the bedroom window in the house next door.

The sun crept through the windows from the eastern sky, not a cloud in sight from this direction. Cassidy Jones stood in the shadows, away from the deadly rays. She stared at the truck below, her heart clenching in her chest when TJ climbed out.

His muscles rippled beneath his dark blue uniform. The fabric hugged his taut buttocks and framed his thick thighs to perfection.

Desire swelled in each molecule of her being, rising like a pulsing wave, engulfing her in a torrent of sensation. Her fingers clutched the cotton fabric of the curtain and her nails dug into her palm as she fought the overpowering surge of need—a need as debilitating as starvation to a refugee.

Not long ago, she'd have rushed out to greet him, inventing an excuse to ask him over so she could test her flirtation skills on the sandy-haired cop. Her college courses hadn't been hard, but she'd insisted she needed his help, wanting his company more than the assistance while she studied. Not that she could study with TJ close by. His presence distracted her in the most delicious ways.

When they'd started the criminology class together last semester, they'd hit it off immediately. He was finishing his last few courses for his degree in criminology, and she was working toward one in forensics. Both were non-traditional students having decided to complete degrees after being in the workforce for several years.

A smile tugged at Cassidy's lips as she recalled her own shy attempts at flirting and how TJ's tender caresses worked into gentle kisses. When they'd finally consummated their relationship, Cassidy had worried her limited knowledge of sex, gleaned from clumsy groping in high school, would turn TJ off.

He'd been tender, trailing his lips and hands across her body, touching her in ways she'd only dreamed about, until he brought her to her first orgasm. That moment was a moving, almost spiritual, experience for Cassidy, and she dared to hope they'd be together forever.

But the night after their "date," everything changed. She'd been giddy with happiness. So giddy, she didn't pay attention. She snorted. Isn't that how it happened to women who don't consider all the factors—dark night, shadowy walkway, walking alone? Hell, as stupid as she'd been, she deserved her fate. She shuddered.

No. No one deserved her fate.

After the attack, her injuries healed, but her life had changed completely. Cassidy wasn't the woman TJ had made love to only a few short days before. Hell, she wasn't even human. She couldn't undo her carelessness and because of it, they could never be together again.

Yearning coiled deep in Cassidy's belly, pressing her to go to him. She hungered for the strength of his arms around her, the touch of his tongue against her breasts and the thrust of his cock filling her. Her panties moistened as the image of him leaning over her, naked and glistening with sweat, wavered in her fevered mind. An image forever engraved in her memories.

When TJ's green eyes glanced toward her window, Cassidy backed away, dropping the curtain over the glass, shutting out the harsh sunlight and her hopeless dreams.

She couldn't trust herself to be with a man again. Her urges were too powerful and she hadn't found the strength to control them. The best course of action was to avoid temptation altogether. With her eyes pressed closed to the darkened room, she could feel the sting of tears pushing against her eyelids, demanding release. Anger knotted her chest and she slammed her fist against the wall, leaving a small indentation in the painted sheetrock. As with her sexual appetite, her physical strength was also a factor she hadn't quite mastered, yet even that was fading with each passing day.

Since the incident on campus, she'd mourned the loss of her freedom, cursing her stupidity for walking alone in the shadowy path between buildings. Her lack of forethought and self-preservation techniques now doomed her to a life secluded from others—a life without TJ and without the ability to bear children.

The heavy weight of depression settled about her shoulders and she trudged down the staircase to the living room. Once a sun-filled space, the curtains were pulled tightly over the windows blocking out every last ray of sunshine—the most deadly poison to Cassidy's body. Only a few weeks ago she'd lazed in the back yard, enjoying the scent of freshly cut grass, allowing the late-afternoon rays to soak into her skin. Now she could only relive those moments in her mind—memories that would have to suffice for the rest of her existence.

Her eyes filling with tears, she stumbled on the antique Persian carpet and knocked a lamp off the end table next to the couch. The lamp couldn't have fallen onto the carpet. No, it had to fall backward onto the hardwood flooring, the bulb shattering into a million tiny shards of razor-sharp glass.

Instinctively, Cassidy bent to retrieve the pieces.

The moment her fingers closed around the largest shard, the doorbell rang. She jumped back, her hand compressed around the glass and the sharp edges pierced her palm.

The pain was sharp, but dissipated by the time she reached the door. Who would be calling on her? She'd cut herself off from all her friends and acquaintances.

Perhaps it was a salesman. She hesitated on the other side of the solid wood paneling, wanting contact with others, but fearing the stream of sunshine that would fill the entranceway.

The doorbell chimed again and Cassidy jumped, her nerves stretched to their limits.

"Cassidy, it's TJ. I know you're home. Please let me in." The low baritone of TJ's voice was barely muffled by the solid wood standing between them, and it poured over Cassidy like hot chocolate.

Cassidy leaned against the wall and sank down to her haunches. A surge of emotions threatened to make her forget herself. She wanted to fling the door aside to let the only man she'd cared for into her home.

No. She bit into her lip, the sharp pain a slim reminder of the control she needed to get through this encounter. If she ignored him, he would go away. Like he had before. Guilt had eaten at her when she'd refused to return his calls. Longing had built like a demolition ball repeatedly slamming against her chest. But she couldn't act on it, couldn't let TJ back in her life. She didn't deserve him.

A soft sob caught in her throat and she willed TJ to go away. As silence settled on the hallway, Cassidy held her breath, straining to hear the sound of footsteps leading away from her front door.

Then the handle twisted and she remembered she hadn't locked the door. With speed born of desperation, she leaped from the hardwood floor and reached her empty hand for the lock. But the door opened and TJ stepped in, bringing with him a flood of sunshine.

Cassidy winced, her eyes blinded by the brilliance. Where the sun lanced across her body, her skin seared.

She staggered backward into the shadows of the darkened hallway.

"Cassidy?" TJ frowned, moving forward to grab her arm. "Are you all right?" He sniffed the air. "What's that smell? Is something burning?"

Her mouth moved, but she couldn't form the words to answer him. The pain of the sun was intense, but no more so than the pain of seeing TJ again.

TJ's frown deepened. "You don't look well. Here, let me help you to the couch."

No. Please go away, a voice screamed inside her head, but her heart refused to let the words past her lips. *Fool! Don't bring him down with you.* Despite her inner warning, she let him lead her into the living room and press her onto the cushions of her grandmother's antique sofa.

All her senses were focused on where his hand held her elbow. The pulse beating in his fingertips pounded through her awareness like the bass drum of a marching band.

She should send him away. Now! Before she did something stupid. Her veins pulsed to the rhythm of his, as if they were one being, connected at a single point, sharing the same blood she so desperately needed.

"What have you done to your hand?" He grasped her other hand and leaned over her.

She hadn't realized she still held the jagged remains of the light bulb. Blood oozed from between her fingers. "It's nothing," she managed. "I can take care of it myself."

"Like hell." His voice was gruff as he pried her hand open and removed the offending glass. "Damn, Cassidy."

Yeah, she was damned all right. Instead of staring at where his hand touched hers, she could only see the suntanned length of his exposed neck, the jugular vein thumping just beneath the skin.

"Where do you keep your first aid kit?" he asked.

She couldn't think past the thrumming of the blood in his veins.

When she didn't respond, he turned her face up to his and spoke slowly, "Cassidy, where is your first aid kit?"

With all the control she could muster, she concentrated on his words. "In the medicine cabinet in the downstairs bathroom."

By the time the last word passed her lips, he'd left her.

Without the warmth of his hands on hers, or his nearness scrambling her wits, she regained a semblance of balance and stood. She had to get him out of the house as soon as possible.

His life and her sanity depended on it.

Two

TJ rifled through the medicine cabinet in the bathroom, his heart beating hard in his chest, forcing blood to slam through his body charged with adrenalin.

As he'd walked across the lawn to Cassidy's house, he'd told himself he only wanted to make sure she left the city. She should have evacuated today. As a cop and protector of the population of Houston, he was only as concerned about her as he was anyone else still left in the city.

So he'd thought.

When she'd refused to answer her door, panic seized him. Was she sick? Was that why she hadn't contacted him? Had he been nursing his bruised ego while Cassidy had been laid up, unable to answer the telephone?

He gripped the edge of the counter and steadied himself. God, if he had been wrong all this time, would she ever forgive him?

Hell, she was bleeding and he was standing in the bath-room berating himself, wasting valuable time. He shook off his thoughts and grabbed a red pouch marked First Aid. As he loped back into the living room, he dug through the package for antiseptic, gauze and adhesive tape.

When he rounded the corner of the hall leading into the liv-ing room, he had his head down and didn't see Cassidy until too late.

He plowed headfirst into her. Tossing the first aid kit to the floor, he grabbed her arms to keep her from falling to the floor. The forward momentum didn't stop them and they ended up slammed against the wall.

A puff of minty air blew into his face when his chest crashed into hers and a soft fragrance wafted up to tease his nostrils. Every nerve ending clamored beneath TJ's skin, sending ur-gent messages to points south. His uniform trousers tightened, his cock springing to attention at the softness of her belly be-neath the rigid row of his fly.

A groan escaped him and he pushed against the wall, brac-ing his hands on either side of her. "Are you okay?" His gaze fell into her bottomless brown eyes, and he was immediately struck by the longing he could swear was shining through. Then she blinked and lowered her gaze to his mouth. Had he only imagined it?

Her tongue darted out tracing a line of moisture over her lower lip, highlighting the deep rose hue with a glistening sheen.

TJ leaned closer, drawn to her despite his resolve to play the unaffected cop. Cop who? He was a man, she was a woman—an extremely desirable woman and all he wanted was to kiss her. To thrust his tongue deep into her mouth and taste the woman who'd been part of his thoughts every minute of every day since he'd made love to her.

For a moment, her chin lifted as if to accept his kiss, then her hands inserted themselves between them and she pushed. "No."

He stood in a sensual daze for a few seconds after her firm refusal. While TJ mentally pulled his brain out of his briefs, Cassidy ducked beneath his arms and stepped out of reach.

Forcing a smile, he straightened, his arms dropping to his sides. "I saw you in the window and wanted to make sure you plan to evacuate soon."

"Evacuate?" Her confused stare looked genuine.

"You must not have been watching the news." Who in this day and age didn't watch the news?

She twisted the fabric of her sundress, crimping wrinkles in the thin cotton. "No, actually, I haven't turned on the television in days."

"You haven't?" He shook his head.

"No."

"Then you might not be aware, the mayor issued a mandatory evacuation order."

"Why?"

"A category five hurricane is headed straight for us." TJ's brows pushed together. "Have you been sick?"

She turned her profile to him, avoiding eye contact as she answered. "Yes . . . yes, I've been ill."

TJ's chest tightened. So she had been sick and he hadn't done anything about it. "Do you want me to drive you the hospital?"

"No!" Her gaze darted toward him, her eyes widening.

He held up his hands. "Okay, okay. So, maybe we won't take you to the doctor." Why was she so spooked by the prospect? Had she had a bad experience with a doctor or hospital in the past? TJ realized just how little he knew about Cassidy's past. At the time he'd taken her to his bed, he didn't think it mattered. In every other way, she'd been his perfect mate. And she made him laugh. Surely he could reach her again, push past this barrier she'd erected between them. "Then tell me, Cassidy . . . what's wrong."

"Nothing. I'm fine." Again, her gaze swept the vicinity of his knees.

When he moved to take her arms, she backed away. "I think you should leave."

"What happened between us, Cassidy?" God, he hated the pleading in his voice, but he couldn't help it. He'd missed her, and he wanted her so much he was willing to plead a little.

Her bunched fist rose to her mouth and her eyes glistened. "Nothing. It just wasn't meant to be."

No explanation, no excuses, just a brush off. So be it. As if pulling a shutter down over his heart, TJ stood taller and nodded. "Okay, I can take a hint." Could he, when all he wanted was to grab her and shake the answers out of her? But that didn't solve anything. "When are you going to evacuate?"

She stared up into his eyes, searching. "Do you think it's as bad as the forecast predicts?"

"You saw what happened with Katrina in New Orleans and the damage Rita did to east Texas. Don't take the chance. Get out."

"I will," she said, her voice unconvincing.

Crossing his arms over his chest, TJ demanded, "When?"

"Tonight."

"Promise?"

"Yeah," she said, chewing at her lip.

"Don't fuck with me. I need to know you'll be safely away from Houston when this one hits."

A brief smile lifted the corner of her lips before she nodded. "Don't worry about me." She pushed strands of her long black hair behind her ear and stared around the room before her gaze returned to him. "By the way, what's her name?"

"Who?" Her softened look and the way her dark hair curved around her earlobe made TJ's thoughts muddy with the desire to fill his hands with all those silky strands.

Again the flitting smile, one like she used to give him when they studied for their criminology class. "The hurricane?"

For a moment, TJ thought the old camaraderie was back. "The hurricane?" He leaned his head back and inhaled. With only a glance, she made him forget himself. Righting his head, he stared back at her, determined to keep this on a professional level. "It's a him. Hurricane Thomas. A cat five hurricane, as of the last report from the weather center, and headed our way."

"When is it supposed to hit?"

"Tomorrow night."

She nodded.

"So, you're going to evacuate?" Once she agreed, he could leave. With Cassidy out of the way, he could concentrate on his job—killing vampires.

She nodded, her hands clasped behind her back.

"Good," he said, although he felt anything but good about her answer.

"Yes, good." Her brows rose in her pale face.

TJ didn't remember her being so pasty-white the last time they were together. It worried him. At the same time he found the pallor of her skin gave her an ethereal quality unlike before. "Are you sure you're all right?"

Emitting a gentle snort, she nodded. "Couldn't be better."

He stood there with nothing more to say. She didn't want him back in her life, having made it perfectly clear by the way she'd urged him to leave. "Then I have work to do to get my storm shutters in place. Do you need help with yours before you leave?"

"I'll take care of them." She held up her hand to forestall his next protest. "Don't worry, they're new and easy to close."

"If you're sure. I don't mind." And if he stayed to help her with the shutters, he'd be around her that much longer.

Pathetic.

"You need to go. I'm sure you have to work tomorrow."

TJ turned to leave, but something stopped him. When he turned back to Cassidy, he caught her staring at him like she wished he wouldn't go, but was unwilling to stop him.

Her chin dipped toward the floor, a soft rosy hue staining her cheeks.

"What happened, Cassidy?" TJ asked. "What went wrong?" He could feel her hesitation and he closed in on her. "Was it something I said or didn't say?"

She shook her head and a single drop slid from the inside corner of her eye all the way down her cheek. "It wasn't you."

He reached out and lifted her chin to look into brown eyes awash with tears. "Did you ever feel anything for me? Or was it all about the sex?" That's what the woman was supposed to say to the man. A laugh threatened to bubble up in his throat. Not that anything was funny about the situation.

Her bottom lip trembled and more tears slipped down her face. "It wasn't you." She twisted free of his hand.

TJ wasn't ready to let her go, the familiar anger rising in his chest. He couldn't walk away without a fight. He ran his finger along her jaw, the moistness of her tears tugging at his heart. "Look at me and tell me you don't care."

With her gaze trained on the top button of his uniform, she said in little more than a choked whisper, "I don't care."

He curled his fingers around her shoulders and shook her gently. "Cassidy, look me in the eyes and say it," he said. When she refused, his control slipped and the frustration of the past lonely days burst out. "Look at me!" His shout sounded harsh even to his own ears.

Cassidy's head shot up, her eyes, sparkling through the unshed tears. "Okay, I felt something! Damn it! I felt something! Are you happy?" She pulled out of his grip and strode across the floor, her back to him. "Now will you go?"

"Not yet." All the resentment drained from him and his heart squeezed in his chest. He closed the distance between them and took her in his arms, slowly turning her around. "Not yet."

His mouth descended on hers and he felt the worry and anger wash away in that single kiss.

When her lips parted in a gasp, his tongue darted between her teeth. He tasted and toyed with her tongue, coaxing her to the level of his passion.

For a moment she stood in his arms unyielding and stiff. Then her hands crept up his chest and circled the back of his neck, pressing his head down toward her and her body relaxed into his.

TJ's hands slid downward, cupping her buttocks and pulling her against his rigid arousal. With his heart beating like a runner in a marathon, he reminded himself to slow down. He didn't want to scare her away again.

The way she moved showed no fear or hesitation. Soon, she took the lead in kissing and caressing, her fingers dancing across his skin, kneading his flesh, digging in to stake her claim. She maneuvered him around until his back was against the wall. Then her hand cupped his face and she bit down on his lip, nibbling and teasing him until his cock pressed painfully against the confines of his pants.

A vague thought skittered by. *How could this be happening when she would have nothing to do with me a moment ago?* What magical cure had righted the wrong he still couldn't name? Whatever it was, he didn't care. Cassidy was in his arms. He pressed his trouser-clad knee between her legs and marveled at the moisture he felt all the way through the fabric.

With deft hands, she unbuttoned his shirt and spread it wide, threading her fingers through the crisp blond hairs sprinkled across his chest. Then her lips joined her hands, teasing the hard brown nipples until TJ moaned.

He reached out, eager to see her naked skin, to touch those places he had only dreamed of a moment ago. With more haste than gentleness, he caught her sundress by the hem and yanked it up and over her head in one fluid movement. Then he tossed it to the floor, his gaze skimming over her, his cock swelling at the sight of her naked breasts and the thin wedge of black lace panties covering the apex of her thighs. "God, I've missed you, Cassidy."

Pulling her close, TJ slanted his mouth over hers in a kiss so deep and tender, he felt it fill the empty space in his chest. This was the woman for him, and now that he had her back in his arms, he'd never let her go.

Cassidy's hands ripped at his shirt, tearing it away from his body. Then her cool slim fingers dove lower, slipping the top button free on his pants. With a slow sexy smile, she dragged the zipper down with one hand while the other glided inside the fabric, following her heated handiwork. The pressure against his penis eased with every inch of unveiling. At the same time, the tension increased until he felt he would explode.

Inside his trousers, her hands slid around his backside to cup his ass. Then she shoved his pants down until they hung to his knees. His cock jutted forward, angling toward her, hard and eager. With only the thin scrap of lace panties between them, TJ was in a frenzy to take it the rest of the way.

But Cassidy had taken full control, and she cupped his balls, squeezing gently, rolling them with the smooth pads of her fingers.

He reached for and captured her hips in his grip, pressing her against his hardness, rubbing the tip of his penis against the erotically abrasive lace.

His breath hissed between his teeth as he dragged in air, reminding himself to breathe.

Cassidy's hand froze in the process of sliding up his shaft. "Did I hurt you?"

"Yes! No! Oh God, that feels incredible." Then his fingers hooked into the lace and dragged it down her legs until her pale body gleamed naked in the shadows of the entryway. With her near-black hair hanging about her shoulders, and the pearly white of her skin beckoning him, he couldn't hold back any more. "I want you, Cassidy. I want to make love to you like we did before."

She closed her eyes and inhaled a shaky breath. Then her shoulders pushed back and she came to him, sliding a sleek feminine leg up his thigh to rest at his hip. Her cunt rubbed against his thigh, the moisture sending shockwaves of lust to his cock. "I want you too, Officer Evans."

His mouth consumed hers and he lifted her legs up around his waist, lowering her until her pussy creamed over the tip of his cock. Hesitating for only a moment, he stared into her eyes. Then he eased into her warmth.

Moaning against his throat, she licked a line from his collarbone to his earlobe. His balls tightened in response, and he lifted her up, taking her to the end of his cock and back down to sheath him again in her creamy depths.

Cassidy leaned into him and practically purred against his cheek. "Stop me now, TJ, before it's too late." While her words said one thing, her hands racing across his skin encouraged him to continue.

With his mind caught in a cloud of desire, TJ couldn't stop. Couldn't pull free of her until he slaked his desire. Tension built, rising in surges, centering on the juncture of their joined bodies.

Cassidy moaned, her breasts bobbing up and down in TJ's face.

He captured one of the pale round orbs in his mouth and sucked hard, drawing the rounded flesh into his mouth, laving the taut rosy nipple.

She murmured her approval and nuzzled his neck, nipping at the skin with her teeth.

The tender bites only fueled the fires and spurred him on. He spun around and pressed her back to the wall where he could leverage her while he plunged deeper inside. He pumped into her again and again, until his entire body tightened into an orgasmic knot.

On his final thrust, he peaked, teetering on the verge of shooting sperm deep inside her.

At that exact moment, Cassidy clamped her legs tightly around his waist, licked his neck in a long, sexy swipe, then she leaned in, her mouth opening to take his throat between her teeth.

The pager buried deep in TJ's trouser pocket beeped, cutting through their labored breathing and vibrating against his knee. The effect was to jerk him out of the sensual haze and remind him they'd used no protection.

"Damn it!" Without pulling out of her, TJ fumbled to reach for the pager around his knees. With his cock still firmly entrenched in her channel, the task was impossible.

When the pager beeped again, Cassidy's lips were sealed around TJ's carotid artery and her teeth were poised to puncture the skin. Holy shit! She jerked her head away. Holy Shit! She'd almost bit him.

"I'm sorry, Cassidy." TJ pulled her close and kissed her open lips.

The touch of his mouth to hers almost stung in its intensity. She could feel every beating pulse in his body, and she was still joined to him. How could she have let it go this far? "Let me down!" She beat her palms against his chest. "Let me down!" She had to get away. Hell, *he* had to get away!

"It's okay, it's just a pager and I didn't cum inside you." But he slid her upward and off his still stiff erection.

As soon as her feet hit the ground, she groped for her clothing and ducked out of reach. With her dress clutched to her chest, she turned to him.

He'd already pulled his pants up, buttoned them and stood with a confused expression denting his forehead. "I didn't come here to do that." He held his hands up. "Not that I'm sorry I did."

She turned away, fighting the desire to climb back onto him and finish what she'd started. "You should go, now."

He stepped toward her, his hand outstretched. "Cassidy, don't shut me out."

"Go. Please!" Her voice caught on a sob, and she spun to race up the stairs.

Three

TJ spent an agonizing night fighting hungry monsters. Damn, he hated vampires, the bloodthirsty bastards. He'd kill every one of them if he could.

When the day shift came on, the night shift was asked to stay and assist in last-minute evacuations. Near dusk, after being on duty for over eighteen hours, rain began to fall, gently at first. As the wind picked up, the droplets became projectiles, blowing in sideways from the south. He'd had to beg the police chief to let him weather the storm at home. Most of the force would be bedded down for the night in the precinct basement.

As he'd left the station, sustained winds blew at fifty miles an hour. Now, based on the way he was fighting to keep his truck on the road, the gusts must be nearing seventy. He hoped to hell Cassidy had gone like she said she would. He'd left so late the previous evening he hadn't had time to check.

All night and day long, his gut kept telling him she'd lied. That she never intended to leave the city. That the crazy fool would try to ride out the storm in her two-story, wood-framed home.

After parking in his garage, he peered through the sheets of blinding rain trying to glean whether or not Cassidy was still there. He couldn't see a blasted thing. With no other way to be certain, he had to go over there and check for himself.

He breathed in the innocent scent of a summer rain, hoping the torrential downpour would slack up, but knowing it wouldn't. The storm was going to get a heck of a lot worse before it got better. He hunched his shoulders and leaned against the wind as he launched into the downpour. With his hand raised before his eyes to ward off the stinging rain, he splashed through soaked grass and up onto the front porch of the old colonial house.

When he shook the water from his hair and eyes, he stared at the house and swore. None of the shutters had been closed and streams of water ran down exposed glass windows. His lips pressed together. Stubborn woman. He would have closed the shutters for her if she'd let him.

Now that the hurricane was at hand, he didn't have time to worry about her shutters. He pounded on the door and waited. No response. Wind and rain beat against his back and made standing still difficult.

"Cassidy!" He pounded again. "You better not be in there!" he shouted, feeling stupid, but not really caring. No one else was around to hear him.

With the rain thundering against the tin porch roof, he couldn't hear anything going on inside to indicate whether or not Cassidy was still at home. His gut tightened when he noticed her car parked in the garage. If she tried to ride out the storm in her house, no telling what would happen.

He hammered against the door again. "Cassidy!"

No answer and he didn't feel any more confident that she'd evacuated. The only other choice was to break the door in and check from room to room. He stepped back, took a deep breath and kicked his heel against the door next to the deadbolt.

The loud sound of wood splitting wasn't followed by the door flying open like TJ had hoped. He snorted. *She would have a good deadbolt.* Hell, he'd helped her install it.

He stepped back again, breathed deeply once . . . twice . . . and kicked the door again. The wood cracked and the door shook but didn't open.

A gust of wind slammed into him and slung him against the hardwood paneling. The weather was getting rougher and the sky darker as night approached. He couldn't stay outside much longer without risking injury from flying debris.

"Cassidy!" He pounded his fists on the door. "Open the damned door!" With his hand raised to pound again, he stopped just as the door whipped open.

The wind jerked the knob out of Cassidy's hand and slammed the door against the wall with enough force the doorknob penetrated the sheetrock.

Cassidy staggered backward as the storm swept through the opening, entering the house uninvited and claiming what it could reach as its own. Before she could object, TJ allowed the wind to push him through the doorway. He turned and forced the door closed behind him, shutting out the sideways rain.

Outside, the storm wailed and thrashed against the house

as if angry it had been cheated. The windows shuddered to hold back the force of nature threatening to break through the single-paned glass.

With the door closed, TJ spun to face Cassidy, anger pulsing through him like a jackhammer through concrete. "What the hell are you still doing here?"

She stood, her shoulders hunched in silence.

"Why?" he asked. "Why didn't you leave when you had the chance? Are you completely out of your mind?"

Her head jerked up and she stared at him, her arms crossing over her full breasts. "You think I didn't want to leave? You think I'm stupid for staying? Well, to hell with what you think, TJ Evans. I sure as hell don't need you telling me what I have to do!"

The fire in her eyes beat the defeated look of yesterday. This was the woman who'd captured his imagination and every sleeping and waking thought, not the one he'd seen hiding in the shadows for the past couple weeks.

TJ took a deep breath and let it out slowly before he attempted to say anything else. He reminded himself he was glad he'd gotten to her before anything happened. "I'm sorry." He scrubbed a hand through his hair. "I was angry and scared for you." He wanted to shout, but he held his voice in check. Before he pissed her off again, he had to get her out of her house and into his. Soon. Really soon.

"Don't worry about me," she said, the anger draining out of her voice. "I can take care of myself."

"I know you can. But you don't have your storm shutters in place. All it takes is flying debris to break through a window—"

At that exact moment, a window shattered upstairs.

Cassidy screamed and threw herself at TJ, burying her face against his chest. "I didn't think about that. I guess I just wasn't thinking much."

"Come on," he commanded in a low coaxing voice, tugging her toward the door. "Let's get to my house before this storm gets worse."

"No!" She pushed against him, her pathetic attempt to break free wrenching at TJ's heart. Her face looked almost gray in the dim hallway and her skin was cool to the touch.

"I should have taken you to the hospital, yesterday." He held her, refusing to let her get away this time. If he had to, he'd pick her up and carry her the short distance to his house.

She mumbled into his shirt.

TJ bent his head to hear her over the howling wind and could swear he heard her say, "It's too late."

"Cassidy, come with me to my house," he coaxed softly.

"I can't," she said, lifting her face to his, her eyes filling with tears. "You're not safe with me. Just leave me alone."

"No. I won't leave you alone." TJ's jaw tightened and his brows lowered over his eyes. "Your house isn't ready for the storm. I can't walk away knowing you'll be hurt."

Past caring, her shoulders sagged. "It doesn't matter what happens to me, now."

"Cassidy, how can I help you if I don't know what's going on?" He pulled her against his chest.

So weak she could hardly hold her head up, she leaned into him and pressed her forehead to his wet shirt. Her knees buckled and before she knew what was happening, TJ scooped her into his arms.

"I'm taking you to my house. No more arguments." With that he flung the door open and launched them out into the rain.

Too weak to resist, Cassidy clung to his jacket, tucking her face against the solid muscles of his chest.

Streetlights barely penetrated the darkness of the night and driving rain, but TJ strode sure-footed across the lawn and into his home. Without loosening his hold, he kicked the door shut behind him and carried her into the living room, switching on the lights as he went.

He sat her on the couch, perched on the cushion next to her and gripped her hands in his. "Now, tell me what's going on? Are you sick?"

She leaned back, enjoying being taken care of at the same time as she worried about what would happen now. "I guess you could say I am sick. But it's nothing anyone can cure."

"Have you talked to the doctors?" he asked, his voice soft, yet concerned.

She rolled her eyes and stared at him. "No. And please don't do the gallant thing and haul me off to the hospital. I'm weak right now because I haven't eaten in three days." Her head fell back against the sofa.

"I can make you some food. Let me help."

His eagerness to help made the tears harder to hide, and one slid down her cheek. "You can't help. What I need, I refuse to eat."

"I don't get it, Cassidy." TJ squeezed her hands. "Why won't you eat? What's happened?"

Cassidy sighed and pulled her fingers free. "I was attacked three weeks ago on campus."

He leaped to his feet, his fists clenched at his side. "Why didn't you tell me? I'm a cop for godsakes!"

"What could you do?"

"Find the filthy bastard and put him in jail, for one."

She shook her head. "Wouldn't do any good. The damage is done."

"What happened, Cassidy?" He gripped her shoulders. "Did the guy rape you?"

"Yes." Her gaze dropped to where her hand pleated the hem of her damp dress. "And worse."

TJ dropped to his knees in front of Cassidy and took her hands in his. "Did you think it would make a difference how I felt for you? I love you, Cassidy. I think I've known it from the day we met."

"Don't." She pulled her hands from his. "You can't love me. I'm tainted. Ruined."

"Not to me."

"Wait'll you hear the rest." She dragged in a deep breath. "The attacker bit me, TJ."

Still kneeling on the floor, TJ's gaze narrowed. "Where?"

"On the neck." Cassidy leaned her head to the side and pointed to the smooth column of her throat.

"You mean like a vampire?" His voice dropped to a low rumble, and he stood.

A chill swept over her body. "Not like. He was a vampire."

TJ's face grew still, the only movement the muscle twitching in his jaw. "And are you?"

"What? A vampire?" She breathed deeply, fighting back the anger and tears. "If not being able to go out in the sunlight means I'm a vampire . . . or craving blood . . . or being unable to control my sexual urges . . . then yes. It's safe to say I'm a vampire." She held up her hand. "Not that I chose to be one."

"Wow." TJ turned away and pushed a hand through his hair.

"Thanks." She pushed to her feet and swayed, her head spinning, reminding her of her need for sustenance. "Now, if you'll excuse me I think I'll go back to my house. Maybe the storm will blow it and me away so you don't have to think about what this means to your job."

TJ spun to face her, his forehead creased in a fierce frown. "This isn't about my career, Cassidy. You were the victim here."

"Yeah, but if I stay around you much longer, you will be the victim." She returned his piercing gaze with one of her own. "That's why I wanted you to leave me alone."

The broad-shouldered cop sucked in a breath and blew it out slowly.

Although she'd expected it, his hesitation hurt.

Then he reached for her hand and threaded his fingers through hers. "You are the victim."

She tried to pull her hand from his, but he held tight. The only defense against a broken heart was to launch her own attack. Schooling her face into a blank mask, she asked, "What do you do on your job, Detective TJ Evans?"

A muscle twitched in his jaw and a long moment passed where the only sound was the wind howling against the eaves.

The outside storm couldn't begin to compete with the internal tempest twisting her in knots. This was the man she'd been falling for since the spring semester began. One night of carelessness had ripped all that away.

TJ stared down into her eyes and admitted, "I kill vampires."

"Yeah." She smoothed a hand over his cheek.

He looked away as if so confused, so lost.

"Don't you see?" she said, turning his face toward her, willing him to look her in the eye. "It's your job and your duty to kill me."

"No!" He grasped her hand and held it to his cheek. "This isn't right."

"Right or wrong, it's your job. You have to keep the streets safe from monsters like me."

"But you're not a monster. You're my Cassidy."

She shrugged. "Not anymore. I crave blood, I need it to survive. No matter how much I want to ignore it, I can't control my blood lust and my sex—"

A spark flared TJ's eyes back to life. "And your sexual lust?" He trailed a finger down the side of her breast. "Is that what happened in your hallway yesterday? Was it all part of the vampire package?"

"There has to be some attraction for the lust, but yeah." His hand did incredible things to her insides. If she wasn't careful she'd lose control again. "Look, I should go." When she took a step toward the door, the room swam and she grabbed for something to hold onto. Her hand found his and she held on until the wave of dizziness passed.

His arm circled her waist and he held her against his damp body. "Let me help."

"What can you do? You don't have a pint of blood handy do you?" Her words were meant to be flippant, but they caught in her throat on a sob. "Oh, TJ, I'm so sorry."

"It wasn't your fault." He pulled her into his arms and pressed his check against her cold one. "After that time we made love, I thought I'd scared you off. That's why you stayed away."

"No way," she said into his neck, her teeth only a breath away from the strong flowing blood beneath his skin.

"Let me help you." He pushed her back and stared into her eyes.

"How? Do you think that you could drive me to the nearest blood bank and I'll just run in and make a withdrawal?" She shook her head. "It doesn't work that way."

His hands tightened. "Let me feed you."

"No!" She tried to back away from him, horrified at how her body leaped at the offer, her mouth watering in anticipation. "I can't. You can't."

"Why not?" He straightened his shoulders. "You didn't ask to be a vampire, but you have to be fed to stay alive, right? I'm offering to help. Let me."

Temptation stared at her in the form of one very sexy, muscular cop. Should she take him up on the offer and slake her thirst? Would she be able to stop at just enough or would she go too far? "I don't know how to control how much I take."

"Have you fed off others?" he asked, tipping her chin up.

"Yes." It cost her to admit to it. She found it disturbing, biting into a stranger's throat. Taking without asking. "I didn't kill anyone or make them a vampire. I stopped in time."

"Then feed off me. I'll take my chances."

The sincerity in his voice and the gentleness of his touch were her undoing. "You don't know what you're getting into. Hell, I don't either. This is all new to me."

"Then let's learn together." He brushed his lips against hers.

The tenderness of his kiss slammed into Cassidy like the wind against the outside of the house. The door to her restraint blew open and all her cravings burst free. "Are you sure?" She gasped as she pressed her breasts to his chest, not convinced she could stop herself, even if he changed his mind.

"Absolutely."

"Will it put your career in danger?" she whispered as her lips trailed along his jaw line and down to the warm pulse in his throat. Hunger surged up from her belly, filling her chest and rising upward. Her mouth opened and her gums stretched allowing the incisors to lengthen and sharpen into gleaming white daggers.

"Just do it, Cassidy. Let me worry about my job." He reached up to cup the back of her head and shove her down on his neck.

Four

$\mathscr{P}$ain ripped through him from the point of penetration to every nerve in his body. Self-preservation instincts kicked in and he grasped her arms to shove her off. Before he could, the pain fell away like so much chaff in the breeze, replaced by tingling warmth. Sensuous heat spread through his body.

Fear fluttered through his belly. For the past weeks, he'd been fighting vampires on the streets of Houston. They were evil, treacherous monsters. Now he'd given his throat to one of them.

No. Cassidy was his girl. His neighbor, human in every way except the teeth penetrating his jugular. What had he been thinking? Was her plea of blood a trick? Would she kill him and have the last laugh on the gullible cop?

Cassidy's hand skimmed down his back to his buttocks, cupping it firmly and pressing him into her pelvis.

His cock jerked to life and swelled beneath his trousers.

Thoughts jumbled in his head as the waves of desire clouded his brain and forged their way to his lower extremities, igniting his senses into a frenzy of lust and a need so commanding he couldn't deny.

The hands he'd gripped her with smoothed down her arms, sliding over moist droplets of rain. Lower still, they traveled to the hem of her dress, lifting it up over her hips.

A loud thump sounded from outside the house, but it barely registered in TJ's head. He couldn't think beyond driving his engorged penis into this incredible woman.

The harder and faster the better. But he was limited to how far he could move without breaking her hold on his neck. Intense waves of pleasure surged from the point her mouth touched him, and he was incapable of turning her away.

With her dress bunched up around her waist, he tore at her panties, pushing the scrap of lace and elastic over her hips and down her thighs.

Cassidy moaned and pressed her furry mound against his pants, fumbling to unbuckle his belt with one hand. Her haste only cost more time.

Shoving her hands away, TJ grabbed for the belt, unbuckled and ripped it from his belt loops.

"Show-off," she said into his neck, her lips brushing against his skin like feathers of a boa.

"I take it you're feeling better?" His fingers worked loose the top button of his uniform trousers.

"Ummmm, you've no idea." Before he could unzip his pants, her hands were there, sliding beneath the waistband, pressing the zipper down at the same time her fingers slid into his briefs.

"I think I do." All the air left his lungs when her hand rolled his balls between her fingers. "Oh, yes. I think I do."

He lifted her legs around him and carried her down the hall into his bedroom. Setting her ass onto the edge of the bed, he eased her back until he lay over her, his chest pressing against hers, the fabric of his shirt and her dress unwanted layers between their skin.

Her legs fell open and TJ pressed his cock against her creamy opening, fighting the urge to slam his way home and fuck her like there would be no tomorrow. And the way the storm raged outside, there might not be a tomorrow for the two of them.

Yet, he held back, knowing how much more satisfying it would be to see her come, to witness her screaming out his name, begging him to take her.

Insinuating his hand between them, he parted her folds and flicked her swollen clitoris.

Cassidy bucked beneath him, her teeth sinking deeper into his neck, inspiring bittersweet rivulets of pain to trickle across his nerves. "Easy, now."

Her jaw loosened and her tongue shot out to lave his skin.

As the pain subsided, his fingers slid lower and dipped into her cunt, stroking the inner walls with first one, then two fingers until he had all four fingers shoved in as deep as they would go.

Another moan vibrated against his neck and her legs rose up around him.

Before she could lock them around his middle, he put out a hand halting her progress. "Un-uh. Not yet."

A mewl of protest gurgled from her throat as she released his throat and licked his blood from her lips.

For all the nights of fighting bad vamps, TJ wondered why seeing a tongue lap at the deep red blood didn't repulse him.

Her heels braced on the edge of the bed, she pushed upward, ramming his hand farther into her.

With his other hand, he cupped her ass and slid a finger down the crease between her cheeks until he found her anus. He dragged her juices downward circling the tight little hole, coating it before he poked in.

Cassidy's fingers raked across his back and kneaded the muscles along the base of his spine. Her strength had returned and she was ready.

A vague thrill of satisfaction filled him knowing he was the one to provide her sustenance. His penis throbbed, demanding release, aching for the smooth, slick walls of her vagina wrapped around him.

"Scoot back," he urged, lifting her to shift her farther onto the mattress.

She inched backward until she lay across the middle of the bed.

The brief loss of connection left TJ breathless and off balance, until Cassidy looked up at him, her hooded gaze beckoning him. She spread her legs wide and ran a hand down over her mons, swirling a finger across the opening to her pussy, coating it with a thick sheen of come. With his blood still staining her lips bright red, she said, "Fuck me."

Unable to resist, and completely mindless of the consequences, TJ climbed between her thighs, and poised his cock at the mouth of her glistening core.

Her legs snaked up and around his waist and slammed him into her at the same time she reclaimed his neck.

A euphoric haze blinded him but for the woman writhing beneath him. TJ rammed into her, lifting her hips to drive deeper until her teeth clamped tight over his throat and her body went rigid.

Blood pounded against his eardrums like a freight train, roaring through his head like a raging storm. His own body peaked and spiraled into a mind-blowing kaleidoscope of exploding sensations. With his cock sheathed to the hilt, he froze, letting his orgasm wash over him until he lay limp against her body.

Sometime afterward, he could feel her teeth retract, slipping free of his skin. Her tongue swept over the wounds, gently laving the punctures, the gesture strangely soothing.

"Wow," he said, nuzzling her ear as he lay on the bed next to her, turning her to face him without breaking their intimate connection.

"Wow," she echoed, a smile curving her lips as she lay with her eyelids at half-mast.

"If I'd known making love with a vampire was so great, I'd have done it much sooner."

Her brow furrowed and she slapped at his arm. "And here I thought you actually liked me for who I am, not what I am."

He pulled her into his arms and held her against his chest. "More than you can imagine. I thought you never wanted to see me again."

Snuggling closer, she unbuttoned his shirt and pressed her cheek to his naked chest. "I wanted to come to you so badly. But I didn't know how you'd react to my . . . er . . . condition."

He nipped at her ear. "I can see where your . . . condition could be an advantage." He pushed his still stiff cock deeper.

"But what about your job, your life?"

Tugging gently, he inched her dress up and over her head.

He loved seeing all of her body and it was even more beautiful with her appetite satiated, her skin pink and healthy. "I definitely have some rethinking to do on this whole vampire thing." His stomach flipped at what his supervisor would say if he knew TJ had slept with the enemy.

She reached up and traced a finger across his lip. "I'll understand if you don't want to see me anymore."

Not see her? This was Cassidy, not a mindless, heartless beast. Had he been wrong all along about vampires?

"Not all vampires are bad," she said, as if reading his thoughts. "Just like not all humans are good."

"True. As it is, I like working nights, and I can't imagine spending my life with a mere mortal after having you." He rocked his hips, his cock swelling within her channel.

"I can never have children," she said, sliding her arms out of her bra.

He pressed a kiss to her bare shoulder and took one rosy-tipped breast between his teeth. "Kids are overrated."

"I'll never die. Unless I stand out in the sun too long or someone stakes me."

"I'll make sure you stay away from sharp objects. And maybe someday I'll join you."

"Would you do that for me?" Her fingers laced around his neck, pulling him down to her lips.

Would he? He stared down at Cassidy, her dark hair fanned across his pillow and couldn't think of another face he'd rather see there, human or not. "We'll take it a day at a time and see what tomorrow brings." Then he kissed her.

Outside, the raging storm spent itself and eased into a gentle, cleansing rain.

MYLA JACKSON is an award–winning, multi-published
author of highly sensuous romances. Ever since she and
her sister, Delilah Devlin, challenged each other to write
romance, neither one has looked back. From kick-ass
action/adventure to character-driven stories, she takes her
readers on wild and sexy rides, garnering fabulous reviews
and rabid fans. Myla atributes her success to her sense of
adventure, a love of fast-paced fantasies, and the synergy
she and Delilah generate as brainstorming partners.

Tempting Grace

Sasha White

To my Allure Sisters,
for their patience, support, and friendship.
You Rock, Ladies!

One

For the first time in over a year Grace Walters didn't want to go home. She didn't want to walk up the brick path and look at the pretty flower bed she'd planted just last week. She didn't want to open the door to the small two-bedroom cottage-style house that she'd bought thirteen months earlier. The one and only place she'd let herself call home since she was fourteen and decided that she was better off on the streets than in a house where no one cared.

She didn't want to go home, because she knew she'd see that small pile of clothes on the dryer that belonged to Chelsea, and then she'd have to accept that Chelsea hadn't felt at home there. That no matter what Grace had done, Chelsea had still gone back to the street, and this time, it had killed her.

Grace didn't want to remember. She didn't want to think.

"Why don't you get them both?"

She started when a deep voice broke through the thick fog coating her mind. "What?" She turned and found Lukas

Martin behind her, less than a foot away. How had he gotten so close without her even noticing? Her instincts for self-preservation had always served her well before.

"You seem to be having a hard time deciding between ice cream flavors, why not treat yourself and get both?" Lukas said with a smile. A pale eyebrow arched and a playful gleam lit up his chocolate eyes as he leaned even closer. "But if you want a real treat you should let me cook you dinner."

Grace started to say no, like she had so many times in the past month when he'd asked her out. But this time, the refusal stuck in her throat.

As if he sensed her weakness, he stepped forward, the playful gleam fading as his gaze took on a more intense heat. "Grace?"

Need blossomed from deep within. One she'd thought was long buried. She swept her gaze over his leanly muscled six-foot frame, and the energizing tingle of sensual awareness she always felt whenever Luke entered a room zipped through her. Grace knew intuitively that he could satisfy that need.

It was a bad idea. Her head knew that, but her heart, her aching heart needed to feel something other than the pain of failure, and there was one thing she'd always been good at. One thing she'd always succeeded at . . . and she was too tired to deny the pull that Lukas' eager-to-please attentions awoke within her. "One night," she whispered.

"One night?"

"One night. You and me. No dinner, and no promises." She met his gaze and let him see the need she felt rising from deep within. "Tonight."

*   *   *

Shock whipped through Lukas. She'd said yes! Adrenaline filled his veins and he fought the urge to shout out. Finally, after so many rejections, Grace had said yes.

His elation faded as her words sunk in. One night.

No dinner.

She hadn't said yes to a date. She wanted a one-night stand.

Disappointment flooded him and he started to shake his head—then he took a better look at her.

"Grace, what's wrong?" Her normally bright green eyes were dark and dull, the skin around them pinched and drawn. "Are you okay?"

She looked at the hand he'd placed on her shoulder, her head turning slowly, as if it took a lot of effort.

"I'm not hurt, Lukas." She looked up at him from beneath those long sweeping eyelashes and his pulse jumped at the raw need there. She stepped closer and placed a small hand on his chest. "I just need to feel something. I need you tonight."

There was no way in hell he was going to turn her down.

They left the grocery store quickly and quietly, neither of them buying a thing. Grace was amazingly passive as he led her out to the car and got her settled in the passenger seat. He'd never seen her so . . . dim before. As if the light from within had gone out.

The drive to her place was silent. Lukas wanted to talk to her, to ask her what had happened. What had made her change her mind about him, finally? But he wasn't sure that was the smart thing to do.

He'd never been attracted to tough girls before, and when his father had told him Grace's story it never occurred to him he'd be interested in her. But when he met the ex-stripper, he'd fallen hard and fast. The vibrancy of her personality softened the hard edges he knew she'd developed in her youth, and her love for the troubled kids she worked with was obvious to anyone with eyes.

The vibrancy was gone right now though. And so was the hardness. As a defense attorney he worked with all types of people and saw all sorts of things, and it almost seemed like Grace was in shock. If she wasn't technically in shock, she was certainly close. Making her talk about whatever set her off wasn't the smart thing to do.

And taking advantage of her vulnerability by sleeping with her wasn't the right thing to do.

He'd been enthralled by Grace ever since he met her. Her personality, her background, her attitude . . . the whole package had hooked him from day one. Not to mention she was the first woman he'd met that had made his cock stand at attention just by being near.

Lukas wasn't a fan of one-night stands. In fact, he wasn't even sure what the big attraction to sex in general was. It was nice, but it never made him feel the way he thought it should. So in the five minutes it took to get to her place, he made a decision. As much as he wanted Grace in his life, he wasn't going to change his ways.

Grace unlocked the door and entered her small house. She didn't look around, she didn't want to see what was there. Instead, she stepped inside, waited for Lukas to enter, then closed the door behind him. "Follow me," she said.

"Grace," he spoke softly as he followed her down the small corridor to her bedroom. "I don't think this is—"

She spun around just inside the entrance to her bedroom, stopping him cold. "Then don't think." She stood on her tiptoes, wrapped her arms around his neck and pressed the full length of her body against him. "Just feel."

Two

*H*e tasted good.

Grace swept her tongue across his full bottom lip before delving deep into Luke's mouth, enjoying his smooth clean flavor. His hands circled her waist, and for a minute she thought he was going to push her away. Then his grip on her tightened, pulling her closer. The hardness of his muscles against her had heat thrumming through her body, attacking the cold knot of failure that had settled deep in her chest hours ago.

She pulled back, twisted her hands in the front of his shirt, and stepped backward, pulling him into her room. His warm hands covered hers, and he tried to pull them away gently. "Grace." He shook his head at her. "This isn't right. It isn't what I want."

"It's what I want." She looked into his eyes as she walked. When the edge of the bed hit the back of her knees, she stopped. "I need to feel something warm, Lukas. I need you."

She pressed against him, kissing her way up to his ear. She nipped at his earlobe and ran her tongue gently around the rim. "This is what I want. What I need."

He pulled back slightly, and the emptiness inside her spread. She thought he was going to walk away. Their gazes locked and she knew the minute he gave in. His eyes darkened, softening as he lowered his head and pressed his lips to hers.

He was smooth and gentle when she wanted hot and hard. His tongue slipped between her lips, searching out her secrets and soothing her soul. His touch, his feel, his flavor was so much . . . *more* than she'd anticipated. A shiver danced down her spine and for a brief second she wondered if she'd made a mistake.

Then *she* stopped thinking.

A sigh of satisfaction welled up within her, and she reveled in the warmth his touch imbued. It seeped into her body, into her soul, reminding her just how good human contact could feel.

She wrapped her arms around him and fell back onto the bed, pulling him down on top of her. She'd thought she needed to dominate him; to tease and please him until he begged her to let him come, until she regained some sense of control. But really, what she'd needed instead was to remember what it was to feel. Wanting more of his warmth, she tugged his t-shirt free and reached beneath it to find hot smooth skin that shifted beneath her fingertips with every touch. Lukas nudged her chin, and she tilted her head, moaning at the fire that burned along her skin when he trailed nibbling kisses down her neck to her collarbone.

He was taking things too slow, teasing her when she didn't want teasing. She wanted more, fast. She braced her heels on the bed, and with a heave and a twist had him right where she wanted. On his back and between her legs.

She whipped her shirt over her head, discarded her bra, and leaned forward, placing a ripe pink nipple directly above his lips.

"Take it in your mouth," she told him. "Use your hands *and* your mouth, Lukas. Touch me."

"Grace?" His eyes widened, heat flaring within their depths.

"Please me, Lukas." The soft command echoed in the room.

Large male hands slid up her ribcage and cupped her breasts. When his warm mouth surrounded her nipple and he started suckling, Grace let her eyes drift shut and reveled in the sensations that swelled deep within with each tug of his lips.

She tightened her thighs around him and rocked her hips. Pressing down so the hard ridge beneath his zipper rubbed against her core, and the heat within her spread.

More, she needed more heat.

As if he could sense her thoughts Lukas shifted and sucked on her other nipple. His teeth nipped, his tongue swirled, and then he sucked and laved it. The fingers pinched and pulled at her other nipple and she gasped, her insides melting, her juices starting to flow.

"Oh yes," she sighed. Taking a deep breath she pulled away and shed the rest of her clothes. She glanced back at Lukas to find that he hadn't moved from his position on the bed except to watch her. His heated gaze ran over her nakedness, and a tight knot of arousal formed low in her belly.

"You're more beautiful than I ever imagined."

"Thank you." She stepped to the edge of the bed and reached for the hem of his t-shirt. "Now it's your turn."

When Lukas was as naked as Grace, she straddled his lap once again. This time she braced her hands on his shoulders and pinned him to the bed. He reached for her as she leaned down, and put her lips to his as she spoke.

"Do nothing, Lukas." She moved above him, the hard tips of her breasts brushing against his chest. Her belly rubbed against his as she took the head of his cock and nudged it between her swollen pussy lips. "Just enjoy the ride."

With that she impaled herself on his rigid cock, welcoming the hot hardness inside her body. She closed her eyes, and shut out everything. The sounds of his passion, the scent of sex, the pure desire in his eyes—it all faded away as she concentrated on the heat of him inside her. She rocked her hips, rubbing against his pelvic bone, feeling the head of him nudge her special spot. The hot spot that spread more warmth through her with every touch.

She concentrated all her energy on that spot, panting as she rocked faster, harder. She was so close, almost there. Her muscles trembled, but in a delicious way as she pushed forward. Fingers gripped her hips and pulled her down roughly, holding her as Lukas shouted and arched on the bed, thrusting deep. A spark ignited, and she cried out as it burst into flames that fanned out to every nerve ending in her body.

When the fires inside her faded, Grace found herself cuddled up on Lukas' chest. One of his hands was stroking her hair, the other her back. His heartbeat was strong and steady beneath her ear as he whispered soothing sounds and held her tight. It wasn't until she tasted the tears streaming past her lips that she realized she was crying.

Three

*B*efore Grace opened her eyes the next morning she became simultaneously aware of three things. The warm naked male she was sprawled over, the steady thump of his heartbeat beneath her ear, and an unusual sense of belonging.

Panic hit hard and fast, and she steeled herself to move slowly and ignore the loss of warmth as she eased away from Lukas.

No need to panic, she told herself. She crawled from the bed and padded quietly to the bathroom for her robe. She brushed her teeth and washed her face, avoiding the reflection in the mirror the whole time. With a last glance at the sleeping man in her bed she headed for the kitchen and the coffee pot.

Minutes later she slid the pot back under the still dripping spout and lifted a steaming mug to her lips. Everything would be all right. She'd laid out the rules to Lukas before they ever left the store, so he knew she'd only been looking for one night.

Besides, preacher's son or not, he was male. A one-night stand wouldn't be anything new for him.

Footsteps sounded behind her announcing his arrival in the kitchen, but she stayed at the counter with her back to the room. A well-muscled arm wrapped around her waist and pulled her back against a hard body. A body that instantly awoke a sleeping hunger within her.

"Hmmm, you smell good." He buried his nose in her hair and pressed a kiss to her neck.

She fought to control her body's reaction to his nearness. "It's the coffee."

A rough chuckle sounded, and his chest vibrated against her back. Pretending not to notice the tempting hardness pressed against her butt, Grace shifted away from him and reached into a nearby cupboard.

"Here you go." She handed him a ceramic mug and moved to sit at the kitchen table. He'd pulled his jeans on, but was still barefoot and bare-chested, and the sight was almost enough to make Grace forget why she couldn't drag him back to bed. Their coupling had been almost magical in its intensity. When he settled into the chair across from her, the soft look in his eyes made it clear he wasn't going to let her forget it either.

"Look, Lukas," she said quietly. "I was . . . in a bad place last night, and I want to thank you for being there for me. But it was a one-time thing."

He looked at her earnestly. "Why?"

Grace had expected an argument, maybe even some wounded male petulance. Luke's simple question was a surprise. "Because you're you, and I'm me, and we come from two very different worlds."

His brow furrowed before he waved her words away. "We can talk about that later. I meant why were you in a bad place? What happened to shake you up so much?"

Clutching the coffee mug in both hands to still the minute trembling, she met his gaze and spoke in a flat voice that hid both her grief, and his effect on her. "Chelsea died of an overdose last night, and I had to go to the morgue to identify the body."

"I'm sorry, Grace. I know how much those kids mean to you. My father thanks God in his prayers every night for sending you to his parish."

She nodded. She thanked God every night in her prayers for leading her to Father John's church that night fifteen years earlier. The sanctuary she'd found there had given her a new lease on life, and put her on the path to helping others. But that night was her secret. Hers and Father John's. And as much as she knew Father John loved her for her work with the troubled teens that took part in their after-school program, she also knew he'd never approve of his son getting involved with her.

"It was a tough night. And when I saw you at the store, I was still feeling a little lost myself. You were great, but it was—"

"Don't!" The firmness in his voice halted her. "Don't you dare say it was a mistake."

This was the argument she'd been waiting for. She stared into his darkening eyes and smiled softly. "Okay, it wasn't a mistake. But it can't happen again, Luke."

His cheeky grin gave birth to butterflies in her belly. "That's okay. Because next time we get together I'm going to take you out for a wonderful dinner, and maybe some dancing."

The tension left Grace's shoulders, and she allowed a small

smile when she shook her head at him. He'd been incorrigible before, if she wasn't careful he'd soon become irresistible. "There won't be any of that either. Lukas, you know anything between us is impossible."

"No, I don't know that. And neither do you. I don't understand what you're so scared of."

"I'm not scared," she denied. She got up and moved restlessly to the counter. She dumped the last of her coffee down the drain and rinsed the cup, using her actions as an excuse not to look at him while she spoke. "It's just not smart. Not only is your father my boss, but he's a minister, Luke."

"So what? My father loves you."

She turned back to him, folding her arms over her chest. "He loves me as a teen mentor and probation officer who works hard to help kids find a better life. He won't love me as the older woman fucking his son." He flinched at her harsh words, and opened his mouth, but she pressed on before he could speak. "Neither would the community that I know means so much to both of you."

"You're a part of this community, Grace."

"No." She shook her head. "I'm an outsider. I live here and I serve a function, but I'm not a part of anything."

He was in front of her in a flash. One hand cupped her cheek and the other her hip as he tilted her head up so she'd meet his gaze. "Last night you felt like the other part of my soul."

Her breath caught in her throat. He wasn't laying a line on her, she could see the truth of it in his eyes. Her heart pounded and the shell she kept it encased in cracked before she could shore it up.

"Don't, Lukas." She twisted her head and pulled away from him. "Don't make this out to be more than it was."

"You can't honestly tell me it was just a one-night stand, Grace. This has been building between us since we met. What happened between us was special. It was *right*."

She heard the anger starting to build in his voice and closed her eyes. She didn't want to hurt him, but she had to make it clear that it had only been sex. "Sex is a normal way to reassert life when grieving, and that's all it was."

"Did you learn that in your psychology classes, or are you just trying to make me feel like shit?"

"No! I'm not trying to make you feel bad at all, Lukas. I just need you to be clear on what's what."

"You want it to be clear that you used me?"

Shame made her blush. "I'm sorry, but yeah, I guess I did."

"You need to stop kidding yourself, Grace." He shook his head at her. "You're incapable of using someone like that, and nobody uses me unless I let them. I knew you were hurting over something, and I wanted to be there for you. I've been in love with you since the first day we met, and if you think I'm going to let you pretend that everything we shared last night was only because you were grieving, you've got another think coming."

He reached out and pulled her to him. His hands warm and sure as they smoothed up and down her spine, keeping her body flush against his as his mouth came down on hers. His tongue thrust between her lips and claimed ownership in a primal way.

Grace reached out to push him away only to find her fingers digging in to his shoulders, pulling him closer as she wrapped one leg around his hip and rocked her pelvis against him.

He pulled back and looked down into her eyes. "I'm going to go now, but I want you to know that this is *us*, together. It's not your grief, and it's not going to be only one night."

Before she could protest, he pressed a soft kiss to her lips and walked away. At the door to the kitchen he turned and flashed her a confident smile. "That's a promise."

Four

Lukas shoved his clenched fists deep into his pockets and fought the urge to go to Grace. A week had gone by since the morning he'd left her in her kitchen, looking shocked and a little scared. It had been a hard thing to do, but he knew it hadn't been the right time to force the issue.

That time was now.

She was much too practical to ever believe in love at first sight, so he needed to find a way to convince her it was real.

Maybe if he told her it hadn't really been at first sight?

Sure he'd been instantly attracted to her. She was a beautiful woman with an attitude who had him in an almost constant state of arousal. But it was only after spending that first afternoon with her and four of the kids she mentored, that he'd recognized the tightness in his chest for what it was.

His heart expanding and opening up to a woman that was tough as nails to the world, with a buried heart as soft as kitten fluff. So soft and willing she was to open her home to an addicted teen runaway when the girl refused the shelter of the church basement.

In the last month he'd spent as much time as he could at the church, taking part in the mentorship program, and asking Grace out. She'd refused him every time. She couldn't, she told him. She worked for his father. She was too old for him. None of her excuses mattered to him.

Then he'd been in the right place at the right time to be there for her. He'd never meant to tell her how he felt right away. He knew her well enough to know that it would only scare her away. So, instead of forcing her to listen, he'd tried to stay away, to give her time to notice his absence, and maybe even miss him. A week had been all he could handle, and now it was time to change tactics.

"I hope you know what you're getting into, Lukas." His father's voice was soft.

They stood side by side watching as Grace said good-bye to the last teenager. "I love her, Dad. It's not going to be easy getting past the brick wall she has around her heart, but I know that once I do, I'll find my own private heaven in her arms."

"You have your mother's poetic soul, Lukas." Father John Martin blessed him with a soft smile few people saw. It was a blend of love, pride, and pain. It was the one that told of the loss he suffered since his wife had been killed in a convenience store robbery five years earlier.

Lukas saw that smile and clapped his hand on his dad's shoulder. His parents had been soul mates and partners. When his mother had been killed, he'd worried his father would do something stupid, like hunt down the kids that had robbed the store and beat the crap out of them. Not something a typical priest would do, but his father wasn't your typical anything.

Instead, once he'd gotten control of his anger and hurt, he'd looked for ways to get the street kids in their neighborhood the mentoring they needed. He'd made it his goal to give the kids options so that they didn't get sucked into the shady ways of life that were all too common around there.

His dad met Luke's gaze. "There's a good reason she built those walls, son," he warned.

Lukas let his gaze go to the fiery redhead that had a hold of his heart, before facing his father again. "She thinks you'll never approve of her. Of us."

"It's not for me to approve or disapprove." His father frowned. "But you need to be aware that what Grace works hard to instill in these kids, is something she often lacks herself."

Lukas nodded. It was true. Grace exuded confidence, but he'd spotted cracks in it before, and the fact she denied her own place of belonging in their tight community made it apparent she wasn't aware of her own self-worth. "Thanks, Dad."

He turned from his father and strode across the cement floor of the church basement.

Grace saw him coming and straightened her spine. He'd been in and out of the church a couple of times in the past week, but she'd managed to always be busy, and he hadn't been able to get her alone. No such luck this time though.

"Hello, Grace. How are you doing?" he asked politely when he stopped in front of her.

"I'm good." She caught some movement out of the corner

of her eye, and saw the minister watching them from the stairway. His father. "And you?"

"I could be better. In fact, I was hoping to talk to you about it over dinner?"

Grace's pulse jumped at the request but she met his gaze and shook her head firmly. "Sorry, Lukas. You know what the answer to that is."

He stepped closer, crowding her in the empty basement. "It's just dinner, Grace. What's the big deal?"

"The big deal is you said you were in love with me."

He'd been so firm in his declaration. So confident and sure that what they'd shared had been right. It had been good, but deep down she knew he could never really love her. Not a teenage runaway who had turned to stripping naked and dancing for strangers to earn a living.

"I shouldn't have told you that," he said softly.

A flash of pain flared in her chest, surprising her.

"Well," she muttered. "It seems you've come to your senses, so why the dinner invitation?"

He stepped closer, blocking her view of the room. "My heart hasn't changed, Grace. I said I loved you and I meant it. I just realize that telling you so soon might not have been the best move."

There was a strange flutter in her stomach and warmth spread throughout her body. She clenched her hands at her sides, and bounced her fists against her legs. She'd always felt an attraction to him, but now, after their night together, she was much more aware of him. There was a determination in his dark gaze that she'd never noticed before. The heat of his body reached out to her, giving birth to a yearning deep within to cuddle up to him, to feel that warmth seep through her skin and into her soul.

She shook her head and stepped back, bumping into the wall. "No, Lukas. I told you the other night, I just wanted sex. I just needed to feel alive."

"And you don't want to have sex with me again?" He stepped forward, putting his hands on either side of her head, trapping her against the wall.

Of course she did. She wasn't dead. In fact, every second that went by she felt more alive. Panicked, she looked over his shoulder, but Father John was gone, and they were all alone.

Get a grip, Grace.

She closed her eyes for a brief second and took a deep breath. Big mistake. His scent filled her head, and her body responded with throbbing heat.

Okay. She pressed her hands, palms flat, against the wall behind her, and made a mental deal with herself. If she couldn't control her body's reaction to him, the least she could do was control the relationship. She could maximize the pleasure and minimize the damage to them both.

"I'd love to have sex with you again, Lukas." She met his gaze head-on and spoke in a husky whisper designed to arouse. "But that's it, no more talk of love. Can you handle a strictly sexual relationship?"

Five

His gut clenched and his cock twitched behind his zipper. Damn it, Lukas thought, this wasn't the way the conversation was supposed to go.

He gazed into her eyes, searching for anything other than the lust she hid behind. Nothing. Only heat, and the flicker of something deeper within. Fine, if the way to Grace's heart was through her body, he was willing to do whatever it took.

If he'd had any doubt about Grace being his other half, it had fled when they'd made love. Sex had just been sex before, but with her, he'd felt . . . free. Free to be himself, to experience every touch, every taste, every ounce of pleasure he could. She'd put her hands on him, and he'd finally understood what the big deal was.

They'd communicated with their bodies on a level that words could never touch. They'd connected. Now he just had to convince her of that.

"I can handle whatever you can dish out, Grace." He leaned down and let his lips rub against her ear when he spoke. "I'm yours, however you want me."

He felt the shudder that went through her at his words and stepped back before he could do something really stupid. Like take her up against the wall of the church's basement.

Lukas thought he knew what to expect when they got to Grace's. No talking, just sex. Instead, he got just the opposite. She invited him in, told him to kick off his shoes and get comfortable on the sofa, then disappeared into the kitchen. When she came back it was with a tray of cheese, crackers, and meats, and a jug of iced tea. She tucked one leg under the other as she settled sideways on the sofa, facing him straight on.

Her emerald eyes sparkled and her full lips tilted in a secretive smile. "So tell me, Lukas, what's your favorite sexual fantasy?"

His jaw dropped. Then he burst out laughing. "You never cease to amaze me, Grace."

She leaned against the back of the sofa and sipped her iced tea before replying. "What? You expected me to lead you straight to the bedroom and strip down?"

"Well, you did say strictly sexual. But food, drink, and conversation, is fine by me. You know I'm more than eager to build this relationship on all levels."

"Yes. But what else are you eager to do?"

His body temperature spiked, and his heart skipped a beat.

He recognized her tactic. But her aggression only made him more certain that they were the right fit. He had to trust the interest in her gaze, and the invisible pull between them. It was time to trust his heart.

"I'm eager to do whatever it takes."

Her cheeks flushed and she cocked her head to the side, nibbling on her luscious lower lip. "Whatever it takes for what?"

The way to her heart, is through her body.

"Whatever it takes to please you."

He'd obviously said the right thing. Her reaction was instantaneous, and intoxicating. Her lips parted, her nostrils flared, and her eyes darkened. His cock stiffened at the idea of pleasing her, and he set his drink on the table before reaching out for her.

"Down, boy. We're still talking." Her tiny little fingers wrapped around his hands and pressed them back to his sides.

His cock swelled further at the command in her tone, and he blinked. Satisfaction eased through him, blending with his excitement, heightening it.

"I thought you were only interested in sex?"

"I'm into much more than *just* sex, Lukas. I said that our relationship would be a sexual one. But in order for it to be fulfilling for us both, we need to set some ground rules."

"Rules like?"

"Before we get to those, why don't you answer my original question?" She smoothed her hands up and down her thighs as she spoke, and it was all he could do not to reach out and do the same. His mind was drifting to naked thoughts and the urge to touch her was almost too strong to resist.

"Your original question?"

"Yes, I want to know what your favorite sexual fantasy is." Her voice firmed, her words coming out like a command instead of a question.

Before he could think twice his mouth opened and the words tumbled over his tongue. "I want to be told what to do, like you did the other night. I want to be told how to please you like no other has, or ever will."

Lukas's admission was music to her ears. She'd been right. She'd tried to ignore the signs in the last weeks, but she couldn't do it anymore.

Lukas was a natural submissive, and the temptation of making him hers had become too much to resist.

Rules be damned, she certainly would be for what she was about to do. She stood and held out her hand to him. "Then follow me," she said simply.

Six

Grace led the way down the short hallway to her bedroom. Once inside she motioned for Lukas to stand at the foot of the bed as she flicked on the bedside lamps, bathing the room in an amber glow.

Her fingers hovered for a moment over the dial on the small stereo, but she decided against it. She could hear Lukas' erratic breathing already, and it fueled the erotic haze starting to envelope her. She didn't want any distractions.

With slow steps, she went back to Lukas. She reached out and trailed her fingertips across the width of his shoulder blades, as she passed behind him. She stopped in front of him, leaving almost a foot of space between them. "Strip for me, Lukas," she commanded softly.

He bent down and removed his socks first, then met her gaze while he unbuttoned the simple dress shirt and pulled it from his jeans.

Grace's pulse pounded and saliva pooled in her mouth when the shirt was gone and he reached for the silver buckle at his waist. His eagerness was clear in the quick work he made of his belt and zipper, shoving his jeans and shorts over his hips and down his legs in one smooth move that stole her breath.

He was beautiful.

She knew men weren't supposed to be beautiful, but he was. He stood before her completely naked and eager. His dark eyes glowed and a lovely flush covered his neck and crept up his cheeks. When Grace's gaze landed on his mouth, his lips parted and his tongue darted out.

Unable to resist the unspoken invitation she stepped forward, cupped his face in her hands and brought him down for a kiss.

She nibbled at his lips, before swiping her tongue across them and dipping into his mouth to taste him. He groaned, his breath mingling with hers as their tongues met and danced, tangling and moving together in a natural rhythm that soon had them both panting. She pulled away and became aware of his hands gripping her hips tightly.

"Hands off until I tell you, Lukas."

His hands instantly dropped to his sides and he straightened.

If Grace had any doubts about his willingness to let her take control, they were dispelled then. She stayed where she was, close enough to breath in his scent and see his nipples harden when she blew a soft stream of air at them. "Lovely," she sighed.

She reached between them and wrapped her hand around his cock. Not too tight, but tight enough that she would feel every telltale throb and twitch. "The ground rules are simple, and always in effect, Lukas. I'm not into pain and humiliation so you need a safe word. That word is *red*, as in stop-sign red. If I'm doing something you don't like, you just shout that word out, and I stop. Okay?"

"Okay," he replied, his voice thick with lust.

"And just so you know . . . I love to hear you beg . . . so don't be shy."

A small frown wrinkled his forehead, but he didn't say anything. He was so innocent; the urge to open the doors to a whole new world for him was undeniable.

She stood on her tiptoes and leaned forward, deliberately breathing hotly as she whispered in his ear. "Do you enjoy oral sex, Lukas?"

His cock throbbed in her hand as he nodded. "I'm going to give you some instructions now, and if you follow them well, you will be rewarded."

That made his cock jump. It swelled and throbbed against the palm of her hand and she was tempted to get on her knees and take it in her mouth. But he'd said he wanted to be told what to do. So that was what would happen. She released him and stepped back.

"Undress me," she instructed.

She stood still as he lifted her t-shirt over her head, and his trembling fingers unsnapped her bra. Her nipples ached, begging for attention, but she held back. She wanted all of her clothes off before she let him touch her.

His knuckles brushed against her soft belly as he unsnapped her jeans. He bent at the knees and tugged the denim over her rounded hips and down her legs. A large male hand cupped one calf as he lifted the first leg to remove the pants, then the other. He looked up at her from his crouched position, his hand lingering on her calf as she said a brief prayer of thanks for the urge to shave that morning.

She reached out and stroked her fingers through the shiny locks of his hair. He pressed into her touch just like a cat being scratched behind the ears. "My panties too, please."

Lukas' hands slid up the outside of her legs to her hips. He fingered the thin elastic that held the front and back triangles of cloth together. In a surprise move he pulled hard and the elastic snapped. Her excited gasp echoed through the room as the panties fell to the floor.

His hands cupped her naked rear, and he dropped to his knees in front of her. Leaning forward, he rubbed his cheek against her bare skin and made a show of inhaling deeply before looking up at her. "I can smell how turned on you are. Can I taste . . . please?"

Grace's knees almost buckled. The sight of him on his knees for her, the words he spoke, the fervent hunger clearly stamped on his face and in the tension of his body, it was like a dream.

"Please me, Lukas. Show me how eager you are."

Fire licked at Lukas' insides at Grace's words. Please her. In that moment it felt like that was his whole reason for being. His needs, the throbbing of his cock, and the tightness in his balls slipped out of his consciousness. His fingers flexed, gripping her butt tightly and pulling her hips closer to his mouth. All that mattered was pleasing her.

Burying his face in the juncture of her thighs, he stiffened his tongue and snaked it into her slick heat.

"Oh, yes."

Grace's sigh was music to his ears. He shuffled forward, urging her back until he could lower her weight to the edge of the bed. When his hands were free, he slid them over her curves to her knees, and pressed them apart. He pulled back and looked at the beauty in front of him. Dark red curls were trimmed close to the skin, full sex lips with the tiny dark red nub peaking out. Using his thumbs, he spread her lips and enjoyed the view.

"Lukas," Grace said. "If you don't put your mouth on me right now, I'm kicking you out of my house, and never letting you back in."

The playful note in her command surprised him, and brought a grin to his face.

"Just enjoying the view, babe. You are absolutely perfect."

"Lukasss." Her growl turned into a purr when he took a long slow lick before delving in. She tasted so good, so sweet and true. He stiffened his tongue and slid it inside her, going as deep as he could, before pulling out and circling her rigid clit. He flicked and nibbled at the hard little button and felt her hips press against him. One hand shifted upward, traveling over her belly to cup a heavy breast and roll the nipple between his fingers, while the other hand slid in under his chin to tease her entrance.

"More, Lukas," she encouraged. "Suck my clit." He puckered up and suckled on the button at the same time he slid a finger into her. Her hips jerked and her cunt clenched around him. "Yes, that's it. Don't stop!"

Desperately inhaling through his nose he sucked and then gently nipped at the pleasure pearl with his teeth. Her thighs tightened around his head, muffling the sound of her ecstatic moan as her scent filled his head and went straight south, hardening his cock to the point of pain.

He didn't stop until her fingers wrapped in his hair and pulled his head away. He looked up at her and was happy to see that she was panting as hard as he was.

Her lips curved into a wicked smile and she petted his head lovingly. "Very good, Lukas, but now it's my turn."

His heart pounded and his muscles trembled as he wondered what was next.

"Get on the bed," she commanded.

When she had him positioned on his back, his hands gripping the headboard, she smiled devilishly. "Do not move, until I say you can."

Seven

Grace stared down at the naked man on her bed. Emotions that had nothing to do with sex swirled about her head and made it difficult to breath. She couldn't let herself think . . . she had to turn off her brain. Don't think, just feel. Isn't that what she'd said to Lukas the other night?

She threw her leg over him and straddled his waist. Leaning forward, she braced her hands on the mattress next to him, and licked first one flat male nipple, then the other. She moved her head so that the curtain of her hair brushed against his skin as she went back and forth, manipulating each nipple with her tongue, her teeth, and her lips until they were rock hard and standing stiff like little miniature dicks.

Shifting her weight further back on her heels, she scraped her chest against his belly as she moved lower, nipping at his ribs, tonguing his navel. She stopped when she was between his spread thighs, her breasts surrounding the rigid cock and sandwiching it to his body. He gasped and his hips pressed up.

Grace lifted her head and gazed at his beautiful face. His eyes were watching her every move, but his lips were pursed tight.

"Talk to me, Lukas. I need to hear what you like just as much as you do."

"Everything. I like it all. Nothing feels bad when you're touching me."

"You like this?" she asked and rocked her body forward, his cock stroking firmly between her breasts.

"Yes," he hissed.

"What about this?" She dipped her head and her tongue flicked the head of his cock when it peaked out from between her breasts as she continued to rock.

His moan echoed through the room, thrilling her. Her tongue darted out every time, swiping at the sensitive tip. Through with teasing him, she pulled back and circled the base of his cock with her finger and thumb. She held the rigid length of him away from his body, and swirled her tongue all over him. She licked up the underside, following the throbbing vein there. She wrapped her lips around the head and sucked him like a lollipop. His hips thrust upward, and his sighs turned to whimpers. She waited . . . she knew it was coming.

"Please," he gasped.

"Please what, Lukas?" She squeezed her thighs together. She wanted so badly to climb up his body and impale herself on his cock. She wanted to feel him touch her deep inside, feel his warmth spread through her once again. She wanted to feel . . . alive.

"Please . . . take me."

Lovely, lovely, words. She opened her mouth and took as much of him in as she could. She sucked gently and stroked up to the tip, then swallowed him again. Her other hand cupped his balls, measuring their weight, their feel.

Suddenly the bed shook and Lukas' voice reached her loud and clear. "No, Grace. Please!!"

She kept going, sliding her mouth up and down his cock, tasting his flavor and feeling him swell even larger in her mouth. "Grace, please. Take me . . . inside you . . . ride me . . . fuck me . . . love me!"

An arrow of pure pleasure went straight to her heart. It wasn't that he was begging, it was what he was begging for, it was what she wanted too. Before she could think twice, she climbed on top of him, aimed his cock at her entrance, and sank down onto him. She had to bite her tongue to keep from shouting *yes* as their connection solidified and her world righted itself.

Grace braced her hands on his muscular chest and met his gaze as she began to fuck him. "Touch me," she pleaded.

His hands immediately grasped her hips. He helped her find the right rhythm, before skimming them over her back, her front, her legs, her breasts. His hands were everywhere, but both of them knew that wasn't the touch she'd been asking for.

She wanted him to touch her heart, the same way he had that first night. She wanted the magic she'd felt only with him. The warmth that had thawed her heart and filled her soul. And she got it when one hand cupped the back of her head and pulled her down to him. Their mouths opened, their tongues danced, and their cries of pleasure filled each other.

Eight

The next morning when Lukas opened his eyes and found himself alone in the bed, he wasn't surprised. Sounds of movement reached his ears from the kitchen, and he wondered just how closed off Grace was going to be. He'd meant to keep things light between them the night before. Just sexual. But it hadn't worked like that. Something about that woman reached deep down inside him and made it impossible to hide what he was feeling.

Stifling a groan he rolled from the bed, pulled on his jeans, and padded down the hall to the kitchen. When he got there Grace was sitting at the table in her robe, a steaming cup of coffee in front of her.

He bent down to kiss her on the cheek. When she didn't pull away he nuzzled his nose into her hair and breathed deeply. She smelled of musky raw sex. She smelled of *them*.

He got his coffee and sat down across from her. Silent.

She met his gaze head-on, making his heart pound and his insides quiver. Her eyes were still guarded, but there was something new in them. Something that gave him hope.

"Grace?"

"I'd like to go out for dinner with you tonight."

To an ordinary person, it wasn't much. But they both knew what it was . . . it was the door to her heart creaking open.

Sassy women and sexy men are what Canadian author SASHA WHITE's stories are all about. Gifted with a salacious imagination, Sasha enjoys working in several genres, such as contemporary, paranormal, suspense and science fiction. With a voice that is called "distinctive and delicious" by The Romance Studio, Sasha has over a dozen erotic stories published and is going strong. She loves to hear from readers, and can be found on her website's blog most afternoons.

www.sashawhite.net

A Familiar
Kind of Magic

Sylvia Day

This story is dedicated to two wonderful women—
Lisa Renee Jones and Cathryn Fox.
Lisa, thank you for bringing the Allure Authors together.
Cathryn, thank you for bringing this collection to Lucia.
Between the two of you,
you made my very first writing-oriented dream come true—
to write for Lucia Macro at Avon Books.

Acknowledgments

Thanks go out to my critique partner Annette McCleave (www.AnnetteMcCleave.com), who makes every story I write better, and to my test reader, Alyssa Hurzeler, who lent a fresh set of eyes when I needed them.

One

The Hunter had finally arrived.

Victoria studied him carefully through the closed-circuit feed that monitored her office reception area. The urbane Armani suit he wore did nothing to hide the predator within. Tall and dark, the Hunter moved with a casual arrogance that made her purr. He didn't look around, completely focused on the moment when they would be together in the same room. Alone.

As she rubbed her hands together, a throaty growl filled the air. The High Council was ready to tangle with her again. She smiled and preened, as was the nature of her kind. This Hunter was powerful, she could feel it even through the walls that separated them.

It was a testament to her own prowess that They would send a warlock such as him after her. She couldn't help but be flattered. After all, she'd broken the laws on purpose, deliberately goading the very powers that had stolen Darius from her. And here was her "punishment," walking into her office with that luscious, long-legged stride. She couldn't be more thrilled with their choice.

He flashed a devastating smile at the receptionist before she closed the door behind him. Then he turned his attention to Victoria and removed his sunglasses.

Oh my.

She crossed her silk-stocking clad legs to ease the sudden ache between them.

Piercing gray eyes measured her from a face so austerely handsome she was almost inclined to leave her seat and rub up against him. *That firm jaw ... those sculpted lips ...*

But, of course, she couldn't. She first had to see if he would reveal who he was or if he intended to pretend. The High Council still hadn't realized how much power Darius had bequeathed her. They didn't yet realize how deeply her awareness went.

Her gaze moved to the crystal-framed miniature on her desk and the man with the rakish dimple who smiled lovingly from there. Captured beautifully in oil paints, glints of gold shining in his blond hair, the sight of Darius brought a familiar ache of loss and heartache that firmed her resolve. The waste of his life filled her with a need for retribution.

Rising to her feet, Victoria held out her hand. The Hunter took it leisurely, the palpable force in his touch betraying him.

"Mr. Westin," she breathed, fighting back a delicious shiver. She would have to thank the Council for this gift when she was done with him. He was so dark—his skin, his raven hair, his aura. Sex incarnate. She could smell it, feel it with his proximity. It was obvious why he was a successful Hunter. Already she was wet and eager.

Max Westin held her hand a little too long, his thickly lashed gaze clearly stating his intentions to have her, to tame her. Like all kittens, Victoria liked to play, so she brushed her fingertips across his palm as she pulled away. His eyes widened almost imperceptibly, a tiny sign that she could get to him if she really put the effort into it.

Of course, she intended to do just that. The Council only sent Their best, most prized Hunters after her, and she knew how it chaffed Them when Their elite met with abject failure. It was the only thing she could do to prevent feeling helpless—give Them a harsh reminder of how great Darius had been, and what They'd lost with his needless sacrifice.

"Ms. St. John." Westin's voice was a rough caress. Everything about him was a little rough, a little gritty. A primitive creature. Just like she was.

Victoria waved toward the chair in front of her glass-topped desk. Freeing the button of his coat, Max sank into the seat, his dark blue trousers stretching over firm thighs and an impressive bulge between them.

She licked her lips. *Yum . . .*

One side of his mouth curved in a knowing smile. Max Westin was well aware of how irresistible he was, which made him irresistible to her. Confidence was a quality she held in high esteem. So was a touch of wickedness, and Westin definitely had that. That dark aura betrayed the edges of black magic he skirted. She doubted the Council had any better leash on him than They had on her.

Liking him immensely already, Victoria sank into her own

chair, arranging her legs beneath her black pencil skirt to show them to best advantage.

"The museum offers its sincere apologies for the loss of your necklace," he began.

Her smile widened. He wasn't going to tell her who he was. *How delicious.* "You don't look like the curator type to me, Mr. Westin."

"I'm here on behalf of the museum's insurance company. Obviously a loss of this magnitude requires an investigation."

"That's reassuring, of course."

Observing him through the veil of her lashes, Victoria noted the energy that betrayed his restless nature. His firm, full lips hinted at sinful delights. She liked sinful, energetic men. This one was a bit rigid for her tastes, but that could change with the right persuasion. They all succumbed eventually. It was the only part of the game that disappointed her—the surrender.

"You seem remarkably at ease," Westin murmured, "for a woman who's just lost a priceless piece of jewelry."

Victoria's toes curled. His voice was so deep and slightly husky, like he just rolled out of bed. It was scrumptious, like the rest of him. He was so broad shouldered, yet lean, every movement he made a graceful ripple of honed muscle.

"Fretting won't accomplish anything," she said with a careless shrug. "Besides, you are here to find the necklace and you look . . . capable. What is there to worry about?"

"That I won't recover it. Your trust in my abilities is flattering, Ms. St. John, and not misplaced. I'm very good at what I do. However, sometimes things are not what they seem."

It was a warning, plain and simple.

Thoughtful, she stood and walked to the wall of windows

behind her desk. Despite having her back to him, Victoria felt the heat of his gaze caressing the length of her. She fingered the pearls that graced her neck and stared out over the city skyline. "If need be, I'll simply acquire another. Everything can be purchased for a price, Mr. Westin."

"Not everything."

Intrigued, Victoria turned, surprised to find him approaching. He took a position next to her, his gaze on the view, but his attention fully focused on her. She felt the shimmer of his power sweep over her, searching for her weaknesses.

Unable to resist the danger, she rubbed her shoulder against him and inhaled the rich, masculine scent of his skin—a mixture of thousand-dollar cologne and pure Max Westin. Her breathing became shallow, her heart rate picked up. Losing her perspective, Victoria moved away. It had been a long time since she'd indulged in a powerful man. Too long. The other Hunters had been crafty and seductive. Westin had that and pure magical muscle.

"Max," she called softly, hurrying their familiarity by using his first name.

"Hmm?"

She looked over her shoulder. He was following her. Stalking her. Reminding her that he was the predator here.

Oh, he could be fun. If he wanted to play.

"Have dinner with me."

"My place," he agreed.

She moved to the wet bar and retrieved two glass bottles of milk, a deliberate choice that showed her cognizance. Certainly he knew how she worked. But did he know why?

Did Westin know that with Darius' dying breath he had

transferred his magic to her, making her far more powerful than the average Familiar? Did Westin know that she'd been loved by her warlock, and that it was that love which gave her the ability to make her own choices now?

Before Darius' gift, she had been like other Familiars. The High Council assigned the pairings between her kind and their magical counterparts, regardless of their wishes. Some Familiars were unhappy with their partners. She had been lucky the first time, finding a love for Darius that transcended time. Now, because of that love, she was too powerful to be taken against her will. In the two centuries since she'd lost him, no other warlock had succeeded in collaring her. Westin would fare no better. She had loved once, and deeply. There would never be another warlock for her.

Swaying her hips and offering a seductive smile, she returned to him. "How about my place?"

"No." He took the bottle from her outstretched hand, his fingers deliberately curling over hers and staying there. Pinning her in place. "Victoria."

Her name, just one word, but spoken with such possession she could almost feel the collar around her neck. Hunters did not keep Familiars, they caught them and passed them on to lesser warlocks. She would never allow herself to be distributed in that manner again.

So they stood, touching, sizing each other up. She tilted her head and allowed her interest to show, not that she could hide it with her nipples hard and obvious beneath her green silk shirt. Her chest rose and fell with near panting breaths, her blood heating from both his proximity and his darkly seductive scent. He was so tall, so hard, so intense. Only the silky lock of dark hair that draped his brow softened his purely masculine features. If he weren't a Hunter, she'd be crawling all over him, she wanted him that badly.

As his gaze dropped to the swell of her breasts, his mouth curved in a carnal smile. "I bet I'm the better cook," he rasped softly, his fingers stroking hers, sending sparks of awareness through her.

She pouted. "You won't know if you don't come over."

He pulled away, his charm vanishing in an instant. "My place or I'll have to decline."

Victoria wished she were in her feline form so she could flick her tail at him. Max Westin was most definitely accustomed to getting what he wanted. He was a Dominant, as were all Hunters. Too bad she was, too.

"A pity." And she meant it, her disappointment was painful. His place was not an option. Who knew what spells he'd cast there? And what toys he had . . . ? It would be akin to walking into a cage.

She ignored the thrill the thought gave her.

"You changed your mind?" His surprise was a tangible thing. The man definitely didn't hear "no" often enough.

"I asked you to dinner, Mr. Westin, and you placed restrictions on the invitation." She waved her hand toward the door in a gesture of dismissal designed to rile him. "I don't tolerate restrictions."

A return warning to him.

When he made no move to leave, she purred aloud, a soft rumbling sound that made the muscle in his jaw tic.

So . . . the raging attraction was reciprocated. That made her feel slightly better about waiting longer to have him.

With calm, deliberate movements, Westin lifted the bottle and drank, the working muscles of his throat making her mouth dry. The implied threat in his actions was not lost on her.

Then he set the empty container on the edge of her desk and came toward her, buttoning his coat before clasping her hand. His touch burned, even though his skin was cold and wet with condensation. His gaze was as icy as his grip. He'd regroup and come back, she knew.

And she'd be waiting.

Victoria brushed her fingers across his palm again before releasing him. "See you soon, Max."

Max stepped out of the St. John Hotel and cursed vehemently. Gritting his teeth, he fought off the erection that threatened to embarrass him on the crowded sidewalk.

Victoria St. John was trouble.

He'd known that the moment the Council had summoned him. Taming ferals was a task for lesser, newer warlocks. The request had startled him at first, and then intrigued him. When he'd met his prey, however, he understood.

Sly and playful, Victoria moved with the natural grace of a cat. Short black hair and tip-tilted green eyes made her a heady temptation. He'd seen her picture a hundred times and felt nothing more than simple appreciation for a beautiful face. In person, however, Victoria was devastating, all sensuality and heat. She was a bit thin for his tastes, more lithe than curvy, but those legs . . . Those impossibly long legs . . . Soon they would be wrapped around his hips while he stroked his cock deep into her. But it wouldn't be easy. She made that clear with her smile.

She knew who and what he was, which meant the rumors of her power were true. She was no ordinary Familiar.

He shook his head. Darius had been a fool. Familiars needed the strong hand of a warlock or they turned feral. Victoria was a prime example. She was already too wild, defying the High Council at every turn.

She'd also defied *him*.

Both intrigued and attracted, Max mentally ran through the information he'd gathered before approaching her. Victoria was one of the most prominent figures of their kind, her shrewd business dealings taking her from franchising a motel to owning one of the largest chains of upscale hotels in the country. Up until the death of her warlock, she'd been an esteemed member of the magical community. Her wildness since Darius' passing solidified the Council's position that it was best if the pairings were made with mental calculation, rather than through affairs of the heart. Occasionally, love grew anyway such as happened to Victoria, but this was far rarer with Council intervention.

Max rounded the corner and stepped into a side alley. Using his powers, he bridged the distance across town to his penthouse apartment in the blink of an eye. There he paced the acid-washed cement floors restlessly, every nerve on edge. He had no doubt Victoria St. John had stolen her own necklace. It would have been impossible for a human to accomplish the theft.

The museum's security was too advanced. Victoria had done it knowing the brazenness of the act would bring another Hunter after her. The Council worked tirelessly to keep the existence of their kind hidden from humans. Her reckless disregard of their laws had to be stopped before they were revealed.

But *why* was she acting this way? That was what he didn't understand. There had to be a reason beyond lacking a warlock. She was too self-possessed, too calculated. Yes, she needed some reining in, but she wasn't out of control. Before he released her, he was determined to find out what her motivation was.

Exhaling harshly, Max looked around his home, a sprawling loft cloaked in silence and protection spells. The soft gray walls and dark armless sofas had been called cold and barren by some of his subs, but he found the decor soothing, absorbing the energy of the place with the ease of breathing. It would have been simpler to tame her here, where all the tools of his trade were available for his use. But even as he thought this, he realized something different would be required in order to succeed where others had failed.

Collaring Victoria would take a unique approach. Her power was augmented in some way, he'd felt the charge she carried with more than a little surprise. It explained how she had managed to avoid capture all these years. He would have to take her, not just sexually, but in every way. She had to be dominated, as all good Familiars were, but he would have to make her *want* it. She would have to willingly submit—body and soul—in order for the collar to appear, since her powers prevented the usual collaring without consent.

As Max thought of all the things he would do to her, magic coursed through his blood in a heated wave. He couldn't deny how the thought of the taming ahead filled him with anticipation. Not of the task, as he was used to in his private hours, but for the woman upon whom he would work. Just the thought of Victoria's total submission made every muscle in his body harden. All that fire he saw in her eyes, and her careless disregard of how powerful he was—not from ignorance, but for the thrill of the game. For the first time, there was a remote possibility of failure and that whetted his appetite like nothing else ever had.

Max wondered who she'd be assigned to once he finished with her. She would always be stronger than other Familiars, and he refused to break her. A broken Familiar lacked the vitality necessary to be truly helpful.

The hair on his nape prickled with awareness, warning him of the summons before They spoke.

Have you met with the feral? the Council asked. Hundreds of voices speaking in unison.

"She's not feral," he corrected. "Not yet."

She cannot be tamed. Many have tried. Many have failed.

He stilled, wary. "You asked me to capture her. That is what I agreed to. I won't kill her without trying first. If it's an assassination you want, you'll have to find someone else."

There is no other Hunter with your power, They complained. *You know this.*

"So allow me to make an attempt to save her. She's unique. It would be a waste to lose her." Running a hand through his hair, Max blew out his breath. "I will do what is necessary if it comes to that."

We accept your suggestion.

He should have felt reassured by that. But he didn't. "Have you decided where I'm to take her once she's been tamed?"

Of course.

His jaw clenched at the vague answer, the flare of possessiveness unwanted, but there nevertheless. The Dom/sub relationship was unique to each pairing and required a depth of trust not easily passed to another individual. This would be the first time he attempted it, and he wasn't certain he was comfortable with the idea. "Go, then. Leave me to plan."

As the evanescent presence of the Council faded away, the urge to summon Victoria with his power and begin the taming immediately was strong. But he tempered it. His eagerness was ill-placed and inconvenient. He loved hunting, relished the taming, but was not prone to hurrying matters. A proper domination took time, something the visit from the Council told him he didn't have. He had several weeks, at most.

Max growled as his cock hardened in anticipation. Weeks with Victoria.

He was ready to get started.

Two

℞estless and edgy, Victoria twirled the sapphire and diamond necklace she'd stolen from the museum around her finger, and wondered if she had finally pushed the High Council too far. A little research into Max Westin had revealed that his usual prey was not their kind, but the Others, those who had crossed over into black magic and could not be saved. He was credited with saving thousands by destroying the few who would wreak havoc with their evil.

The knowledge filled her with concern. Was she now an Other? Considering that Max was rarely sent after anything the Council didn't want dead, it would seem she was. He was a legend, a hero, and on the verge of promotion to the Council. She would have known this had she been an active member of their community instead of an outcast. Which left her with a question she'd spent years trying to answer—was her end goal to die? Did she in truth have a death wish now that Darius was gone? She was strong enough to fight off the collar, but she wasn't strong enough to fight off a warlock of Max's considerable power. And yet she had deliberately goaded his pursuit.

Troubled by the direction of her thoughts, she did what she always did—turned her focus to action, rather than reaction. Since she could not go toe-to-toe with Max and win, she would have to get to him another way.

She would have to seduce him, make him care for her. It was fitting that doing so would be a cruel blow to the Council. It would, in fact, be the ultimate revenge. The Council so rarely promoted anyone. In fact, the last to be so honored had been Darius, and he had refused Them because it would have meant losing her. Rejecting the safety of distant command, he had remained a foot soldier and They had punished him with the most brutal assignments. Leading to his death. The Council would regret that, she would ensure it.

She couldn't wait to get started.

Damn Max Westin for being so stubborn! If he'd come to dinner like she wanted, she could be rubbing against that beautiful male body now. She could be licking his skin, nipping his flesh, fucking his brains out.

Avenging her beloved Darius the only way she knew how.

Max was the perfect Hunter with which to goad the Council. Victoria could picture him easily, tied to her bed and prone for her pleasure. All that rippling muscle and voluptuous power. The Council's golden warlock snared by his own trap.

She blew out her breath, the sudden pang of guilt too disturbing to contemplate. Standing, Victoria loosened the buttons of her sleeveless satin pajama top. She prepared to alter to her feline form when the sound of the doorbell stopped her. Padding leisurely across the golden hardwood floor, she sniffed the air.

Max.

Unexpected pleasure warmed her blood.

Opening the door, she was rendered speechless for a moment. In Armani, Max Westin had been devastating. Now, dressed in low-slung jeans and a fitted t-shirt, his feet bared in leather sandals, he was . . . He was . . .

She purred, the soft vibration filling the air between them with lush promise.

Sneaky bastard. He knew her natural instinct at the sight of his bare feet would be to alter form and rub against them, circling his legs in a blatant display of her willingness. Fighting her very nature, Victoria lifted her arm and leaned against the door jam. Her shirt spread with the pose, revealing her tummy and the under curve of her breast. He shot a brief assessing glance at her display, and then brushed her aside, entering her home like he had every right to do so.

As he crossed to the kitchen with a paper grocery bag in his arms, the candles she had spread around the room flared to life in his wake. The stereo came on, releasing a cacophony of garbled reception before coming to a halt on a classical station. The rich sounds of stringed instruments flooded the room, swelling upward through the exposed ductwork ceiling of her contemporary apartment, setting the stage for what she knew would be a memorable night.

She followed him to the kitchen, where he set the bag on the counter and begin to withdraw its contents. Behind him, a pan was magically freed from the overhanging pot rock and settled on the stove.

"The warlock reveals himself," she said softly.

Max smiled. "I am exactly who I said I was."

"An insurance fraud investigator. I checked you out."

"I've recovered on every case."

"So I learned," she said dryly. "You're determined to save the world from evil-doers, both magical and otherwise."

"Is that such a bad thing?" he challenged softly. "Once, you did the same."

He pulled out a pint of organic cream, and she licked her lips. Perceptive, as all Hunters were, he beckoned a bowl from the cupboard with a flick of his wrist and poured her a ration. Victoria freed the last button on her shirt. A moment later, it and her drawstring pants were pooled on the marble kitchen floor. She waited a second longer, giving him a quick glimpse of what he'd get his fill of later, and then altered shape. With a fluid spring of her feline legs, she made the high leap to the butcher-block counter and crouched over the bowl.

Max ran his hand over her soft black fur. "You're beautiful, kitten," he rumbled in his delicious voice.

She purred in reply.

As she lapped up the cream, Victoria curled her tail around his wrist. His large hand dwarfed her, but she felt safe with him, unusual for an uncollared Familiar around a warlock who lacked a guide.

Hunters were the most powerful of magicians and didn't need the augmentation Familiars provided. They kept the magical world clean, tracking down and dealing with any deviants who fought the command of the High Council.

Others like her.

The blunt tips of his fingers found the spots behind her ears and rubbed. She melted into the countertop.

"Let me finish dinner," he murmured. "And then we'll play."

Max turned away to tend the stove, and she fought the urge to go to him. She lay on the countertop, her chin on her paws watching the muscles of his upper back flex as he chopped vegetables and seared fish. Studying him, she noted the ebony hair that shined with vitality and the firm, proud curve of his ass. She sighed.

She missed having a steady man in her life. Lately the loneliness seemed worse than ever, and she blamed the Council for that. They should have waited until a second witch or warlock/ Familiar pairing could have joined them against the Triumvirate, but They failed to temper their eagerness. Unwilling to fail in so important a task, Darius had lost his life in order to succeed. And she had lost her soul mate.

With her heart weighing heavily, Victoria jumped to the floor and circled Max's feet, purring and preening to win his attention. He was, astonishingly, too busy taking care of her to have meaningless sex with her. Too busy cooking for her, and soothing her with music and candlelight.

Her weary soul soaked up the attention greedily.

Moving through eternity without a partner was taking its toll. She couldn't date humans, and she was exiled from her community. There was no one to wait for her or worry about her.

Her work was fulfilling and her success a source of deep pride, but often she wished she could curl up on the couch with a man who cared about her. Loved her. Max was not that man, but he was the first of all the warlocks sent after her who took the time to woo her. Part of her appreciated his efforts. The other part of her understood that he had ulterior motives.

So she wooed him right back, rubbing against his powerful calves with soft, tantalizing purrs.

The road to failure began thusly with all her Hunters. She promised them delight with every brush against their legs, her pheromones scenting the air until they were mad to have her. Due to Darius' gift, she was able to alter her scent from one of submission to one of carnal demand, a primitive challenge to a Hunter's need to be dominant. In effect, a waving red cape to a raging bull.

"It's not so bad," Max soothed in a tone that made her spine arch in pleasure. "There is joy in submission."

Piqued that he remained so casually unaffected, Victoria sauntered away, her tail held high and her head lifted proudly.

Submission. She wasn't suited to it. She was far too strong willed, far too independent to bow to a man's demands. Darius had known this. He had accepted it, and made exceptions for her so they could live in harmony.

Victoria altered form, and sprawled on the couch naked. From his position in the kitchen, Max had only to turn around and he could see her. His self-control disturbed her, as did the quiet air of command and the steely determination in those gray eyes. He was not a man to be led around by his dick.

She sighed, and waited for him to come to her. No man or warlock could long resist a naked, prone, and willing woman.

Leaning heavily into the counter, Max stared down at the

cutting board and exhaled his frustration. At this moment, he wanted nothing more than to show the beautifully bared woman on the couch all the things he could do to her. For her. It took far more restraint than he was used to exerting to prevent tossing the knife into the sink and doing exactly that. A hard, heavy fucking would help her forget, for a while, the sorrow he felt in her.

His eyes closed as he focused on that faint hint of sadness. The bond between Familiar and warlock always began with this tiny thread of awareness. It was early, too early, for the connection to be there, but it was. There was not enough of it yet to discern the cause of her unhappiness, but Max knew it was not a new distress, but one she'd carried for some time.

Strangely, it was that deeper knowledge of her that attracted him now. More so than her beauty. Lust goaded by tenderness was a new sensation for him, one he savored slowly, as he would the first taste of a fine wine. Soft and mellow, it heated his blood just as liquor would.

As he continued to cook, he held on to the feel of his kitten, fostering the bond that he would use to bring her in from the fringes and back into the fold.

"Dinner's ready," he called out after a time.

Victoria stared up at the ceiling and wondered how Max could be so indifferent to her brazen offering of sex. Petulant, she said, "I want to eat in here."

"Suit yourself," he answered easily. She heard one of the dining chairs pulled away from the table, and a moment later the clink of silverware against china. Mouth agape, she bolted upright.

"Ummm . . ." Max's deep hum of enjoyment made goose

bumps race across her skin. Then the rich scent of seared ahi and cream hit her nostrils and made her tummy growl.

She stood, and stomped into the kitchen where she found only one setting—the one Max was seated in front of. Hands on her hips, her feline sensibilities offended, she snapped, "What about me?"

"Do you intend to join me now?"

"I planned to."

Pushing away from the table, he rose to his full height, dwarfing her, a difference made more noticeable by her own state of undress. He offered her his chair, his apparent indifference to her bare body making her fists clench. Victoria plopped into the seat with an audible exhalation. This was not at all how she'd planned to corrupt him.

He reached for the long-tined fork. Spearing a piece of the nearly raw fish, Max dipped it in cream, and brought it to her lips. Startled, she stared up at him.

"Open."

Before she realized it was a command, her lips parted and accepted the offering. Designed for her palate, the tastes blended together to form a delight for her senses. Max stood beside her, one hand on the back of her chair, caging her in while he prepared another bite. Her eyes met his in silent query.

"It's a warlock's duty to care for his pet."

"I'm not your pet." *But it felt wonderful in any case.*

"For now, you are."

She hated to admit it, but his unwavering confidence aroused her. Her small breasts grew heavy, tender, the nipples peaked hard for his touch. Obligingly, his hand left the chair back and cupped the soft swell. Victoria gasped at the unexpected intimacy, and Max slipped the next bite into her mouth. As she chewed slowly, savoring the singular meal, his skilled fingertips toyed with her nipple.

"To submit is not to be weak," he crooned in a husky, hypnotic tone. "You would not be less of a woman, kitten, but so much more of one."

She shook her head fiercely even as she squeezed her thighs together, fighting the aching depth of lust she did not want to feel. The soft rolling and tugging of Max's fingers on her nipple made her blood hot. As his arousal rose to meet hers, his skin warmed and filled the air with the faint scent of his cologne. The prominent bulge of his hard-on was eye level, and she couldn't help but stare. The danger inherent in wanting him and his implacable arrogance turned her on to such an extent that she was panting in her chair. Her back arched helplessly, begging for more.

"It's in your nature," he murmured, his mouth to her ear. "The desire to be taken. To have the choice ripped from you so all you have to do is feel. Imagine my hands and mouth on your breasts . . . my fingers, tongue, and cock thrusting between your legs. . . . Your only task would be to enjoy the pleasure I can give you. Imagine the freedom in that."

Freedom. Submission. The words could not be used together. They were mutually exclusive, but every time Victoria opened her mouth to retort, he filled it with food.

He continued to feed and fondle her until she writhed in the seat. Her skin was hot and tight, her cunt wet and creamy. Max knew all about her. He would have studied Familiars with precision and her in particular. It was his mission to hunt those who defied the Council. He knew Familiars craved to be touched and well fed. His approach was unusual, and therefore caught her off guard. They usually tried to fuck her into submission, not coddle her into it.

Soon her belly was full, which normally made her sleepy. But not tonight. The burning lust in her veins kept her from napping. But still she was languid. Pliable. Max lifted and carried her to her room, and she was unable to protest. She wanted to feel him inside her like she wanted to breathe. Still, she wasn't a fool. With a softly spoken word, Victoria bound his powers.

His smile told her he felt what she'd done. It wasn't just any smile, but one that promised she'd pay.

It only made her hotter.

Max set her on her feet, and turned her to face away from him. Anticipation rippled down her spine, making her shiver and breathe shallowly. With a firm, irrefutable hold on the scruff of her neck, he pressed her forward until she bent at the waist, face down in her bed.

"Max?"

As he pulled away, his teeth scraped her shoulder with seductive portent and before she could blink, her hands were bound behind her.

"What the hell?" Her heart raced in near panic. She couldn't believe he would move so quickly. She had never been bound. The sudden feeling of helplessness reminded her of the way she'd felt when Darius stood in the midst of deadly swirls of magic and she could only watch, useless. "No!" Victoria struggled wildly.

"Hush, kitten." His large body came over hers, a warm physical blanket. With his hands on either side of her head, he nuzzled his cheek against hers, his voice far huskier than usual. "I won't hurt you. Not ever."

"I—You—"

"You can't bind my powers," he murmured. "You're strong, but not that strong."

"I don't like this, Max." Her voice was a plaintive whisper.

Then one of his hands lifted from the mattress. She felt it working against the curve of her ass just before she heard the slow rasp of his zipper lowering. To her amazement, the arousal that had died flared to life again.

"You're so tense." He licked a slow, wet trail along the length of her spine. "All you have to do is lie there and come."

Suddenly, she couldn't see, her vision blocked by some spell he'd cast. Victoria went completely still, her breath caught in her throat. She'd never felt so completely at the mercy of someone else.

Between her legs she ached with an arousal that made her writhe. Despite what her mind said, her instinctual nature could not be denied.

"Look how ready you are." His fingers stroked between her legs, gliding through the creamy evidence of how excited she was. "It must be exhausting fighting against yourself all the time."

"Fuck you," she spat. Though his tone was matter-of-fact and not smug, she still felt suppressed. Restrained.

Dominated.

"Actually, I'm going to fuck *you*. And you're going to trust me enough to enjoy it."

"I can't trust you. I don't know you. I only know what you want, which is the exact opposite of what I want."

"Is it?" he asked patiently. "You'll know me by the time I'm done. We'll start with sex and work our way out."

Victoria snorted. "How original."

He paused, and she knew she'd scored a direct hit. She thought that would be the end of it.

Then against the back of her legs she felt the roughness of his jeans. "Aren't you going to undress?" she breathed, her already keen senses now painfully acute from her blindness.

"No."

One word. No explanation. She struggled, but was stilled by the warm, broad head of his cock stroking against her clit.

"Spread your legs wider, Victoria."

She didn't move. Damned if she'd help him tame her, arrogant bastard.

He sank in, forcing her slick tissues to spread for him, to accept him. Just an inch. Then he withdrew. Rubbing the now creamy tip against her, Max teased her, and then pressed inside her again. Just that one inch. She buried her head in the comforter and groaned, her cunt spasming, trying to pull him in to where she needed him.

"If you spread your legs, you can have what you want."

Victoria lifted her head. "I want *you* tied to the bed so I can torture you. Not the other way around."

His rumbling laughter made her shiver. The fact was, no matter what Max did or said, he attracted her. "But you wouldn't be enjoying that nearly as much as this."

"Screw the games, Max. Can't we just fuck?"

"I want to fuck you like this, angled just the way I want you."

"What about what I want?" she complained.

"You want the same thing, kitten. You just wish you didn't.

You're so tight like this, your cunt is like a velvet fist. I'll have to work my way into you . . ."

Max waited with the same studious patience he'd displayed since meeting her, all the while the head of his cock stroked into the mouth of her pussy in silent enticement. Her traitorous body beckoned him with a soft ripple. She was soaked and hot, more than ready.

She briefly considered altering and walking away, but then she wouldn't have sex with Max and that just wouldn't do. So, with her pride smarting, Victoria widened her stance. He'd pay later.

Immediately he surged inside, going deep and then deeper still until she couldn't breathe, couldn't think, every part of her focused on the thick pulsing cock that filled her too full.

Gasping, her back arched as his short nails scraped lightly across her hips. He leaned over her. Dominated her. As his rippling stomach touched her bound hands she felt the dampness of his sweat through his t-shirt.

The warlock was not as controlled as he appeared.

Taking what little power she could, she clutched his shirt in her hands, holding him to her.

Hands on the mattress to support his weight, Max began to shaft her cunt in long, deep drives. The angle of his penetration stroked with tantalizing pressure inside her, and he varied his thrusts, rubbing high and then low in an expert inner massage.

It was slow and far too easy, his hips pumping in timed, measured rhythm. Unable to see, she pictured how it must look, Max fully clothed, his ass clenching and releasing as he fucked her bound body. She quivered and began to purr. He growled in response, the vibration traveling the length of his body and into his thrusting cock.

"Do you feel weak?" he asked, his voice guttural and taunting. "Do you feel reduced because your body serves my pleasure and not your own?"

She wanted to retort, to argue, to fight, but she couldn't. It felt too good doing nothing but taking what he gave her. She was a cat after all and inherently lazy.

"Inherently submissive," he corrected. He moved one hand to cup her thigh and pulled it wider so he could fuck deeper. Now every plunge of his cock brought his tight, heavy balls against her clit.

He'd read her thoughts, she thought with what part of her brain was still functional.

The taming had begun.

With a soft hiss, she tightened around him. He cursed softly and shuddered, his body betraying him.

Suddenly, she grasped that he was as helpless as she. She'd attempted to use her body to entice him, and he'd succumbed. Despite the outward control he displayed, Max had started the evening with an entirely different approach and had dissolved from that into lust that could not be denied. Even now, his fingers bruised her hips, his thighs strained against hers, his labored breathing sounded loudly in the room.

Realizing that she was not alone in this unexpected physical fascination, she relaxed, sinking into the bed with a moan. It was not surrender. It was a stalemate.

Victoria's mouth curved in a catlike smile.

Three

Max lifted the cup of coffee to his lips and stared out the window at the St. John Hotel directly across the street. He took deep, even breaths, his thoughts fully focused on clearing his mind. Excitement and anticipation coursed through his veins, and he studiously worked to temper them.

Control. Where was his? It was undeniable that when he was with Victoria hunger drove him, not his mission.

His kitten was a tigress in bed, one who rolled, scratched, and bit with abandoned fervor. Tying her to the brass headboard had been a necessary delight. One he'd repeated often over the last two weeks.

I don't like this, Max, she'd said every time. But with her nipples hard against his tongue, he'd known the truth. She quaked, cursed, writhed, and the sight always made him so hard he'd have to grit his teeth to hold back his lust. Then he'd give up and fuck her for hours, long past exhaustion, abandoning his assignment in favor of overwhelming pleasure.

And the Council knew it.

Your lack of progress displeases us, They'd complained just an hour ago.

"You've given me very little time," he'd retorted.

We think no amount of time will be sufficient for taming the feral. She is beyond rehabilitation.

"She is not." He'd exhaled sharply. "You've never rushed me like this before, and she's the toughest case I've ever been given."

Decades have passed. Our patience is thin.

Turning away from both the window and the memory with a low curse, Max caught up his coat and left the café. Time had just run out. He couldn't fail in this. Failure would cost him more than loss of pride. It would cost Victoria her life.

He crossed the busy thoroughfare and entered the St. John by way of the revolving glass doors, waiting until he was mid-rotation before using his power to move up to the top floor where Victoria was hard at work. The thought of her occupied at her desk made his dick ache. He adored intelligent women, and Victoria was more cunning than most. She was also tough as nails.

The only time she'd been truly vulnerable was on the brink of orgasm, so he'd kept her there, time and time again, absorbing the sudden flood of her thoughts and recollections. Feeling the love she'd once had for Darius and the aching sadness of loss. Those glimpses of her soul always moved him to orgasm, the feeling of connection so profound it stole his breath.

He grit his teeth as his cock swelled further. He'd cum more since meeting her than he would have thought possible. It was why he had made so little headway. A proper taming required restraint on the part of the Hunter. He should have been finding his release elsewhere, tempering his desire, but no other woman appealed.

"Good afternoon, Mr. Westin," the receptionist greeted with a come-hither smile.

With a snap of his fingers, she had no recollection of his visit, her memory wiped clean in the blink of an eye. All she knew was that her boss was too busy to be disturbed, and she would take messages and deny visitors until she was told otherwise.

Max entered Victoria's lair without knocking, setting in place a simple glamour that prevented any passerby from seeing their coming activities through the glass office wall.

She looked up, arched a brow, and set her pen down. "Max."

His name. One word. In that soft purr, it was an aphrodisiac and he was not immune as he should be.

"Hello, kitten." He smiled at the soft shiver he felt from her. She was not immune either.

"I'm busy."

"You're about to be," he agreed, setting aside his coffee and summoning a beautifully wrapped box on her desk.

Her mouth curved in a sensual smile that made his blood heat. "A gift? How delightful."

Long, elegant fingers plucked at the lavender iridescent ribbon and tore at the royal blue wrapping. Inside rested an ornate wooden box. He watched as her fingertips drifted over the phrase that was carved there: *Only within my bonds will you truly know freedom.*

Victoria said nothing, but he watched her with a Hunter's perception and noted the sudden appearance of erect nipples beneath her white silk blouse. Her hand lifted to engage his vision, holding aloft a set of velvet-lined nipple clamps connected by a delicate gold chain.

"I was wondering when you were planning to get around to the toys," she said, a tad breathlessly. "You've waited longer than most."

The intimation that he was nothing special, merely another in a long string of annoyances, forced his hand. Furiously swirling air filled the room, scattering the papers on the desk and thrusting Victoria backward. Max stalked toward her, his gaze narrowed, his open palm closing swiftly into a fist, bringing her to an abrupt stop just a scant inch away from the window.

Her green eyes were wide, her lips parted on panting breaths, her chest rising and falling in apparent fear. He, however, knew it to be intense arousal. He could feel her in his thoughts, their bond building with every moment spent together. The surge of power inside her, a careful blending of magic and Familiar enhancement, made him groan aloud with his own overpowering lust. Never in his life had he felt this way about a woman. It felt almost as if he'd found the perfect fit to a puzzle piece. His fingertips itched with the magic coursing through him— magic strengthened by his proximity to Victoria.

"Kitten," he growled, reaching her. He thrust his hands into her cropped hair and pressed her back against the glass, her feet suspended a few feet above the ground. Eye-level with him.

She purred and nuzzled against him, her silver hoop earrings cold against his cheek, and then too hot. He stepped back, his power pinning her to the scenic view of the city behind her. Her arms were held motionless beside her head, her breasts thrusting wantonly toward him in the submissive pose. Only here, in the seat of her corporate influence, would a true taming be possible. She was ruler here. Until he arrived.

That was the lesson to be learned.

As he reached for the buttons of his shirt and freed them, magic mimicked his movements with Victoria's blouse. He smiled as he felt his belt loosen, pleased with her initiative in exerting her own power to undress him.

"A nooner?" she murmured, before licking her lips.

"An all-afternooner," he corrected, shrugging out of his shirt.

"You're insatiable."

"You love it."

Max watched with heated anticipation as the bra clasp between her breasts snapped open and then separated. The nipple clamps rose up from the floor and then clipped into place, her reaction to the sudden pressure a low hiss from between clenched teeth. The sight of those pale, firm breasts capped with swollen, reddened nipples and the slender chain made freeing his cock from its confinement necessary.

"Oooh, Max," she purred, moving sinuously against the window as he dropped his pants. "What a big cock you have."

He gave her his best wolfish grin, enjoying her playfulness in the face of her helplessness. "The better to screw you with, my dear."

The side zipper of her thin skirt lowered and then the garment fell to the carpeted floor along with her black lace thong and stiletto heels. "After," he summoned the remaining contents of the box into his open palm, "I screw you with this."

Victoria swallowed hard at the sight of the slightly curved dildo in his hand. It was long and thick, close in size, shape, and coloring to Max's cock. He lubed it generously, his gaze never leaving hers.

She pouted. "I don't want that thing. I want you."

Max faltered a moment at her words, then moved quickly, taking her mouth with deep-seated hunger, distracting her from the tightening bond between them.

I want you. Such simple words, but for her, the words imperiled. It wasn't quite the "needing" required to make the collar appear, but it was close enough to cause a quickening inside him. He shouldn't feel anything more than triumph at her words, but he did. Much more.

It was what he'd hoped for, the result he had set out to achieve, but he hadn't expected it to happen so fast. He had been certain he'd have to drive her mad first. He couldn't do it while he was inside her, like he had done with every other Familiar he'd tamed. When he was joined to Victoria, the Council faded from his perception, leaving just the two of them lost in each other. The only needs he cared about were his own, and the Council could go to hell.

As he breathed deeply of her scent, his eyes squeezed shut, his chest heaving against hers, his fingers slipping between her legs to rub her clit. He felt possessive and needy. God, all morning since he'd left her he'd wanted her. Only hours apart. Too long. Knowing their time together was temporary, he coveted every moment and hated to share her with work or anyone else.

Irreverent, saucy, mischievous—she was a cat through and through. She both soothed and incited him, a dichotomy that left him satisfied on every front.

And he was preparing her for an eternity with another man.

The knowledge made his jaw ache, and his chest tighten painfully. He shoved the thought away, and concentrated on the here and now. At least she'd be alive. If he had to lose her, better to another warlock than to death.

Whimpering into his mouth as he stroked her slick cunt, Victoria tried to writhe, but couldn't fight the force that held her. "Max," she breathed into his mouth. "Let me touch you."

He shook his head, unwilling to break away from the kiss.

"I want to touch you, damn it!" She jerked her mouth away.

"You should want what *I* want." His voice was rough, harsh. "My pleasure is yours. My hunger is yours."

"Is your need mine, too?" Victoria asked softly, her gaze riveted to the large man who stood before her. She heard his teeth grind in response to her query and his touch left her.

There was an urgency to his seduction that had never been there before. To come to her during the day, when they would have been together within hours . . .

She inhaled sharply. How often had she caught herself daydreaming about him, reliving moments from the long night before? He cooked for her every night, and fed her by hand. He showered with her, and washed her hair. There were rough moments, too, along with the tender. Moments of high passion—like when he'd come through her front door and dragged her to the floor, saying hello with guttural cries and drugging thrusts of his beautiful cock deep inside her. Never asking permission. Taking what he desired as if the use of her body was his right.

The attention had seduced her, reminding her of the intimate connection between warlock and Familiar. But the woman within her had also been captivated. She wielded great power in her human life. She was responsible for the thousands of employees who worked under her command. There was relief and pleasure to be found in turning herself entirely into Max's dominant keeping. Darius had treated her as equal. Max never let her forget that he held the power.

But now his words betrayed him, revealing the depth of his affection for her.

You should want what your Master wants. His pleasure is yours. His hunger is yours. His need is yours.

But Max had inserted himself as her Master. And the need to accept him was nearly overwhelming.

When she was with him, the restlessness that had plagued her for so long was soothed immeasurably. She wasn't alone when she was with Max. Aside from Darius, he was the only man to ever make her feel that way. She'd put on needed weight, finding joy in sharing her meals and life with someone who wanted her to be happy. And she was, because he made sure of it. Yes, the single most important aspect of their relationship was satisfying him, but what satisfied Max was pleasuring her.

Victoria watched him warily as he approached. The dildo, glistening with lube, was aimed straight at the juncture between her legs. Max leaned forward and licked across her lips. "Open up, kitten."

Mutinously, she defied him. "Make me."

With a slight flick of his hand, magic forced her legs apart. She creamed, softening further, some traitorous part of her heritage relishing the taming, knowing she was about to be pleasured beyond bearing, and she didn't have to do a damned thing.

"Look how wet you are," he praised, rubbing the smooth tip up and down her drenched slit. He pressed his mouth against her ear and whispered, "You love a hard cock in you."

"I love *your* hard cock in me." She gasped, her pussy clenching tight in an effort to capture the thick head that teased her opening.

"Let's play first," he rumbled, sliding the dildo a scant inch inside her. She tried to grind her hips down onto it, but couldn't.

"Max!"

"Shush, I'll give it to you." With deft twists of his wrist, he pumped it softly, working it inside her, his other hand catching the chain between her breasts and tugging gently. A deep ache built within her breasts, spreading through her torso, making her cry out.

"Easy," he crooned, thrusting gently, finally spearing home with breathtaking expertise.

Her eyes met his, trying to understand why he took her like this, what it was he wanted from her so she could give it to him. Then she gave up, her eyes drifting closed, her body shuddering with pleasure as he fucked her with long, smooth strokes.

"Please," she whispered, her hot cheek pressed to the cool glass.

"Please what?" His tongue swiped across the pinched tip

of a tormented nipple, then his mouth closed around both it and the clamp, sucking in rhythm to the rutting between her thighs.

"I want you."

Max released her breast, and quickened his pace. Her hips rocked as much as they were able, her cries desperate, her clit swollen and throbbing for the slight touch that would send her into orgasm. Deep inside, the feel of the wide, flared head stroking along the walls of her cunt made her head thrash from side to side, the only part of her body she was allowed to move.

He groaned and leaned against her, his skin coated in a fine sheen of sweat. His tongue licked the shell of her ear and then thrust inside.

"Don't you want me, Max?" she gasped, dying from the need to climax, to move, to have more than a fake cock could ever give her.

"You drive me insane." He nuzzled his damp forehead against her cheek.

"Is that a 'yes'?"

If it was . . . if he felt the connection she did . . . What she wouldn't give to find love a second time. Perhaps, in the end, it wouldn't be with Max, but this was the closest she'd come to that emotion in over two centuries.

Suddenly his hand was at her throat, his mouth over hers, his knees braced against the window to support the thrusts of his hand.

Give me what I want.

The melding of his thoughts with hers was all the impetus she needed. Part of the taming was his ability to read her thoughts, but for her to know his meant the connection ran both ways.

The tension fled her body. Her cunt spasmed with want, clutching greedily for what it *needed* . . .

"Please," she breathed, aching to hold him. "I need you."

Max tilted Victoria's head back a split second before the collar appeared. The thin black ribbon looked so innocuous, but it bound her more than chains ever could. It would fade when she was paired with a warlock, become a part of her, just as her new master would.

The sight of the collar and the submission it signified made cum dribble from the head of Max's aching cock, every cell in his body flaring with masculine triumph. He yanked the dildo free and tossed it away, releasing her from his spell, catching her limp, willing body in a protective embrace.

He'd almost given in, he had wanted her so badly. Feeling her body grasping for him, hungry for him, had driven him crazy. The only thing that held him back was concern for her. If he failed to bring her back from the edge, They would kill her. And that would kill him.

Clutching her close, Max used his powers to take them home—his home. There he lowered her gently to his velvet-covered bed and then cupped her thigh, spreading her wide. The sight of the glistening lips of her sex and tiny pussy made his balls draw up. The look in her eyes made his heart ache.

Hours. That's all they had left.

He climbed over her, admiring the new curves she'd acquired with careful tending. Under his care, she'd lost the signs of neglect. As he caught one of her wrists and pulled it over her head, he never took his eyes from her, using magic to pull the velvet rope from the bedpost and bind her.

"Max." A whisper, no more than that, as she lifted her other arm without urging and used her own power to restrain herself.

Victoria was the most powerful woman he'd ever known, both in their world and the world they shared with humans. Her submission of that power to his demands was a gift of such magnitude it captured his heart. His eyes burned, his throat clenched tight.

His kitten. *His*.

He took her then, in a swift sure thrust that joined them so tightly there was no separation. A raw sound tore from his throat as she climaxed instantly, sucking his cock with ripples of pleasure, luring him to cum in her with hard, fierce spurts. Holding her shivering body tightly to his, Max pumped gently, draining his seed while prolonging her pleasure, absorbing her cries with pure infatuation.

Later, he laced his fingers with hers and rode her bound body again. Harder this time, releasing his passion in a brutal taking, his hips battering hers, his cock plunging deep.

Victoria accepted his lust with such beauty, her voice hoarse, her words barely audible over his labored breathing.

"*Yes . . . yes . . . yes . . .*"

Taking all that he was, blossoming like a flower beneath him, lush with such promise. The places he could take her, the things he could teach her, the freedom he could give her . . .

But he was a Hunter groomed to join the Council, and They didn't keep Familiars.

So Max took what he could, his tongue and lips working

at her breast, drawing on her with hungry pulls, worrying the hard nipple against the roof of his mouth. His hands pinned her down, kept her still for the steady rise and fall of his hips, his cock working her into endless pleasure, giving her no rest, afraid to stop touching her. Afraid to lose her.

Keep her.

The compulsion rose up so unexpectedly that his rhythm faltered, suspending him at the deepest point of a downward plunge, his cock scalded by the hot clasp of her cunt.

"No!" she cried, struggling beneath him. "Don't stop. Please . . ."

How could he walk away? She'd sacrificed the life she'd built for herself to reenter his.

He would do the same for her. He *needed* to do the same for her.

"Never." He growled and crushed her to him, resuming his claiming, his flushed cheek pressed to hers. "I'll never stop. You're mine. *Mine.*"

Victoria summoned the black robe Familiars wore when facing the Council and dressed silently. She'd preserved the garment all these years, saving it for the day she would face Them and exact her revenge. Now she donned it with a different purpose in mind.

As she prepared to leave, her eyes never strayed from the sleeping form on the bed. Max's powerful body sprawled face down, the red satin sheets riding low on his hips. Gorgeous.

She ached to touch him, to wake him, to look into those molten silver eyes one last time.

How dangerous he was, even in slumber.

Tears fell unchecked.

Lost in her, his mind had lowered its guards, his thoughts and feelings pouring into her in a flood of longing and affection that destroyed. He was willing to give up all that he'd worked for to keep her, and she couldn't let him do it.

She couldn't lose him like she lost Darius. The Council would be furious at being thwarted a second time. Their spite had cost her one love. She refused to let it cost her another.

Better to lose him to a life apart from her than to death.

So she covered her mouth to muffle her pain, and left him.

Four

The moment Max woke from the depths of sheer physical exhaustion, he knew she was gone. Their connection was such that he had felt Victoria inside him ever since the collar had appeared. Now the warmth she gave him was no longer there, leaving him cold.

But he wasn't alone.

Once again, you exceeded our expectations, the Council said, in a tone laced with satisfaction. *The Familiar is returned to the fold, a result she says would not have been possible without your power and expertise. We are pleased.*

Rolling out of bed, Max tugged on a pair of loose-fitting trousers, his heart racing in near panic. "Where is she?"

She is preparing for the joining ceremony.

"*What?*" He paused and glanced at the clock by his bed, his fists clenching. Two hours ago he'd been balls deep inside her. Now she was bonding forever to another man? "What's the goddamned rush? I just collared her! The training wasn't finished."

How could she?

Black rage rolled over him.

We felt it would be safest, and most effective, to partner her quickly. Her warlock will train her to suit him.

"Who is he?"

Gabriel was selected. He was the only warlock strong enough, aside from you.

Max's jaw ached from gritting his teeth. Gabriel was powerful, considered handsome, as popular with women as Max was, but the other warlock stayed far away from the darker edge of magic. To Max it was a weakness. Gabriel had a line he wouldn't cross and it opened him to failure. Weakness like that would give Victoria too much leeway. She needed an iron fist. Craved it. Max had only one vulnerability, and it was one he needed to control her.

Victoria herself.

There was no line he wouldn't cross to achieve his aims.

And he proved it by abandoning his home, his ambitions, and the life he knew to go after her.

Victoria stared at her reflection as the handmaidens adjusted her robes for the ceremony ahead. Her eyes were red-rimmed, bloodshot, bruised from lack of sleep and too much crying.

She'd forgotten who Max was, seeing him only through smitten eyes, failing to remember that he was a Hunter and next in line to ascend to the Council. He'd spent centuries working toward his goal, and two weeks working on her—one of many assignments in his past, with more to come in his future. He would forget her in time.

The thought made her heart hurt, the pain so piercing she panted with it.

Waving her attendants away, Victoria caught the edge of the vanity and gulped down desperate breaths. She'd been out of the loop so long, she had no idea who Gabriel was, but the handmaidens raved about her luck. Yes, she would pine for the man who'd taken over her body and filled it with mind-numbing pleasure, but perhaps, in a decade or two, she could come to tolerate Gabriel's touch . . .

"You'll never know, kitten," rumbled a deep, familiar voice behind her.

Her gaze lifted and met stormy gray.

"Max," she breathed, her palms growing damp at the sight of him. Bare-chested, barefooted, wearing only trousers that hung low around his lean hips. His shoulders so broad, his golden skin stretched over beautifully defined muscles. A predator.

Her mouth dried, her breasts swelled with desire, as if he hadn't just fucked her into exhaustion mere hours ago.

He came toward her with his sultry, long-legged stride. She was held motionless by his stare, forgetting to breathe until her lungs burned, then she gasped and cried out as his hand cupped the back of her head. His strong fingers pinched strands of her hair and tugged roughly, bending her to his will. She stared up at him in a haze of fear and desire, the flush of anger on his face enough to frighten her. And arouse her.

"I'm keeping you," he rasped, just before he took her parted lips with possessive hunger.

Having thought him lost to her, she melted in his arms. He anchored her, even as he brought her to heel. His breathing labored, he turned his head, his cheek rubbing against hers, absorbing her tears.

"The Council will punish you," she cried, her voice breaking. "I-I can't bear to lose you."

"But you were about to." He licked deep into her mouth, making her moan and open to him, silently begging for more. He obliged her, groaning, his tongue stroking along hers with so much skill it left her breathless. One arm supported her back, the other hand cupped her breast and kneaded it with the aggressive pressure she'd come to relish and crave.

"Let me be the instrument of your revenge," he whispered darkly, his lips moving against hers.

A gift. For her.

Victoria swallowed hard, stunned by his statement and the ramifications of it. "Max."

He held her gaze. "You have your business interests to occupy your daylight hours, but your private hours are mine. You will serve, obey, and please me. You will never question an order or deny me anything. I'll do things to your body that will test your limits. Sometimes, you'll want to tell me 'no,' but you'll do what I want regardless. That is your commitment to me."

He hugged her tightly to him, burying his face in the tender space between her neck and shoulder. His voice lowered and came gruffly, "My commitment is to care for you, and provide for you in every way. If you need your revenge to be free of the past, I will deliver the means to you. You are my greatest treasure, Victoria. I will always value and treat you as such."

Her arms came around him, her lashes wet and vision blurry. "I want the Triumvirate."

To give her this, he would have to skirt the very Council

he'd aspired to for so long. There was more to that long ago night than she knew, and the danger was mortal.

Max nodded his understanding and agreement without hesitation, but the tic in his jaw betrayed him. "Will you love me like you loved him? Can you?"

She released a deep breath in an audible rush. Her heart reached out to him, revealing the many facets of her affection and adoration, the feelings she had for Max so different from what she'd felt for Darius, but just as powerful, and growing every day. She was beginning to see how much of herself she'd kept away from Darius, and how much of herself she'd already shared with Max—the man who'd shown her how to embrace her nature and revel in it. Safe in his embrace.

"Yes, Max," she promised. "So much."

His power swelled in response to her passion, flowing into her, and she enhanced it. The soul-deep thrumming that coursed through them was almost overwhelming. They would have to train, relearn everything they knew, find a way to control it. Together.

I can't wait to get started. Max's confident voice in her mind gave her courage.

The task ahead wouldn't be easy . . .

You don't like things easy, kitten.

Victoria offered her mouth to him and he took it, his chest rumbling with laughter as her lips curved against his in a cat-like smile.

SYLVIA DAY is the multi-published author of erotic romantic fiction set in most sub-genres. A wife and mother of two, she is a former Russian linguist for the U.S. Army Military Intelligence. Her award–winning books have been called "wonderful and passionate" by *WNBC.com* and "Shining Stars" by *Booklist*. They also regularly appear on bestseller lists, such as Bookscan and Barnes & Noble. Please visit her at www.SylviaDay.com.

Quick Silver

Vivi Anna

One

As the communicator buzzed in her ear, Sangria Silver pulled her Hummer off Ventura Boulevard and onto the shoulder, knowing the significance of the call. Only important, influential clients had her private number.

After adjusting the miniature microphone attached to her ear down toward her mouth, she pushed the red connect button on the dashboard. "Yes."

"I have a package for delivery." The feminine voice was commanding and cold. Sangria noted that the caller was certainly no underling but most likely the main contact herself. This was indeed an important call.

She was used to dealing with intermediaries when it came to pickup and delivery. Usually the cargo that she transported around the country was illegal in some manner. She didn't know that for sure, and she didn't ask. Her discretion was the reason she was the number one Conveyor in the New States of America.

"Size?" she asked.

"A metal case. Six feet by three feet by four."

Sangria sketched out the measurements on a pad of paper she had lying on the passenger seat. She had to make sure it would fit into the false bottom in the back of her Hummer. "Weight?"

"About two hundred and fifty pounds."

She scribbled that down. "Explosive or toxic?"

"Neither."

Sangria breathed a sigh of relief. She hated those jobs and was planning to avoid taking on any more. About a year ago, she transported a toxic case that was supposedly airtight and safe. When she arrived at the designated address, she was whisked inside a large warehouse by two men in white suits and facemasks and put into a detox station.

There she spent the next two hours naked, under scalding hot water, while two other men scrubbed her body with hard bristled brushes. She had been sore and raw for weeks afterward. However, she had a sneaking suspicion that whatever they were trying to get off her skin made its way inside anyway. She'd been feeling weird lately.

"Pickup and delivery addresses?"

"Pick up at the corner of Rochester and Selby; deliver to 1020 East Bonanza Road, Las Vegas."

Sangria punched the addresses into her GPS system mounted on the dashboard. Instantly she had the distance calculated and the time estimation of how long it would take her to go from one place to the other if the traffic was flowing and she drove the posted speed limit.

"An approximate driving time of four hours and ten minutes. I can pick up the package early in the a.m."

"Now," the woman demanded. "I need you to pick it up now."

Sangria didn't like the way this conversation was going. Something about the woman's voice bothered her. Too icy, too controlled. A woman without emotions was a very dangerous person.

"That will cost you—"

"Two million."

Fingers poised over the GPS system, Sangria froze. That was more money than she hoped to make in the next two years. Her usual transporting fee was twenty thousand. She made a comfortable living on that, with a job or two a month. With two million from one delivery, she could actually retire from the job and settle down in a Caribbean country like the one she always dreamed of. But there had to be a catch.

"Excuse me?" Sangria choked.

"I will pay you two million dollars to come now, tonight, to pick up my package and deliver it to Vegas."

"My usual fee is twen—"

"I know what you usually get paid, Ms. Silver," the woman interrupted.

Sangria swallowed hard. The woman knew her name. She went to great pains to be anonymous. Her vehicle was registered to a company with three bogus owners who didn't exist. Her modest house was leased under a false identity that Sangria had created online, complete with birth certificate and social security number. Being an orphan and having run away from every foster home she'd been sent to, she had no family to speak of. And she had no friends and no regular lover. Sure, she had a couple of acquaintances who owed her favors, but it was strictly business not personal.

How did this woman know who she was?

Before she could speak, the woman continued as if reading Sangria's thoughts. "Yes, I know who you are. I wouldn't be in *my* position if I allowed people I come in contact with to remain anonymous." She chuckled. "But I have to admit it did take longer than usual to uncover who you really are. You're very good at hiding." There was a long pause and then, "I'll have to remember that."

"What do you want?" A sense of dread started to wash over Sangria. She was never any good at dealing with glitches in her system. Her attention to detail and organization made her feel safe, secure. Now, she felt anything but.

"Your silence."

"If you've called me then you must be aware of my reputation for discretion."

"I am quite aware," she stated icily. "But I am not some drug dealer moving H across state lines, or an arms dealer moving guns from New Mexico to Texas. I am so much more dangerous than that, Sangria."

All the air left her lungs, and she had to close her eyes to stop from panicking. The woman knew about Sangria's other conveying jobs. How was that possible? Unless she had been watched for the past year? But why?

Sangria's hands were trembling, and she had to squeeze them together to stop from shaking. She couldn't take this job. She had a frightening feeling that it would be her last. And not in a good, retirement type of way. Somehow, though, Sangria knew refusal wasn't an option.

"I figured that out the moment I heard your voice," Sangria answered trying to keep her voice from trembling.

"Good girl. I knew you were smart." The woman chuckled, but it brought no warmth to Sangria. "Take the turnpike off Ventura and make your way to Rochester. Someone will meet you there."

Sangria turned in her seat, scanning the boulevard, looking for parked cars, or buildings from which someone could be watching. She saw nothing but passing vehicles and large flashy billboards. Maybe her vehicle was tagged with a tracker.

"This will be the last communication we have." The woman paused, and then stated acidly, "Unless there is a problem. And Sangria, you better hope that never happens."

The woman clicked off, leaving Sangria close to hyperventilating. Ripping the communicator off her head, she shuffled across the seat, opened the passenger door, and jumped out onto the shoulder. Instantly the oppressive heat suffocated her. Although it was nearing dusk, there was no relief to the stifling summer weather.

As she took in some cleansing breaths, sweat started to dribble down Sangria's face and neck, soaking the collar of her white cotton t-shirt. But she knew it wasn't just because of the temperature.

She knew there would come a time when she wriggled into something way over her head. A person didn't do the job she did and not know that they teetered on the edge of immorality and danger. She just didn't realize how instantly it could sweep over her, pulling her down into a terror-filled void.

Leaning against her vehicle for support to try to ease her strangled breathing, Sangria quickly went over her options. And realized she pretty much didn't have any. If she didn't show up at the pickup address, she knew that no matter where she went, the ice woman on the phone would track her down and eliminate her. The fact that Sangria didn't know the woman's identity and hadn't taken any money seemed to her inconsequential.

The only thing she could do was to pick up the package and safely deliver it to the Vegas destination. She had executed thousands of deliveries without issue. There was no reason that this one wouldn't be the same.

Pushing away from the vehicle somewhat relieved, Sangria almost believed that. If it wasn't for the cold creeping along her spine that ended on her skull, causing her short bone-white hair to stand on end, she could almost believe anything.

Two

The pickup had gone smoothly.

She met with two burly men dressed casually in shorts and tank tops at the corner of Rochester and Selby just as she was instructed. When she pulled up to the curb, they hefted the shiny metal case into her Hummer and handed her a black duffel bag. Without a word, they walked around the corner, jumped into a nondescript four-door sedan, and drove away.

After they had driven away, Sangria had jumped out of her vehicle again and slid under it on her back to check the undercarriage for any tracking devices. She had found two.

Swearing that she'd been so reckless and stupid for not inspecting her Hummer every day, Sangria had smashed the metal devices off with her tire iron. Although she knew it wouldn't matter. Certainly, the case had been installed with a tracer.

She had jumped back into the vehicle and checked the bag.

It was full of money, but not nearly enough for two million. There was a typed noted inside stuck to one of the money stacks. *Fifty thousand now ... the rest on delivery.* Zipping up the bag, she sighed angrily. Figures. She wondered what other surprises were waiting for her. Sangria had the distinct feeling that this trip was going to be anything but a regular everyday delivery.

The sun was down by the time Sangria turned onto the I-15 heading toward Las Vegas. So far, everything was going as planned, and she managed to relax a little and enjoy the ride. Pushing a button on the dash, classical music blasted from her four built-in speakers. The Hummer's controls were programmed to respond to her moods. And right now, she needed the soothing sounds of Mozart.

Humming to the music, Sangria didn't see the semi that jumped the meridian and came barreling toward her with its headlights off.

The next few moments were mostly a blur. She didn't remember jerking on the steering wheel and ramming into the side of the semitrailer. Or the flipping of the vehicle, as it turned over and over, landing—remarkably—back onto its wheels in the ditch. All she could remember were the grunts and groans she heard resounding in her ears. Surprisingly, it had sounded like more than one voice echoing around her.

Sangria didn't know how long she sat still strapped into the driver's seat, blood dripping down her forehead, until reason and awareness slapped her in the face. Putting a hand to her aching head, she surmised that she had a large cut on the crown. Looking at the red-splattered spider-webbed windshield, it wasn't hard for her to guess from what.

Turning in her seat, she took inventory of the damage to her vehicle. The black bag was still there, jammed under the passenger seat. Her personal effects were strewn on the floor and seat from the glove compartment that had flown open. Seeing that triggered a horrible thought, and she spun in her seat.

The trunk door of the Hummer was open, and so was the hidden door in the floor. Damn it, she'd forgotten to padlock it!

Unhooking her seat belt, Sangria tried to open her door. It wouldn't budge. The frame was bent inward, and she was very lucky that it hadn't rammed into her side. Shuffling across the passenger seat, she tried that door, and discovered the same damage. She slid between the front seats, crawled into the back, and peered down into the false bottom of her vehicle. The compartment was empty. The case was missing.

With a cry of alarm, she jumped out of the back. Pain—immediate and sharp—ripped up her side, making her head spin. Looking down, she noticed blood blossoming on her t-shirt from under her arm. She lifted her shirt and noticed a long cut on her left side. *Guess the car door didn't miss.*

Letting her shirt fall, she scanned the surroundings near the accident. The semi was nowhere to be seen. He obviously fled the scene. The driver was probably driving drunk, or had fallen asleep at the wheel. But when her eyes settled on something only three feet away, her injuries and everything else was immediately forgotten.

The case lay on its side all banged up, with the lid wide open.

She stumbled toward it, realizing that the cut on her head was making her a tiny bit woozy. As she neared, all the breath left her lungs, and she doubled over almost throwing up. She was in deep shit, and she didn't have a shovel.

Lying on the ground a few inches from the case was a man. Bound and gagged but alive, he looked straight at her with wide vivid blue eyes.

"Fuck," she whispered as she collapsed to her knees beside him. Her legs were quivering too violently to support her any longer.

Rolling over, he shuffled to her on his side, his eyes beseeching her to end his misery. Blood streaked his chiseled face and dampened the cloth gagging him.

With a trembling hand, Sangria reached over and pulled the gag out from between his full lips.

He sighed. "Oh thank God." He moved his mouth open and closed, stretching out, what she assumed, were cramped jaw muscles.

"Who are you?" she asked, shock slowly creeping over her.

"Vance Verona." He raised his bound hands behind him. "Can you cut these, please?"

"What—" She paused, rubbing a hand over her face in frustration, and then started again. "Why . . . what the fuck is going on?"

"I have a one-way ticket to the Blue Room district in Vegas," he explained as he tried to pull apart the ropes binding his hands. "I'm a sex worker. Usually I entertain the most powerful women in the country, but I must have pissed someone off."

"Do you think?"

Chuckling, he continued to squirm, jarring his shoulders back and forth trying to free his hands. "I do believe Lady Maxine Madison is mad at me."

Gasping, Sangria made a grab for his gag. "No, no, no. Stop fucking talking." He moved his head, but wasn't quick enough. She shoved the cloth back between his lips and scrambled to her feet.

She marched back to her vehicle, mumbling under her breath. This could not be happening. The man did not say what she thought he did. He must have been mistaken. There was no way in hell that the First Lady, Maxine Madison, was involved in the sex industry.

Crawling back into the Hummer, Sangria slid into the front seat and turned the ignition. Nothing. The engine wouldn't turn over. She tried repeatedly, to no avail.

"Fuck!" She banged the steering wheel with her fist. The situation was getting worse by the second. And she had no idea what to do about it. She didn't have the contact's number, and even if she did, using it might not be the wisest course of action, if she wanted to stay alive. She had broken her number one rule, and the only thing that could get her killed . . . she had seen what was inside the package.

Glancing in her side mirror, she could still see him on the ground near the case. He had ceased his futile efforts to release his hands and was just lying there staring toward the vehicle. Sighing, she glanced toward the road. So far, no other vehicles had stopped to inspect the accident. Didn't surprise her, not in this day and age. No one stopped for anything.

However, it wouldn't be long before her smashed-up vehicle attracted attention from the law. Unwanted attention that could get her killed.

She crawled into the back of the vehicle and lifted another hidden door in the floor. Pulling out a black bag, Sangria unzipped it and took inventory. She had her passport, some clothes, a roll of cash, a first-aid kit, and a gun. All the things she packed in case of emergencies. This was definitely one of those times.

Reaching over the passenger seat, she started grabbing the items spilled from her glove compartment and shoved them into the bag as well. When she was finished, she took a cloth rag and wiped down every inch of the vehicle, erasing her fingerprints. She took the moneybag and her pack, and jumped out of the vehicle. Bending down, she used her pocket screwdriver to take off the license plate. She shoved that into her bag too. It wouldn't keep her hidden for long, but at least it was a start.

Marching back to the package, Sangria knew without a doubt that she was going on the run. There was no other way to avoid the inevitable. No matter her excuses, Ms. Madison would not keep her alive. She had seen too much. By accident mind you, but still she didn't think the First Lady was going to care much about that. Her position was much too powerful and influential to have Sangria running around with the knowledge of her involvement in illegal sex trading.

Staring down at the cargo, she took in his handsome face and lean sculpted body. He had obviously been taken from his bed as he wore only a pair of black silk boxer shorts. Disheveled dark hair curled around his ears and hung over his forehead, covering one of his beautiful blue eyes. He was indeed exquisite to look at. He had probably been one of Ms. Madison's prized studs.

Maybe I should leave him here. The thought crossed her mind then fled just as quickly. It didn't matter anymore. She was a dead woman. She might as well have company along the way.

Using the pocketknife she had strapped to her ankle, Sangria cut through his ropes at his wrists and his ankles. Breaking free, he quickly sat up and pulled the gag out of his mouth.

"I thought you were going to leave me," he sputtered.

"I thought about it." She slung the moneybag over her shoulder. "Can you walk?" She held out her hand to him and pulled him up.

Standing, he flexed both his legs, rotated his shoulders, and then nodded. "You wouldn't happen to have a t-shirt in that bag would you? I'm feeling a little vulnerable right now." He splayed his arms out, indicating his bare chest. He didn't need to do that for her to notice. He was the kind of man that *all* women noticed.

She unzipped the bag, and tossed him one of her tank tops. "I didn't think that would bother you."

Smirking, he yanked the shirt over his head and pulled it down over the straining muscles of his chest. "Why? Because women pay me to service them?" The shirt was tight and clung to every ridge and ripple he had. Smiling he cocked his head. "Honey, that just means I'm good at what I do. It doesn't mean I don't have any humility."

"Sorry," she said grudgingly.

He shrugged. "What's the plan?"

"The plan is to get the fuck out of here and stay alive. Valley Wells Station is just over that rise. I know of a little shack we can hold up in. Then we split up. The rest is up to you, cowboy. You'll be a free agent."

With that, Sangria turned and walked toward the road, not caring whether he followed or not. She wasn't any good with other people. She'd been alone for most of her life. She liked it that way. Fewer attachments, less complications.

But as he moved in next to her and matched her stride for stride, she felt a strange feeling of comfort wash over her. She was almost elated to have a companion. An emotion she couldn't recollect ever experiencing.

Three

The shack barely lived up to its name.

There were four wooden walls, dilapidated but still intact, a single lumpy mattress with surprisingly clean sheets on the dirty floor, a cracked linoleum table with one equally crumbling chair, and a bathroom, consisting of a toilet sans lid, and a shower stall without a door. The amazing thing was, the place had running water.

Sangria tossed her bag onto the floor and sat with an exhausted sigh on the chair. In the throes of lust, an old lover had told her about this place. He had been a gunrunner and had used the place years ago when he had to disappear for a few weeks. He had invited her along. She had refused. And that was the last time she'd ever heard from him. She wondered how long he lasted out here, with his big mouth that couldn't keep his own secrets.

Vance glanced around the room and grimaced. "It's lovely."

"It's for one night. You'll live." Rotating her shoulder, she realized how stiff and sore she was. And that she'd forgotten about the big gash in her side. If she didn't look after it, it would get infected.

Vance must have noticed her wince, because he came to her side and touched her arm. "You're hurt."

She flinched from him and stood. "I'm fine. I just need to wash it and bandage it up."

"I have first aid skills."

She glanced at him, her brow lifted in question.

Lifting his shirt, he said, "I had a client who liked it rough." He drew his finger over a small scar on his abdomen. "I stitched it up myself."

Although his voice was cool, she could see the emotion in his eyes. They flared like blue flame when he spoke. The man had obviously suffered.

"I'm fine." She turned and marched into the bathroom, shutting the broken door behind her. It creaked and groaned as it moved, and didn't completely close, but it would have to do.

Stripping off her clothes, Sangria reached for the shower taps and turned on the water. To her surprise, the water came out hot and relatively clean. She stepped into the stall and submerged her head under the spray. The water felt heavenly sluicing down her skin. Lifting her arm, she moved to the side to allow the cleansing effects of the water flow over her wound. Pain immediately seared through her, but soon healing warmth spread over her. Minus the blood, the cut didn't look too tragic. Nothing a bandage and time wouldn't heal.

She closed her eyes and tilted her head back, enjoying the hot water playing over her body. It was then that she felt the gentle scrape of a sponge on her back.

Jolting, she turned quickly and nearly collided with Vance, who was naked and trying to rub her back.

"What the fuck are you doing?" she spurted.

"Washing your back."

"Get out," she demanded, trying to cover herself and look indignant.

"Let me do this, please. You freed me. I need to pay you back."

She stared at him and noticed the emotions swimming in his eyes. She couldn't imagine what his life must have been like. And to be shoved in a case and transported to another city like chattel . . . she could just imagine the humiliation he must be feeling.

"Fine," she conceded. "But it's just washing."

He smiled and his eyes danced with mischief. "Hey, I'm a professional, remember? I'm not even aroused. See?" He tilted his head down.

Sangria followed his gaze to his cock. Even flaccid, he was well endowed. Tingles of desire spread over her thighs as she stared at him. His hand moved over to his cock and he wrapped his palm around it sensuously while she watched.

"Like what you see?"

Her head snapped up and she met his smoldering gaze. "Maybe."

With his hand still on his member, Vance took a step forward. "I'm very good at more than washing, honey."

"Don't call me honey."

"Well what should I call you? You never gave me your name."

Suddenly, Sangria felt ashamed. Not because she was naked, standing in a shower stall with an equally naked stranger, but because she'd been rude to him from the get go. She could feel her cheeks redden, and she hated that. No one ever made her feel embarrassed before.

"Sangria." She averted her gaze. "My name is Sangria."

"A beautiful name for an equally beautiful woman."

Raising her eyes, she caught his saucy grin and the way he looked at her with a promise of something swirling in the bright blue depths. "Keep your flirtations to yourself. I'm not one of your clients."

His grin never faltered as he spoke. "Turn around, Sangria. I'll wash your back."

Cautiously she turned, giving him her back. She hated that her name on his lips gave her pleasure. A warm tingling sensation started deep in her belly as he touched her on the nape of the neck with the sponge. With slow firm circles, he made his way over her lean muscled flesh. Sighing, she let her head fall forward and enjoyed his attentions. Past the point of stress and uncertainty, she was surprised that her brain could still function. If she could let go for a little while and revel in this pleasure, she would. For she didn't know when she would ever get another chance.

As Vance neared her ass, her pussy started to purr in delight. Without thinking, she spread her legs apart to ease the ache. It had been a long time since she felt desire. Her last lover had been almost a year ago, and then he hadn't been that memorable. A porn video and a vibrator would have been more inspiring.

When she heard a groan of appreciation, Sangria glanced over her shoulder at Vance. He was grinning again, but this time there was no humor in his eyes, just brazen lust.

"You have an amazing ass."

"I told you to save your words."

Shaking his head, he stared down at her rounded flesh. "I can't help it, Sangria, this is the firmest, most delectable ass I have ever come in contact with."

She laughed then. He sounded sincere as he gazed at her backside. But when he lifted his gaze to hers, her grin faded. She could see the desire in his eyes, pacing like a caged animal eager to escape and hunt. She swallowed hard as he leaned into her, resting his sensuous lips beside her earlobe and whispered. "I want to lick your flesh. Allow me to pleasure you."

She nearly moaned as his lips tickled the sensitive skin on her ear. She'd never been with anyone eager to please her. Deep down she knew that he was a professional, that he was trained in the art of seduction, trained on how to make a woman feel desired, lusted after. But she didn't care. For once, she would take what was offered without question, without a thought of reciprocation. She would take what he offered her, selfishly.

In answer to his plea, Sangria braced her hands against the shower stall and spread her legs farther apart. With a feral growl, Vance tossed the sponge over his shoulder and dropped to his knees behind her. She closed her eyes in ecstasy as she felt his hands kneading her ass cheeks, his thumbs feathering against her throbbing intimate flesh. Need, hot and delicious, licked at the insides of her thighs, making them tremble and making her sex weep with want.

Vance brought his hands down and wrapped his palms around her vibrating flesh. "Your quivering excites me, Sangria. Like a virgin on her first night."

"I'm no virgin," she growled.

"You are with me." And with that, he moved his hands up, separated her cheeks with his thumbs, and slid his tongue into her pussy.

She jerked violently, as surges of intense pleasure smashed into her, surprising a loud moan from her lips. "Ah, fuck," she groaned as another wave of glorious rapture swept over her.

Vance was doing incredibly delectable things to her sex. While his tongue lapped at her inflamed clit, causing sizzling jolts to shoot up and down her body, he circled her anus with his finger. Every so often, he pushed the tip in and then out, teasing her with every movement.

Intense pleasure built up deep in her belly and between her legs. Sangria could feel the liquid heat swirling around deep within preparing to explode. She didn't think she could handle it. Too many violent sensations bombarded her at once. Shaking her head, she ground her teeth and clenched her legs against the onslaught.

"Open for me, baby," Vance cooed, stroking her anus and vaginal opening with his fingers.

She shook her head back and forth, panting like a dog.

"Let go, Sangria. I won't hurt you." He inserted a finger into her and swirled it around, exploring every inch of her. "Let go and I promise you more pleasure than you've ever felt before."

She didn't want to let go. She'd been so uptight and guarded for all her life, how did one just let go? Vulnerable as a child, jumping from foster home to foster home, Sangria vowed never to feel that way again. But the promise of what Vance offered pulled at her insides, and tugged at her legs. Could she finally just let go and feel real raw emotion?

With sounds of encouragement, Vance eased her legs even further apart, and pushed her forward forcing her to arch her back. She allowed him to maneuver her, to control her. He was the expert and she put herself in his capable hands, literally.

"That's it, baby," he purred as he slipped another two long fingers into her, pumping them in and out at a tortuous lazy pace. "You feel like liquid silk. So soft and wet."

His words inflamed her even more. Even without the hot water still pounding down on her skin, she'd be drenched. Everything he was doing to her ignited passions she hadn't felt in a long time, maybe not ever. And she craved more. So much more.

"Oh fuck, yes," she hissed as he circled her anus with a finger.

"Hang on, sugar." He pressed his long digit into her virginal opening, filling her slowly, inch by inch. "Deliciously tight, just the way I like it."

Sangria clamped her eyes shut as a sizzling whip of electricity shot over her body. She was very near to climaxing. All her muscles started to tremble and quiver in anticipation. She bucked against Vance's hand as he picked up his pace, thrusting his fingers into her pussy and ass in a delicious rhythmic pattern.

"That's it baby, come for me," he panted, adding his tongue to the ménage of parts fucking her hard and fast.

All it took was one final lick on her clit, and Sangria orgasmed. In an explosion of white light and total rapture, she cried out. "Yes! Oh, my, God, yes!"

Her legs shook violently but Vance held her up, his fingers still pumping inside her, prolonging her orgasm. She could barely see, nor hear, nor think. All that crossed her mind was total bliss. Slowly, her climax ebbed, but he was still there at her pussy, licking her, keeping the shocks and jolts of pleasure searing through her like lightning. She wanted to push him away to allow her to think, but at the same time, she wanted him to keep his assault going so she would never have to again.

"Oh, baby, you taste so fucking good." Finally, he relinquished his hold on her sex, but gave her quivering flesh one final lap with his tongue.

Eventually, reason came back to her in a rush, and she was able to draw air without panting. Clawing her way up the shower stall, she managed to stand. Every muscle in her body still trembled with exertion and spent passion. Every nerve ending still pulsed with want and desire. She turned just as Vance stood and she stared him in the face.

Good lord, he was gorgeous. Silky dark hair plastered to his chiseled face from the water, his lips flushed and swollen from sucking on her pussy, and his eyes still aflame with lust. She gazed down his lean slick body until she found his cock. He was erect and glistening from the water still spraying on them both.

With a cheeky grin, Vance touched his cock, sliding his hand over his shaft. "It seems I'm not so professional after all."

Four

Unable to control her hunger any longer, Sangria launched herself at him. He must have anticipated it, because he wrapped his arms around her, pulling her close, and crushed his mouth to hers. A surplus of tastes circled in her mouth as they kissed, including her own lusty juices. It tasted like ambrosia on his lips and tongue. Moaning and groaning into him, she raced her hands over his body. Up his back, down to his ass. She searched everywhere for his flesh, something to hold onto, something to dig into while their tongues tangoed in her mouth.

Sliding his hands down, Vance grabbed her ass and lifted her up into his arms. Wrapping her legs around his waist, Sangria didn't miss a beat as he carried her into the other room. She continued to feast on his mouth, nipping and tugging at his full bottom lip.

She nearly squealed when he dropped her onto the mattress

and covered her wet throbbing body with his own. Nestling his cock between her legs, he nibbled on her chin and neck, while his hands were busy at her breasts, squeezing and pulling her nipples into aching rigid peaks.

Spreading her legs wide, she tried to capture his cock with her slick inner folds. Eager to have him sheathed inside, Sangria nudged her pussy against him repeatedly. Groaning, he finally acknowledged the hint, and guided his cock into her, sliding in with one hard thrust.

She ground her teeth against the urge to scream as he filled her completely. She thanked the lord that she was already sopping wet or he would have never slid in so easily. Even now, she felt overstuffed with his long wide cock moving inside. She could hardly breathe with the delight of it.

"Oh god, you're still so tight," he panted through clenched teeth. "You're like crushed velvet against my cock."

"Shut up and fuck me," she growled against his throat. "You talk too much."

He ceased all movements and grinned down at her. "Hmm, sounds like someone's pretty eager." He slipped out of her and sat up.

"What are you doing?" She grabbed for him, but he slapped her hands away.

"I want to know how much you want me."

"Fuck that."

Still smiling, he sat back against the wall and stroked his cock lazily. "Then you'll get none of this."

Leaning on her elbow, Sangria couldn't help but watch as he touched himself. Furious that he denied her what she wanted, she couldn't turn away. He was an exquisite example of male perfection. Even his cock was perfect. And she wanted it, she wanted him.

She knew he was playing a game with her. She hated games especially when it came to interaction between the sexes. But something about this man made her want to play. It was more than the gorgeous cock between his legs, and the way it filled her up. Here was a man that only the rich, the privileged, and influential touched. He was a man she would never have thought of approaching, never dreamed of being with. Her past lovers had always been just as serious and uncomplicated as she was. Not someone to laugh with, or to share comfortable silences. As she watched Vance, eyed him up and down, taking in his smoldering eyes, handsome face, and playful smile, she realized that she could do that and more with him. That she wanted to.

Getting to her knees, Sangria crawled to him. "I want you."

"What was that?" he murmured. "I couldn't quite hear you."

She shuffled up to him, straddled his lap, and nuzzled her pussy against his cock. "I said I fucking want you." She licked his lobe. "Can't you tell?" She growled as she ground her sex onto him.

"Mm, yeah," he moaned while he aided her hips back and forth lubricating his member. "I can feel your sweet juices dripping onto my cock."

Nibbling her way over his chin, Sangria covered his mouth with hers, pushing her tongue between his lips. On a chuckle, he opened and swept his tongue over hers teasingly darting in and out.

She loved his playfulness. She couldn't remember the last time she relaxed enough to enjoy sex this much. It was always hurried, more like a necessity than a luxury. But this, with him, was all lavishness, and she was going to revel in every moment of it.

As they kissed, she could feel Vance's fingers exploring her. He slid them between her ass cheeks and into her soft wet folds. Trailing his fingers back and forth along her cleft, he finally slipped them one at a time into her pussy.

"Mm, I love how you feel inside. So fucking hot," he said while nibbling on her bottom lip.

"Fuck me, and you'll see how much hotter it can get."

She wanted his cock inside her now. She was burning for him. If he waited much longer, she might just self-combust.

Without another word, he slid his fingers out, lifted her up, and pulled her down onto his rigid length. As he filled her, Sangria bit back a cry of pleasure. She mounted him perfectly. A deliciously snug fit.

Once he was fully sheathed inside her pussy, Sangria held still, clutching her vaginal muscles around him, enjoying the way he felt. Savoring every ridge, every vein of his glorious cock.

He groaned against her neck as she clenched and un-clenched her muscles, squeezing him tight. "Oh, God, woman. You're killing me."

"Well I can't have that," she chuckled. "I'm not nearly through with you." And with that, she started to rock back and forth.

Gritting her teeth, she pushed up with her legs, stopping right at the tip of his cock, and then slammed back down. Each time she moved, Vance groaned, his jaw clenched tight. She knew she was driving him insane because she could feel it in the way his muscles bunched and twitched. He was reining it in, trying to stay in control. She wondered what it would take to send him over the edge.

While she pumped up and down, Vance pulled her close, nibbled on her neck, and ran his hands up and down her back to end up on her ass. He squeezed and kneaded her flesh, brushing his fingers in the valley of her cheeks, circling her anus. Each time he did this, the breath caught in her throat. An explosive orgasm was kindling inside. She was afraid of its intensity, knowing it was going to be fiery and overpowering like a raging inferno.

Vance ran his tongue up and down her neck and ended to suckle on her earlobe. "I love how you feel, Sangria. So soft, so silky," he groaned. "I want to fuck you so hard that you scream."

His words sent ripples of pleasure over her. She grabbed hold of his dark silky hair and crushed her mouth to his in answer to his statement. *Oh, God, yes, fuck me hard!* She wanted to scream.

Gripping her ass cheeks tightly, Vance lifted her up, but keeping his cock still buried deep, and flipped her onto her back. Once there, he grabbed her legs and pushed them back, spreading her wide. Her knees touched the mattress and she had to take in a few ragged breaths as he began to slide his cock out, and then back in.

In this position, she was completely stretched open and exposed. She could feel every glorious inch of him thrusting in and out of her. At first, his rhythm was leisurely and controlled. However, that didn't last long.

Soon, he was plunging into her. Flesh slapped against flesh. Their pants mingled together with each thrust. Sangria whimpered as he rammed into her pussy again and again. She could feel him deep inside, as if pushing at her very soul.

Tears welled in her eyes, as her climax quivered on release. She couldn't take much more. Every nerve ending in her body was firing. She felt like she was ablaze.

Reaching down, she brushed her fingers over the hood of her slit, pushing it back to find her inflamed nub. All her muscles flinched and bunched as she stroked her clit. That was all it took to send her spiraling over into bliss.

Crying out, as starbursts exploded in her eyes, Sangria came hard. She tried to push her legs back, but Vance held her still, held her open as he continued to thrust his cock into her contracting pussy.

She thrashed about on the mattress as delicious wave after wave of pleasure surged over her. She nearly lost her breath with the power of it. Crying out again, she ran her hands over his chest, raking her nails over his skin. She couldn't do anything else but hang on as her orgasm took her under into the rapturous deep.

Groaning loudly, Vance finally released her legs and fell forward, wrapping his hands around her head, digging his fingers into her hair. With one final deep thrust, he came in a rush of heat and violence.

Sangria wrapped her arms around him and held him as he came, enjoying the way her hands slid over his slick, sweaty skin.

"Oh fuck!" he moaned as he emptied himself utterly.

They laid there for what seemed like an eternity, pressed together, sweat mingling, juices flowing. Finally, Sangria began to stir, testing her limbs for the strength to move. Everything felt like rubber. Soft, hot, pliant rubber, but rubber all the same.

Vance's body began to twitch on top of her. She was alarmed at first, until she realized that he was laughing.

"Holy fuck, woman, I think you just about killed me."

Sangria swelled with pride. She never almost killed someone with sex before. A knife possibly, her Hummer most certainly, but never had that pleasure with her body.

"Maybe you should think of getting into the sex trade. You'd make a million."

She brushed her hand over his sweaty brow, pushing his hair to the side. "I'll take that as a compliment."

He pushed up onto his elbows and smiled down at her. "It was meant as one."

As she gazed up at his perfectly sculpted and flushed face, she could almost forget that they were a few hours away from officially being on the run. That she had fifty thousand dollars of the First Lady's money for a job she didn't finish, and that she'd just fucked the woman's prized stud in a rundown hovel. Other than all that, Sangria felt damn good.

"You look pleased with yourself," Vance commented, his brow arching playfully.

"Yup. I am." She traced her finger over his full sensuous mouth. His lips were designed specifically for kissing. And she wished she could stay attached to them forever or at least for another few hours.

But she couldn't. Their union was to be brief.

She dropped her hand and turned her gaze from his face. She started to wiggle underneath him so he would move.

He didn't. Instead, he cupped her cheek and turned her face back to look at him. "What happened there? Everything was spectacular."

"Yes, it *was*. But now, now it's back to reality."

"Screw reality. Let's flow with this for a while."

She frowned at him. "We've had our while. Now, it's time to make plans to get the fuck out of here."

Vance leaned down and pressed a soft kiss to her pouty lips. "You're so quick to get out of here, that you can't enjoy it. We only have this moment once, Sangria."

She paused and stared into his sparking blue eyes. He was right. She'd always been quick to decide, in a rush to move on. Not once had she'd enjoyed a moment just for the sake of satisfaction. And she might not get another chance for a long time.

Nodding, she smiled. "You're right."

He tapped her on the nose with his finger. "Of course I'm right."

Laughing, she snapped at his finger with her teeth. But she didn't get a chance as he rolled over onto his back pulling her with him. Once settled, he nuzzled her into the crook of his arm and sighed.

"Ah, this is the life. Lying on a lumpy mattress, in a rambling old shed with a gorgeous woman still soft and pliant from some fan-fucking-tastic sex." He closed his eyes and sighed again. "It can't get any better than this."

Chuckling, Sangria felt her eyes begin to droop. She yawned and snuggled into his body, finding his presence rather comforting and safe. She closed her eyes and drifted. The last thought to cross her mind was one of Vance. He'd make for an interesting traveling partner.

Five

The metallic sound echoed in Sangria's ear. She knew that sound all too well.

Opening her eyes, she had the displeasure of staring into a barrel of a handgun. By the shape and size, most likely a 9 mm Beretta.

"Good morning, sunshine," the big brute holding the gun chirped.

Vance, who had been underneath her, finally opened his eyes and flinched. "Oh fuck!"

Sangria slowly sat up and surveyed the situation. There were two of them. The hulk holding the gun, and the shorter chubbier brute leaning against the wall by the door, a smug smile on his round pudgy face. Leg-breaking goons, if she ever saw any. They were in deep shit.

"Hello, Vance. Nice to see you again," the hulk said.

Rubbing a hand over his face, Vance sat up and sighed. "What's up, Leon?"

"It seems you missed your appointment in Vegas."

Sangria cleared her throat. "I can explain that. A semi hit me and flipped my vehicle. The case broke open and . . . well, Vance fell out."

The guy at the door started to laugh. "You're kidding?"

Vance shook his head. "It's true."

Leon looked over at Sangria, and then did a long thorough perusal of Vance. Sangria thought she saw something feral in his eyes as he scrutinized Vance's body. Hmm, was there something there? Lust, affection?

"We did find your Hummer. It looks pretty banged up, as do the both of you." Leon lowered his gun and took a step back as if to assess the situation.

"I didn't know what to do." Sangria sat forward and tried to convince Leon. He was obviously the one in charge. "I didn't have the number, and as it stood, since I saw what was inside the package, I didn't think Ms. Madison would let me live."

Leon gave her a half-smile. "You got that right."

Sangria glanced at Vance. He reached over and grabbed her hand, squeezing it tight. "So, what are you going to do, Leon?"

"My job for one."

Sangria watched Leon. Although he looked like a killer, he didn't look like a stupid man. In fact, the way he eyed Vance convinced her that he was not pleased with his assignment. Obviously, the two men knew each other, and by the way they spoke, even had once liked each other. Maybe, there was hope yet, that they could get out of this alive.

"Take the money," she blurted.

Everyone looked at her.

"What?" Leon responded.

"Take the fifty thousand and pretend you couldn't find us."

Leon shook his head. "I get twice that much for killing you and taking Vance back."

"Okay, take the fifty thousand and give us twenty-four hours. Then come after us."

Vance squeezed her hand in question. She glanced at him and shrugged. She was making it up as she went. Anything to get them out of this predicament.

It was working. She could see Leon start to waver. He was definitely thinking about it.

"Six hours," he countered. "We'll give you six hours to run."

"Eighteen."

"Twelve."

"Deal," she said and held out her hand to him. Grinning, he took it and shook, sealing the bargain.

"You got balls, girl." Tucking the gun back in its holster, Leon looked around the room. "Where's the money?"

Sangria nodded to the black bag on the table.

Leon unzipped it, looked in, and then zipped it back up. He slung the strap around his shoulder and tipped his head to Sangria and Vance. "We'll be seeing you in twelve hours. Enjoy it while you can."

With that, the man at the door exited, and Leon followed him out, shutting the door behind him.

When they were gone, Vance grabbed her and pulled her to him, wrapping his arms around her. "I thought we were dead," he whispered into her neck.

"Not yet we're not."

He kissed her on the side of her neck under her ear. Shivers rushed over her again. Damn it! Even in moments of severe panic, he could make her squirm with lust.

Obviously sensing her growing desire, he moved his lips down her throat to her shoulder and lightly nipped her there. He ran his hands down her back to her ass, and kneaded her cheeks firmly.

Wriggling, she tried to push out of his hold. "Vance, we need to get our shit together and go."

Slipping his hands lower, he slid two fingers into her still sensitive pussy. "We have twelve hours," he murmured while trailing his tongue down her shoulder to her breast. "Lots of time."

She sucked in a breath as he pushed his fingers deep, swirling them around inside. She couldn't deny her desire to fuck him again, but they needed to get going. She bought them twelve hours; they needed to make the most of it.

When Vance reached her breast and sucked in a nipple, she closed her eyes and arched her back, pushing her breast into his hot wet mouth.

"Okay, you have twenty minutes," she moaned.

"Twenty minutes? That's hardly enough time for foreplay."

Opening her eyes, she glanced down at him. "Twenty minutes, take it or leave it."

"I'll take it." Vance pushed her back onto the bed, grabbed her around the hips and flipped her over onto her stomach. "On your knees, woman."

Laughing, Sangria obliged him. The moment she was on all fours, he gripped her hips tightly and thrust into her pussy, hard and quick. Gripping the sheets on the bed, she held on as he rammed into her. Already she could feel an orgasm quickening deep inside her sex.

Sweat dripped off him as he slammed his cock into her. He went so deep she swore she could feel him in her throat. Panting, she reached back and slid her fingers into her open wet sex, quickly finding her clit. Pressing down, she rubbed at it hard.

Within minutes, that hard ball of pleasure at her center exploded into a million little pieces of delicious delight all over her body. Crying out, she pushed back into Vance driving him so deep she came again, harder, faster.

Clamping her eyes shut and twisting the sheets in her hands, Sangria groaned as wave after wave of intense pleasure crashed into her. She could barely breathe as the sensations whipped at her like electricity. Each time she thought she was done, another swell surged through her, pulling her down. Drowning her in its delicious torment.

Vance cried out as he thrust once more into her, digging his fingers into her hips. "Oh shitfuckdamn!" He flung himself forward over her back, pushing her down into the mattress.

She didn't know how long they laid there but it felt like an eternity before she could move again. Testing her limbs, she wiggled her fingers, then her toes. *Good, both still working.*

Vance groaned and slid his hand up to cup her breast. Where he got the energy, she'd never know.

"I think we still have ten minutes left. Time for another round."

She burst out laughing. She couldn't help it. The man was incorrigible. "You're a nymphomaniac."

He raised his head and grinned at her. "Yeah, hello, I'm a man, aren't I?"

She crawled out from underneath him and slid off the bed. "We need to get going." Shaking her head, she padded over to her duffel bag on the floor, unzipped it, and made sure she still had everything they'd need to disappear. She pulled out a slim black leather book and her cellphone. She still had a few tricks up her sleeve.

As she punched in some numbers, she glanced over her shoulder at Vance. He was lying on his side watching her, heat still evident in his eyes. She didn't think she could ever get tired of seeing that particular look.

"How's the Caribbean for you?"

He smiled. "I think I could get used to lying around on a beach every day." Then his eyes sparkled. "A nude beach?"

Laughing, she put the phone to her ear. "I'll see what I can do."

"What are you doing?"

"Calling in a favor." She only had to wait three rings before someone picked up. "Carlos? Remember that thing I did for you last year? Well, I'm calling in my chit, amigo."

A few seconds later she flipped the phone closed and tossed it back into her bag. Turning, she stared at Vance who was still lounging on the bed, like a pleasure God. She shook her head. How did she get so lucky to have this sexy man fall out of her vehicle?

"Now what?" he asked.

"We wait for the helicopter."

He chuckled and held out his hand to her. "That's convenient."

She took his hand and allowed him to pull her down to the mattress. "Yup."

"How long do we have?" he asked, while trailing a naughty finger back and forth across her thigh.

"Hmm, I'd say about another twenty minutes."

Laughing, he grabbed her around the waist and flipped her onto her back, settling between her legs. He pressed his lips to hers. "Just enough time."

A bad girl at heart, VIVI ANNA likes to burn up the pages with her original unique brand of fantasy fiction. Whether it's in ancient Egypt, or in an apocalyptic future, Vivi Anna always writes fast-paced action-adventure with strong independent women who can kick some butt, and dark delicious heroes to kill for.